BROKEN PROMISE

M. JAMES

Copyright © 2021 by M. Jones

All rights reserved.

No part of this book may be reproduced in any form or by any electronic or mechanical means, including information storage and retrieval systems, without written permission from the author, except for the use of brief quotations in a book review.

This is a work of fiction. Names, characters, businesses, places, events and incidents are either the products of the author's imagination or used in a fictitious manner. Any resemblance to actual persons, living or dead, or actual events is purely coincidental.

SOFIA

1

I wake up to fluorescent lights above me and the scent of disinfectant filling my nose. For a moment, I'm completely disoriented; my last memory is of spooning fruit onto a china plate in the banquet room of the hotel.

Then I open my eyes fully, and I realize where I am.

I'm in a hospital, lying in a hospital bed. I feel something tug at my arm, and when I look over, I can see there's an IV in my arm, some other machine hooked up to me monitoring my heart rate with small, steady beeps that speed up as the memories start to flood back in. An explosion—glass shattering and smoke filling the room, chairs overturned, and guests screaming.

Luca's body on top of mine, bleeding from his mouth and nose. And more blood on his side—

I gasp, pushing myself up as much as I can. My first, overwhelming fear is that he's dead. I don't even take the time to examine why or to wonder why I would care after everything that's happened.

My husband might be dead. Inexplicably, the thought fills me with sadness, maybe not deep enough to be called grief, but something aching and hollow in my chest.

If I'm a widow, Don Rossi will kill me.

I'm glad that wasn't my first thought, but it's definitely my second. If Luca is dead, there's no one left to protect me. It's not the only reason I hope he's alive, but it's definitely one of them.

And I can't help but wonder why he threw himself over me at all. If I'd died in the explosion, it would have solved two problems for him—he wouldn't have had an unwanted wife any longer. He also wouldn't have had to feel responsible for *letting* me be killed by Rossi. It would have just been an unfortunate casualty of—whatever the fuck happened at the hotel.

There's a knock at the door, and an older blonde nurse walks in, a slight smile on her face. "Oh, Mrs. Romano. Good to see that you're up!"

Mrs. Romano. It's the first time I've heard someone refer to me like that, and for a brief second, I have the urge to say *no, I'm Ms. Ferretti, you must have the wrong room.* And then I remember that I *am* Mrs. Romano, Luca's wife—in every single way.

The memory of our wedding night sends a flush through me that makes me feel uncomfortable. Everything about that night felt wrong and confusing—and then the betrayal of finding out that I didn't have to at all and Luca cutting my thigh as a last resort instead of a first.

I can't even feel the sting of the cut now, but reflexively I want to reach down and touch it. I don't, though; instead, I look up at the nurse as she approaches my bedside.

"How are you feeling?" she asks pleasantly, checking the clipboard at the foot of my bed. "You're lucky, Mrs. Romano. Your injuries were minor. Some bruising and a light concussion, but that will resolve itself fairly quickly. There's no internal bleeding, and the damage to your inner ears seems to be minor as well. You have some scratches and cuts, but it's all pretty superficial." She smiles at me. "You were very lucky."

The way she says it makes my stomach clench. Something in her voice implies that others weren't as lucky. "What about my husband?" I ask, my voice a hoarse croak.

"Mr. Romano's injuries were more severe—but he's alive," the nurse adds quickly at the end, seeing my face.

"What do you mean, *more severe?*"

"He had a deep laceration to his side, and we found some shards of glass in there. He also had a perforated eardrum, but it will heal within a couple of weeks, and he should be able to go home soon. He's sedated right now, after the procedure to remove the glass and stitch up the laceration on his side."

"Can I go see him?" The question even surprises me—I'm not sure why I *want* to see him. Maybe it's because I feel guilty that the relief washing over me upon hearing that he's alive is at least sixty percent because I now know that I'm safe—or at least as safe as I can be. My husband is still alive.

The other forty percent is because he had a split second to make a decision, and he chose to protect me.

I don't know why, but I'd like to. And as angry as I still am over the events of our wedding night—I'd like to at least be able to thank him.

"I can walk you down to his room," the nurse says after a moment's thought. "But you can't go in just yet. And not for long—you need to rest as well."

"Alright," I agree quickly. "Not long. I just want to see him."

The nurse beams at me, no doubt thinking that I'm a new bride in love with and missing her husband. It doesn't hurt to let her believe that, and I don't bother saying anything to make her think otherwise as she helps me get out of the hospital bed, undoing the connections to the monitor and showing me how to wheel my IV stand along.

I hate all of this. Even the penthouse is preferable to being in here, with tubes coming out of my arm and a hospital gown on. I feel sick and weak, and it reminds me too much of the last time I was in a hospital with my mother, in the months before she died. I try hard not to think about that, not to remember the way she went from a beautiful, vibrant woman to a shell of herself, her glossy blonde hair gone, her perfect skin dry and cracked, her once healthy and strong body frail and skeletal. I didn't even recognize her by the end, and a part of me was glad that my father wasn't there to see her like that. That his last memory of her was the woman he'd married, that he'd often hinted he'd risked a great deal for, because he loved her so much.

At least part of that was simply because she was Russian; I know that. But there was always a hint of something else, some reason that he should never have married her but did anyway.

She was glad that he hadn't been there to see it, either. She'd said as much to me, not long before she'd died. And then she'd given me her necklace and told me that she hoped she'd see him again soon.

But there had been something in her eyes that had told me she didn't really believe that. That whatever she'd tried to believe all her life, growing up in the Orthodox churches of her home, had been leached away by the illness like everything else.

I don't believe it either. Just like I don't believe in fairytales anymore. If there's a heaven or a hell, it's the one we make here and nothing more.

I'm still not sure what my life with Luca will be like. Not heaven, I'm certain of that. But if he cared enough to throw himself on top of me during the explosion, maybe a tentative middle ground. A purgatory, if you will.

The nurse walks with me all the way to the window of Luca's room. He's in a bed, hooked up to the same sorts of tubes and wires, and asleep just like she'd said. He looks paler than usual, and I can see the bruises around his eye and the side of his face, cuts on his neck and hands.

"He was lucky, too," the nurse says quietly as she follows my gaze. "If something as large as what embedded in his side hit his neck, he wouldn't be here now."

That sends a chill through me that I didn't expect, and I'm not sure if it's for him or me. Me, at least partially, because of how tied my life is to his. But also him—and I don't want to admit that I care. That even if I don't want to be married to him, even if I do hate him more than a little for all of this and blame a good deal of it on his willingness to go along instead of finding some other way out for me, I don't want him to *die*.

He looks almost that peaceful, lying in the hospital bed with the sheet tucked up underneath his armpits. His face looks softer like this, younger, the harsh lines of his jaw and cheekbones more relaxed in sleep. He seems more like a man I might run into on the street or swipe right on Tinder, not a hardened criminal. Not the second-in-command of the most notorious, powerful organization in the world.

I'm his wife. A Mafia wife. It makes me feel cold all over. I don't want any part of this, and yet I *am* a part of it and always have been. I'd tried to get out, but I'm getting sucked in deeper and deeper every day.

"What about the others?" I ask quietly. "The Rossi's—Caterina and her mother, and—"

"Ms. Rossi and her fiancé Mr. Bianchi are well. I'm told Mr. Bianchi wasn't even in the room, so he, of course, didn't sustain any injuries. Ms. Rossi had some bruising and mild eardrum perforation as well, but she'll heal quickly. As for Mr. Rossi—" The nurse takes a deep breath. "He's in critical condition. I can't give exact details as you're not a member of his family, but we're not sure—"

My heart is beating so hard that I can hear it. "Not sure?"

"His condition is very critical," the nurse says again. "It's really all I can say."

"And his wife? Giulia?"

The nurse's silence tells me the answer before she ever speaks. "Mrs. Rossi did not survive the explosion," she says quietly. "I'm very sorry. I'm guessing they were friends of yours?"

"Of my husband's." I feel numb. I didn't know Mrs. Rossi well, but nothing about her ever came across as particularly malicious or unpleasant to me. She was cool and formal around me, and I got the impression that she was happy to live the life she'd married into and enjoy the perks, turning a blind eye to her husband's crimes and dalliances. She hadn't looked overly pleased when they'd come in to see the bed the morning after the wedding, though, and I'd gotten a distinct impression that she'd thought it was an outdated and ridiculous ceremony. She'd been polite to me and loving towards her daughter.

She hadn't deserved to die. Especially not with someone like her husband in the same room, a man who *is* truly evil, who would have me killed just for his own peace of mind, who threatened Luca, the man he's supposed to trust more than anything, if he'd refused to rape his bride on her wedding night. I'd consented in the end—but still, I know Rossi hadn't cared. He wouldn't have cared if Luca had bound and gagged me, as long as it was done.

He should be dead, not Giulia. I can feel my throat tightening, my eyes burning with tears as the nurse helps me back to my room. *Caterina.* I wish more than anything that I could go to her, help her through this in any way that I can right now. *And I will, as soon as we're all released from the hospital,* I promise myself. I know exactly how much it hurts to lose a parent. And Caterina has only ever tried to be kind to me since we've met.

"You need to rest," the nurse says sternly. "You might not have been badly hurt, but you've been through a lot, Mrs. Romano. It'll take some time for you to process the shock."

"I—"

"I'm going to give you a sedative," she says. Before I can argue, she's already injecting something into my IV line. "Get some rest, Mrs. Romano."

I don't feel like I can rest. My stomach is in knots, my throat and eyes burning with unshed tears, and I feel like everything has gotten so much worse. I can feel some of that shock setting in, the realization that if we were attacked—and we must have been, it can't be a coincidence that there was a random explosion at the hotel where we happened to be staying after the wedding—it could happen again. It could happen *here.* At Luca's penthouse. How will I ever really feel safe?

The wedding was supposed to push the Bratva back as well as satisfy Rossi. It seems to have done the latter, but not the former. And if I'm honest, I don't know who terrifies me more.

* * *

WHEN I WAKE UP AGAIN, I feel groggy, probably from the aftereffects of the sedative. My mouth feels dry and cottony, and I desperately want a drink of water. I blink rapidly as I try to sit up a little, wincing at the stickiness of my eyes.

"Glad to see you're awake."

The sound of Luca's deep voice jolts me fully into consciousness. I look over to see him sitting at my bedside, fully dressed in a pair of charcoal slacks and a burgundy shirt undone at the collar. Even like that, though, it's the least polished I've ever seen him. The shirt is a bit wrinkled, and his hair is messy, once again making him look younger and more approachable.

The sleeves are rolled up to his elbows, and I can see a few bandaged patches on his arms, as well as the one on his neck. He half-smiles at me, and for once, it doesn't seem calculated or guarded. He seems genuinely happy to see that I'm awake and alive.

"Can you get me some water?" I ask tentatively, nodding towards the side table that's just out of reach, where a plastic pitcher and cups are sitting.

Luca nods, getting up without a word and pouring some water into a cup. Just the splashing sound makes my mouth ache and my throat contract—the IV might have been pumping fluids into me, but I still feel as parched as the Sahara—and I take the cup gratefully when he hands it to me, gulping it down.

"Easy," Luca says, sitting back down. "Don't choke."

He says it casually, but there's a hint of actual worry in his eyes. For just a second, I catch another glimpse of what it would be like if we were a normal couple—if Luca were just an ordinary husband getting some water for his ordinary wife, both of us recovering from the trauma that we'd just shared.

"How are you feeling?" I manage once I've finished with the water. "The nurse said—"

"I'm alright," Luca says abruptly. "Some scratches and bruises, but mostly fine."

"She said you had a pretty bad injury to your side. I saw it when—when you were on top of me." I swallow hard, knowing exactly what that last sentence sounded like. It brings back the memory of the *other* time he was on top of me, when I learned what it felt like to have him inside of me.

"I've had worse," Luca says grimly. "You don't make it to your thirties in the mob without getting shot at least once."

I stare at him. "You've been *shot?*"

"A couple times." Luca shrugs. "It happens."

And just like that, any illusion that we could ever be normal is shattered all over again. Not that I legitimately thought that was possible. But the moment had almost been nice.

Thinking about Luca being shot doesn't quite elicit the same response I'd had when I thought he was dead. The other night, I'd kind of wanted to shoot him myself. Just not fatally.

"I am glad you're alive," Luca says quietly, leaning forward in his seat. "And uninjured. I'm grateful for that. The nurse says you'll be able to go home now that you're awake."

Home. I don't have a home anymore. But I know what he means—the penthouse, even if it will always be his home and not mine. Soon, hopefully, I'll be able to at least have my own apartment, even if I'm not sure that will feel like home either.

"You saved me." I blurt out the words that have been on the tip of my tongue since I woke up and saw him sitting there. "You threw yourself on top of me when the explosion happened. Why did you do that? You could have died."

His features go carefully blank; I see it happen. "You're my wife," he says coolly.

"And you could have solved two problems in one go by letting me die," I point out. "You're free, without the guilt of letting Rossi kill me. I'm sure your widower's grief could have gone a long way towards warming your bed, too."

"I don't need help warming my bed," Luca says tightly. "If I want another woman, I'll get one. If I want you, I'll have you. As far as what I did, I went this far to protect you. Why stop there? Might as well see it through to the bitter end."

The words ring hollow even as he says them. I know as well as I'm sure he does that it's just a cover for the actual truth—that he doesn't understand why he instinctively protected me. His answer just confirms that for me.

But I'm not letting the rest of what he said go so easily.

"You can't have me whenever you want me," I say quietly. "Just because of what happened on our wedding night—that's not going to happen again, Luca. There's no reason for it now. You proved to Rossi that you *fucked* me—" I grind the word out bitterly, "but I'm not going to be some toy for your pleasure. That one time was it."

"Sure." Luca shrugs. "It wasn't exactly the best fuck of my life, Sofia."

I flinch. The words shouldn't sting—I shouldn't even care—but they do. It's just another confusing reaction to him in a long line of them, ever since I woke up in his bed after he rescued me. I should be glad if he didn't enjoy himself, happy that he'll be inclined not to try again—not to push me up against doors and kiss me wildly or bend me over couches and bring me so close to orgasm that I feel like I might die if—

Jesus, Sofia, get a grip. I swallow hard, and I can feel my face flushing. My skin feels hot just at the memory, and I try as hard as I can to push it out of my head, to forget about the mingled pleasure and denial and embarrassment of that night.

"Don't take it so personally," Luca says easily. "You were a virgin, and you didn't even want it. I expected you to be a cold fish."

His words feel like daggers, sharp and cutting, even if they're not meant to be insulting. He says it so casually, and I've never felt less like a wife, let alone a cherished one. I feel like something he's finished with and ready to discard now that he's done his duty.

Which is exactly what I should want, I remind myself. The sooner I have my own place and can put some distance between him and me, the sooner I'll stop feeling all these awful, conflicting, confusing things.

"The nurse told me about the others," I say quickly, changing the subject. The moment I think about that—about Mrs. Rossi's death, Caterina's grief, I feel guilty for even caring about Luca's insulting comments. Caterina has just lost her mother, and I'm in my feelings because my new husband insulted my—admittedly nonexistent—skills in the bedroom. "About Don Rossi, I mean, and Giulia. What does that mean for you—for us?"

Luca's face goes very still. "Don Rossi is in very critical condition," he says quietly. "The last I spoke with the doctor just before coming in here, he's awake, but they're keeping him for an indeterminate amount of time. There was—severe damage to his legs and possibly his spine, as well as head trauma. He'll have to have extensive surgery if he's going to walk again, and there was internal bleeding and damage. He's far from out of the woods."

It's so unfair. There's something slightly poetic about Don Rossi suffering in a hospital bed after all he put me through. Still, I can't help but feel that it's an awful injustice that he's alive at all when his wife is dead. I try to imagine him grieving for her, and I can't. I can't imagine any real emotion from him at all.

"He's not in any shape to continue at the head of the family as don," Luca continues. "We'll be going in to see him before I take you back home, and Caterina and Franco will be there as well. Franco will be stepping into his new role as underboss—the role I inhabited up until now." He takes a deep breath, his green eyes meeting mine.

"And I'll be the new don."

SOFIA

I feel as if all the breath has been sucked out of my body.

I'd suspected something like this when the nurse had said Rossi was in critical condition. But I hadn't wanted to think about it. With Luca in charge—I don't want to think about what will happen next. If he'll become harder, crueler, and impatient with me, if he'll expect me to fulfill the same kind of role that Giulia did, that of a good mafia don's wife. I know he'd hoped, even expected for it to be years before anything like this happened.

"I thought I'd have more time to prepare you," Luca says quietly, confirming my suspicions. "I will be don—at least acting, but most likely for good, even if Rossi recovers. It's doubtful that he'll be able to take up his duties again."

Looking at his face, I can't tell if he's happy about it or not.

"You'll have responsibilities too," he says. "Although I don't expect that you'll willingly take up many of them," he adds, a touch of bitterness in his voice. "But if you can at least try to be a good friend to Caterina during this time, it would help."

"I'd already planned to talk to her," I say defensively. "After all—"

"You know about dead parents. Yes, I'm well aware. As do I," Luca reminds me. "I need you to think less about your issues with me in the coming days, Sofia, and more about all of our survival."

"Who was it?" I manage to keep my voice from trembling. "Do you know?"

"Not for certain, yet. But I would put money on the Bratva," Luca says tightly. "It's them that we're fighting with, after all. Boston has no reason to bother us. If it didn't have something to do with Viktor and his men, I'd be shocked."

I'm a little shocked, too, if only because that's the most open he's been with me since the day he brought me back to his penthouse. "So what now?"

"Now," he says, standing up and smoothing his hands down the legs of his pants, "we go see Rossi. And then we go home."

Something in my stomach clenches every time he says *home*. I do a decent job of hiding it, though, looking away as the nurse comes in to get me ready to leave. Luca brought my bag in with him, and I manage a mumbled "thank you" as I grab it and head into the bathroom. I feel overcome with nerves suddenly, facing going back to the penthouse with him and seeing Rossi before that. All of this has been some kind of awful, escalating nightmare ever since the Bratva kidnapped me, and I can't take anymore.

But clearly, things are going to get worse before they get better.

I emerge a few minutes later, in jeans and a blue sleeveless top, my hair scraped up into a ponytail. I desperately need a shower and feel worse than I have in recent memory. I'm almost grateful to be going back to Luca's place if it means I can wash my hair and get a good night's sleep in a real bed.

Luca is waiting for me when I step out, and he takes my hand without bothering to ask, holding it tightly as we walk out into the hall. It's not so much a romantic gesture as a possessive one, and even when I try to wriggle my hand free of his grasp, it's clear that he has an iron grip on me. "I'm not going to run away," I say through gritted teeth. "I'm not that stupid."

"You might," he says coolly. "Rossi is in the hospital, and I'll be the don shortly. You might decide that now is as good a time as any to make a run for it. But I'll warn you, while I wouldn't have you killed, I can certainly have you picked up and brought back to me. Just about every cop in this town is on our payroll. No one in this hospital will help you either," he adds, seeing me look around. "Our grip on this city is strong, Sofia. You can't escape me, just as you couldn't escape Rossi. The difference is that he would have had you killed. I'll simply make you regret trying to leave."

The cool indifference in his voice chills me as much as his words do. I have to almost trot to keep up with his long strides as we make our way towards the elevator, and I feel like I might be sick. I'd thought that Rossi dying would mean I might be able to get out of this, but I can see that tiny loophole narrowing until I'm not sure if it even exists anymore. This really might be for the rest of my life—or at least until Luca dies.

I hadn't known *until death do us part* was supposed to be something I wished for. Ten minutes ago, I'd been glad he survived. Now I'm not so sure anymore.

Luca doesn't say a word to me as we ride up to the floor Don Rossi is staying on. He remains silent until we walk into the room, where Caterina and Franco are already waiting for us. Franco is uncharacteristically somber, giving Luca a quick but tight hug, and Caterina is visibly a mess. I've never seen her without makeup before, but she's completely bare-faced, her eyes red and swollen from crying, her lips bitten, and her face deathly pale. I notice that she's standing a little apart from Franco, who doesn't seem to be paying much attention to his grieving wife at all. I can feel how lonely she is just from looking at her. It radiates off of her like an aura.

I remember that feeling all too well after my own mother died and left me all alone. It breaks my heart to see her like that, especially when Franco should be the one who's there for her through this. He's not even injured, not a scratch on him, since he was still in his hotel room when the attack happened—too hungover to come down. *Lucky him*, I think bitterly. I wonder how Caterina feels about that—glad that her fiancé is unharmed, or bitter that out of all of us, her mother is the one who had to die?

"Luca." Rossi's voice is hoarse and cracked, but it still retains some of its old power nonetheless. "Come stand by me."

Franco goes with him, standing at Luca's side as they walk around to the other side of the hospital bed, leaving me next to Caterina. She glances over at me, and I reach out instinctively, taking her hand. I wonder if she'll pull back—we're not that close, after all, but her fingers lace through mine instead, squeezing back. Her face is still pale and somber, but when her eyes meet mine, I can see that she's grateful for the support.

"If circumstances were different," Rossi says, "there would be a formal ceremony to pass the title on to you. But since they're not, and I'm not leaving here anytime soon, this is the best we can do." He takes a deep, rattling breath, and I wince just hearing it. I can see from everything about him that Luca was right when he guessed that Rossi probably won't ever be in any shape to lead again. Even if he survives, he won't ever be strong again. He's already an old man, and this was a massive blow.

"I, Vitto Rossi, in the presence of these witnesses—my daughter Caterina, your wife Sofia, and my consigliere Franco Bianchi—renounce my seat at the head of the family and my title as Don. I pass it on to you, Luca Romano, son of Marco, heir to my place. You will hold this title, preserve and defend it and the family you lead, until such a time as you pass on or see fit to step down. You will pass it on to the first son of my blood, born of the union between my daughter and Franco Bianchi."

He tugs at the ring on his finger then, a thick band with a ruby embedded in the top of it, and I swallow hard. The energy in the room is tense. Everyone focused on the two men—one in the hospital bed, one standing beside it—and the transfer of power taking place there.

"I, Luca Romano, accept this title and the place that it gives me at the head of the table. I vow to uphold the alliances you have built, defend against all enemies, and give my blood and life if need be in defense of the family. I will hold, preserve, and defend all who serve with and under me, and when the time comes for the title to pass on, I vow to give it to the first son of your blood, the child of Caterina Rossi and Franco Bianchi."

Those last words, repeated by Luca loud and clear, are a cold reminder of the contract I signed and my place in this family. A reminder that I won't even have children to love, no family to console me while my husband is off killing and torturing and fucking other women. Mrs. Rossi had that, at least, a beautiful daughter to love and cherish even if she couldn't have a husband who cared for anything other than his power and greed.

I'll have nothing. No husband, no children, barely even my best friend. No real purpose other than sitting down and shutting up and holding onto Luca's arm in public when need be. I'm a trophy wife, a decoration, a means to an end. A card taken out of play.

My happiness doesn't matter at all.

I hear Caterina's breathing, and I glance sideways to see her hand pressed over her mouth, tears gathering on her lower lashes. But neither Luca nor Don Rossi is paying attention to any of us. Franco stands at his elbow as Luca takes the ring, sliding it onto his first finger and gripping Don Rossi's hand.

"You've been like a second father to me," he says quietly, his voice low enough that I have to strain to hear it. "I'll do my best to be worthy of the trust you've placed in me."

"I have faith in you, son." Rossi smiles weakly, gripping Luca's hand until his knuckles turn white.

"He needs rest," Caterina says suddenly, stepping forward. Her voice is shaky, and her face is very pale, but she looks firm. "Please, this is enough ceremony."

"Quiet, woman," Franco growls, and I look over sharply at him, surprised. I've spent very little time around him, but on the few occasions that we have met, he seemed the most lighthearted and boyish of them, not someone who takes life all that seriously. But now I see someone else underneath that, someone capable of snapping at his fiancée on one of the worst days of her life, someone who might have a side to him as brutal as any of these other men.

It's a reminder to me all over again not to let my guard down. I can't trust anyone—least of all, my new husband.

Caterina visibly flinches, shrinking back next to me, and it makes my heart ache to see it. Everything about her so far has shown me that she's kind, that she at least wants to try to be my friend, even if it's hard for me to let her in. Seeing Franco be so cruel to her makes me hate him. At least Luca speaks to me politely in public, even if we fight behind closed doors.

"I want Giulia avenged," I hear Rossi say quietly, still gripping Luca's hand. "Those bastard dogs killed my wife. That's not something that can go unanswered."

"We don't know for sure that it's the Bratva," Luca replies quietly. "But rest assured, Vitto, we won't allow her death to be ignored."

"I won't be able to be at the funeral. Make sure—"

"I'll handle all of it, papa," Caterina says, stepping forward again with her chin lifted. "Don't worry about a thing." She walks to his bedside without looking at Franco, taking her father's other hand. "I'll make sure mama is laid to rest properly."

I realize then, with a little bit of a shock, that she really does love her father. It shouldn't have surprised me, I suppose—I'm sure there were many things my own father did that were as violent as anything Rossi has done. He worked for him, after all—served him, really. And I loved my father deeply. But I wasn't aware of the things he did, everything he was a part of. Caterina surely knows more—she was raised to be a part of this, marry the right man, and be a good mafia wife. But she still loves him.

And now he and Franco are all she has left.

"Come on," Luca says tersely, letting go of Rossi's hand and crossing to me. "It's time to get you home and safe."

The words should be reassuring, but they're not. I know I don't have any choice, though, so I follow Luca obediently out of the hospital room and to the elevator, staying silent the whole way.

The ring on his finger glimmers in the light, the red ruby gleaming. It sitting on his right hand represents every bit as much of a commitment as the gold band on his left does, and I can't help but wonder if it comes down to it, which commitment will win out? He's promised to keep me safe, made me his wife to accomplish exactly that, and yet—if the title he's just vowed to uphold demands otherwise, what would he choose?

It makes me feel more uneasy than ever, and I can't shake the feeling as we get into Luca's car and ride the blocks back to the towering building that he—*we*—live in. It persists all the way up to the penthouse, and as we walk into the living room and he presses the button to pull the blinds back and flood the room with light, I turn to face him.

"So what now?" I swallow hard, looking up at my new husband. "When will the funeral be?"

"It's tomorrow," Luca says tightly. "But you won't be going."

"What? But surely, since we're married, people will expect to see me there—"

"There will be plenty of times you're expected to be seen, but I'm not particularly concerned with this one." The words are cold and clipped, curt. "You'll be staying here. It will reduce the likelihood that the Bratva will try to hit us at the funeral, although I hope Viktor might have enough respect to hold back from that."

"And what about me, here?" Cold fear winds through my belly and up my spine—has Luca decided I'm too much trouble? Would he rather the Bratva come for me here than put everyone else in danger again? And if that's the case, why not just go ahead and hand me over?

"You're not to leave the penthouse for any reason. My security will be doubled, and I'll assign you a personal bodyguard."

"Until when?" I can feel the panic rising. "This wasn't the deal, Luca. I'm supposed to be given my own apartment, so we don't have to stay here together—"

"Until the Bratva are pushed out of the territory." He strides towards me, that hard glint in his green eyes. He looks as handsome as ever—sometimes I think, traitorously, that he looks the *most* attractive when he's like this, cold and angry and almost terrifying, but hard and chiseled as if made from granite. This hard and cold man only burns hot when it comes to me, only ever softens a little when we touch.

But I can't think like that. I can't think about him in any way that might make me want him more, let my guard down, feel things towards him that aren't cautious, and even hate. I can't allow myself to soften towards this man who has now become even more powerful than before, who might have to be and do even more awful things in order to keep it.

"How long will that take?" My voice trembles as much as I try to keep it from doing exactly that. I don't want Luca to know how afraid I am—of him, of them, of all of this—but I can't stop it.

He shrugs nonchalantly as if it doesn't matter. "Who knows? Weeks? Months? Years? I can't possibly know the answer to that, Sofia. They will be beaten back when they realize they can't win, and no sooner than that. Viktor won't give up easily."

Panic floods me. I can feel my rational, logical thought slipping away in the face of being kept a virtual prisoner in this penthouse—however luxurious—for an undetermined amount of time. "No!" I exclaim, shaking my head and stepping back, trying to put some distance between us. "You promised, you told me if I married you that I'd be safe, that—"

"You will be," Luca says patiently, but I can hear it eroding from his tone. "In time."

"But you can't tell me how much time!" I swallow hard, feeling the lump in my throat swell and choke me. "Rossi couldn't even protect his wife, and now you want me to feel safe when you're saying I can't even leave this apartment?"

"Rossi is not the don now!" Luca thunders, taking two strides towards me. Before I can so much as try to dart around him, he scoops me up into his arms as if I weigh nothing at all, bridal-style. The irony of it isn't lost on me, and I wriggle in his grasp, trying to squirm free as he carries me up the stairs. Halfway up, I almost manage to get loose, and Luca growls with frustration, a sound that sends a shiver down my spine that isn't entirely unpleasant.

What the fuck is wrong with me? Why do these fights turn me on? I'm not winding him up on purpose—or am I? Luca's anger both scares and arouses me, and I don't understand it. It's almost as if a part of me wants him to take control the way he did the night before our wedding, to make me feel the things I can't allow myself to feel with him.

"It would serve you right if I pitched you over the side of this staircase," Luca snarls, setting me down briefly. I think for a moment that he's going to let me walk the rest of the way up. Instead, he just scoops me off of my feet once more, tossing me over his shoulder so that I'm draped over his back, staring at the gleaming hardwood stairs as he starts his ascent once more.

"Put me down!" I shriek, slamming one fist somewhere in the range of where I think his kidney might be. My legs flail, and I hope vaguely that one might connect with his balls, but Luca wraps an arm around my knees, holding them firmly to his chest. Something about that sends another shock of pleasure up my spine. I can feel to my horror that I'm starting to get more than a little turned on, the thin fabric of my panties clinging damply to my skin as my body flushes with heat.

"Not a chance," Luca says flatly, carrying me straight towards the double doors that lead into his bedroom.

He deposits me unceremoniously onto the bed, and I spring up immediately, strands of my hair coming loose from my ponytail and floating around my pink face.

"I'm not fucking you again." I lift my chin, hoping I look more sure about it than I am. I'm painfully aware of the huge bed behind me, the empty penthouse, and the fact that Luca could do anything he wanted to me—has the *right*, in his own mind, to do anything he wants to me. And watching him shrug casually out of his suit jacket isn't helping. His muscular forearms flex as he rolls up the sleeves of his shirt, and I feel my mouth go dry as he undoes the top button of his shirt, revealing a sliver of chest that makes my knees feel a little weak.

I'm suddenly reminded vividly of our wedding night, of him circling around behind me as he started to undo my dress, of how different it could have been if I hadn't told him to get it over with. What would he have done if I'd let it be something else? Would he have used his hands on me, like he did when he bent me over the couch? His mouth?

Oh god. Just the thought of that sends a wave of something I don't totally understand through me, a tight feeling in my stomach that makes my skin prickle and flush.

Luca probably wouldn't even do that. He likes having you under his power, not giving pleasure without getting some back.

"I'm not asking you to," Luca says, raising an eyebrow, and I feel a flush of sudden embarrassment.

"You didn't ask the first time, either," I snap.

"Well, I'm not telling you to. Is that good enough for your virginal sensibilities? I thought I fucked those out of you last night." He smirks. "Sofia, like I said in the hospital, I'm not interested in a poor lay. If I want to get my dick wet, I'll do it with someone who actually knows what to do."

And just like that, my humiliation feels complete. I don't even bother trying to work out why his rejection feels worse than his demands. All I know is that my husband is, for some reason, pretending that he doesn't even want me now that he's had a taste, that one night with me turned him off completely.

"Then why did you drag me in here?" I cross my arms, glaring up at him in an effort to conceal the riot of feelings tangling up inside my chest. "What was the point?"

"The point, Sofia, is that you won't have your own room any longer. You'll sleep in here, with me, like a good wife should and where I can keep an eye on you. I can't make certain that you're safe if you're down the hall. So you can move whatever things you like in here today, and leave the rest in your old room. They can stay there. The room won't be used by anyone else." He clears his throat, looking at me sternly. "If you sleep, it's in here. If you take a shower, it's in the master bathroom there. If you—"

"I get the idea," I say quickly. "So what? I'm supposed to just stay locked up here, never leave, sleep next to you and be fine with it?"

Luca's eyes glitter dangerously. "That's exactly what I expect you to do, Sofia," he says, his voice low and dark as he walks towards me.

"Because I'm keeping you safe. I'm the don now. This family is under my control. I will do *everything* I can to ensure that nothing like what happened at the hotel *ever* happens again. But I can't focus on that if I'm too busy making sure my little hellion of a wife *obeys my fucking orders.*" He grinds the last words out, punctuating each one, and I can see his anger rising.

It terrifies and excites me all at once, and I don't understand it at all.

"I'm not one of your little soldiers," I hiss, unable to resist the urge to fight back. "I don't take your orders."

Luca takes one more step forward, bringing his body very close to mine, and he looks down at me with that chiseled face, his green eyes dark and furious. His hand flies out, grasping my chin to tilt it up so that I can't look away, and even though his touch isn't painful, there's no questioning the meaning behind it. "You will take my orders, Sofia. Or maybe you'd rather take something else?" He smiles coldly. "If fucking you into compliance is what I have to do, then perhaps it's a duty I'll have to take on. Just like protecting you. Unpleasant, but necessary. Maybe we should find out if your mouth is any better at pleasing me."

He's lying. I know he is. I'd felt him inside of me, felt the way he'd lost control at the end, his mouth devouring mine as his hands roved over my body, his cock hard and throbbing as he came. I *know* he enjoyed it. But for some reason, he's bent on insisting that he doesn't want me, that sex with me is distasteful to him.

"No." I swallow hard, wrenching my chin out of his grasp and backing away. If there's one thing I *know* I don't want, it's Luca fucking me while acting as if he doesn't want it. That would make it so much worse. It's confusing enough the way he makes me feel without complicating it even more. "Fine. I'll stay here until the Bratva is no longer a threat."

"Good." Luca straightens, his expression pleased. "Now that you're my wife, Sofia, and I've taken on my new responsibilities, it's important that you know the high-ranking members of the family, their wives, and their positions. I'll leave an iPad for you that Carmen can upload all of those details to—study it the way you would for an exam," he adds, "because I'll expect you to know every word. It's important that you not embarrass me at any events we might have to attend together. Charity galas and the like." He frowns. "I hope you aren't going to argue with me about that?"

His voice is cold again, reserved and formal, and I swallow past the lump in my throat. My husband has so many different sides to him, and I don't understand any of them—what makes him switch from one to another.

"No," I say quietly.

"That's good to hear," Luca says, looking sideways at me as he strides to the closet. "I have a great deal of responsibility now, Sofia. I need a woman who can be at least a *decent* wife to this family and me."

His cutting tone tells me everything that I need to know about how much faith he has that I can do that. And the truth is that he has every reason to feel that way—I don't want to be here, I don't want to be his wife at all, let alone a *good mafia wife*. But for some reason, the way he said it made me feel even worse than before.

I sink onto the edge of the bed, sitting there speechlessly as Luca gathers up his suit and goes into the bathroom to change. When he emerges, he barely even looks at me. "I'll have Carmen send that information for you to study. I'll ask you about it when I return." He glances over at me then, his expression flat and emotionless. "Don't try anything stupid, Sofia."

And then he strides out, leaving me there without another word, a goodbye, or anything else. It underscores more than ever what a sham this marriage is, how behind closed doors it's nothing but a lie, one constructed to protect me that might not even be able to do that now.

When I hear the front door shut and I know I'm truly alone, I can't help myself. The weight of everything that's happened in the past days comes crashing down, and I roll over onto my side on the bed, burying my face in my arms.

And just like that, I burst into tears.

LUCA

3

The fight with Sofia leaves me feeling exhausted.

If I'm being honest, it's not just the fight with her. It's everything else that's happened too—the drama of our wedding night, the attack on the hotel, the injuries that put me in the hospital, the sudden transference of Rossi's title from him to me, and everything that entails.

But in the end, that all circles back to one person—Sofia. Without her, none of this would have happened. And although I'd never want to or sanction killing her, I can suddenly see why Rossi felt it was the most expedient solution. The fight we just had only made me more frustrated with her and her inability to stop being contrary over every single fucking thing I tell her to do.

It doesn't help that just being near her is enough to turn me on, and fighting with her—seeing her skin turn that pretty shade of pink, seeing her eyes blaze and that delicate pointed chin turn up, seeing the way she quivers with rage—all of that makes me harder than I've ever been in my life. Now that we've gotten past the hurdle of taking her virginity, all I want to do is toss her into my bed and spend a solid weekend inside of her, doing nothing but fucking her in every possible way until we're both wrung completely dry.

This is why I need to do anything but—exactly why I've made a point of making her think that I'm completely turned off by her innocence and lack of experience, when in fact, it's the exact opposite. Because I don't need the distraction. It's hard enough for me to keep my lust for her under control. So every time we wind up face to face, it's just a case of me protesting too much that I want nothing to do with her sexually.

When in fact, I want to do *everything* with her sexually.

Sixteen years of fucking every woman I can get my hands on, and no one has ever captivated me like Sofia Ferretti—no, make that Sofia *Romano*. She's got my last name now, which is yet another thing that drives me absolutely mad when it comes to her.

I've given her everything—my protection, my name, my home, my security and wealth, my cock, and anything else that she might need to keep her safe and protected. Yet, she acts as if I'm torturing her by insisting she follows a few simple instructions. It's maddening, and it makes me want to strangle her.

Something that could just as easily be accomplished with my cock down her throat instead of my hands around her neck.

I shake off the thought, gritting my teeth as I try to put Sofia out of my head. At least by the end of this particular argument, she seemed to be leaning towards compliance. I'll see how well that went when I go back home. But before then, I have any number of things I need to deal with—and the first is visiting Rossi before I go to his wife's funeral and having a discussion without so many ears in the room.

"He needs rest," the nurse tries to tell me as I stride towards his room, but I can see through the window that he's awake, and this can't wait. He'll agree with me, so I simply ignore her and reach for the door.

She nearly slaps my hand away, and I turn to glare at her, pinning her with my icy green stare. "Do you know who I am, Ms.—" I look down at her nametag. *"Browning?"*

"No, but I assume you must be family if you were allowed up here—"

"I'm Luca Romano," I tell her coldly, my voice stiff and

commanding. The authority of it feels good. "The new don for the American branch of the Italian mafia family. And if you don't know what that means, I suggest you go find your superior and tell them what I just said so that they can educate you on how to speak to your betters."

The nurse goes bone-white, and I allow myself to enjoy it for a moment. There are benefits to my new title that goes beyond wealth, and one of them I'm seeing in real-time right now.

"Of course, Mr. Romano," she says quickly, backing up so that I can walk into the room.

"Flirting with nurses again?" Rossi jokes as I stride towards his bed, pulling up one of the chairs so that I can sit.

"I'm a married man," I say mock-gravely, and Rossi snorts, pushing himself up a little.

"You know as well as I do that doesn't mean shit. I fucked more women after I was married than before, I think." He grins. "The more power and money you have, the more they line up to fall into your bed. Mark my words, you'll get more pussy now than you ever did before you took my title."

"I didn't take it," I point out. "You handed it over. I'd have been happy to keep waiting."

"Well, what's done is done." Rossi frowns, the light mood dissipating. "What did you come here to talk about, Luca? The funeral is tomorrow, yes?"

"Yes. The viewing is in the morning, the service in the afternoon." I lean forward, looking at him intently. "We need to discuss the Bratva threat and what to do about it. I know you may not like how I want to handle it, but—"

"What is there to discuss?" Rossi's voice rises. "They killed my fucking wife, Luca. We go to war and kill every last Russian dog with her blood on his hands until they're driven so far back they won't crawl out of their dens for another decade."

Well, that's about the answer I expected. I take a deep breath, steeling myself for the fight that I know is going to come. "That's not how I think we should handle it. I understand the desire for vengeance—" I

M. JAMES

say quickly, "—but that doesn't end, Vitto. It never ends. I want to take us down a different path."

"What other path is there?" Rossi growls angrily. "They killed your father, Luca. They killed Sofia's father. Your mother killed herself because she couldn't handle the fear of wondering when you'd be next. How much more blood does Viktor have to order spilled before you'll decide that they all need to die?"

"Vitto. Be reasonable." I grit my teeth, trying to keep my voice measured and the frustration clear of it. "What do you think happens if we kill Viktor Andreyev? We should take out some of his soldiers, yes. Maybe even a brigadier or two. But we can't slaughter the head of the Bratva and everyone else along with him. What does that say, to the other territories, to the Irish that we drove out of New York decades ago and have tentative peace with now if we just kill another leader? Spill his and every other Russian's blood in the streets until they're red with it? There will be no trust anymore. No reason to make treaties. It will be an all-out war, and no one will believe us when we try to make deals. Our business relies on *deals*, Vitto. Hell, we've been working with the Irish on guns for the last seven years, and it's made you a wealthy man."

"I don't give a fuck about any of that. They killed Giulia." Rossi's face reddens with rage, and for a minute, I worry he might push himself over the edge into a heart attack or something equally as bad.

"Forgive me for saying this, but I didn't think you were *so* in love with her, Vitto," I say calmly. "They killed her, yes. It will not go unpunished. If you want the men who planted the bombs dead, I will ask Viktor to hand them over. We'll throw them off a dock and watch them sink. But you're talking about violence on a scale that hasn't been seen in—Christ, I don't even know when. Before I was born. Maybe before my father was born."

"For Marco's son, you're more like Giovanni," Rossi says with a growl. "It's not about love, you fucking child. It's about *vengeance*. It's about them killing what was mine. Taking something that belonged to me. How would you react if it were Sofia?" He narrows his eyes. "I so much as threatened her life, and you threw away all that bachelorhood you so cherished and rushed to put a ring on her finger like a lovesick boy. And you're telling me you wouldn't paint the streets red to avenge her death."

I try to think of it, just for a moment. And I know he's not wrong. I think of the blood splattered across the hotel room walls when I went in to rescue her from Mikhail, the dying gargles of all those men, the teeth on the concrete floor when I tortured one of Viktor's soldiers to get the location. Would I do that and more if she were dead?

I want to say that I'm not sure. I want to say that I know it wouldn't bring her back, that I'd think of the good of the family, that I'd remain clear-headed and try to do the same thing I'm doing now—make peace and bring order back to our streets.

But the truth is that I'd murder every last man who so much as thought about harming Sofia, all the way to Viktor Andreyev, and then I'd pull him into pieces and feed them to the dogs.

None of that helps now, though. None of it changes the fact that war isn't going to fix anything. It's only going to make it worse.

"I wish Giulia were still here. I do," I say calmly. "I see your pain, Vitto, and I understand your desire for revenge. But how many civilians were hurt in that explosion?" I pause, looking at him. "We're going to have the law down on us too if there's too much collateral damage. And a war with the Russians will mean people dying who have nothing to do with this."

"The cops are in our pockets or theirs," Rossi says with a wave of his hand. "There will be no heat, and you know it."

"There's always a few who insist on doing their job. And if we escalate this to the point that the Feds get involved—"

"So what? Do you want to roll over and show your belly like a whipped dog? To the *Ussuri*? Fuck that," Rossi spits.

"I'm not rolling over." I can feel the last shred of my patience ebbing thin. "You made me don, Vitto. So let me be don.

"I didn't know I chose an heir who would be so weak." Rossi's voice is cutting. "I thought you were your father's son."

"I am," I say coolly. "And in many ways, yours as well. I'm not weak, Vitto. I'm trying to be practical."

There's no question that he's trying to get a rise out of me, to piss me off enough to follow his lead, but I'm not about to take the bait. I hadn't intended to rise to this position so soon, but I've always intended to lead in my own way. I'm not about to change that now.

"Hmph." Rossi snorts, turning his face away. "I'm tired. Make sure they do right by Giulia tomorrow. We'll talk about this later."

It's a clear dismissal, and part of me seethes at how he thinks he can still wave me off so easily. But I'm not about to dwell on it. I have the ring and the title now, and I intend to proceed in my own way for as long as possible, regardless of how Rossi seems to want to continue to rule through me. That will only happen if I allow it, and I don't intend to.

I decide to spend the night away from Sofia. I need time to process, to think about everything that's happened in the last forty-eight hours. So instead of going home, I send Carmen a message asking to have a fresh suit delivered to the hotel where I'll be staying. Then, give my driver the location before leaning back in my seat and pouring myself a generous slug of whiskey. I'm not usually one to drink in the afternoon, but I think now is as good a time as any to make an exception.

The hotel room is cool and fresh-smelling, perfectly made up and cleaned, one of the finest suites that they have available. I strip out of my suit immediately and hang it up, pouring another shot of whiskey from the minibar before striding into the large bathroom and turning on the taps in the shower. I down the golden drink as I wait for the water to heat up, enjoying the burn of it spreading through my chest, the smoky taste at the back of my throat.

Finally, some fucking peace and quiet. I feel more drained than I have in years; the load of responsibility on my shoulders increased tenfold. I need a moment to breathe, remember who I am and why I've done all of this for so long.

But the truth is too simple. I was born into it. I know no other life, and I don't think that I want to. And now Sofia has thrown a wrench into that. I had my future planned—continue my wealthy playboy lifestyle until the day that the title passed to me...and then keep on being a rich playboy, but with more responsibilities. Children had been out of the question, which meant a wife wasn't necessary. And love?

Love is for other men. Lesser men. My father hadn't loved my mother. Even as unsure as I am of what love really means, I know that much.

But from what I'd heard of Sofia's family, her father *had* loved her mother. And look where it had gotten them—where it got *all* of us. Sofia's father was murdered by the Bratva, my father murdered to avenge him, my mother, dead, Sofia's mother, dead. Both of us are orphans. And if Sofia's father hadn't insisted on marrying a Russian woman?

Maybe they'd all still be here. Giovanni, Marco, their wives. My parents.

Sofia wouldn't exist, though. Not without all of that.

"This is getting too fucking philosophical for my blood," I mutter aloud to the empty room, pushing the thoughts out of my head. There's no point in mulling over the past. What's done is done, and the dead are dead. They can't be brought back. All I can do is make certain that the carnage is stalled and that more don't follow them to early graves. Whatever Rossi says on the matter, I don't want war.

Rossi believes that we aren't meant to be men of peace; I've always known that. He thrives on it. But I've never been that man. I believe peace is possible for all of us if we work together. We have the same interests, after all—Russian, Irish, Italian. We want money, and power, to live life on our own terms and fuck those who want to say otherwise. We want to choose our lives and choose our ends.

So what's necessary is to find that common ground and work out among all of us how to achieve that without stepping on each other's toes. *Easier said than done.* And with Rossi trying to still rule through me, it adds another layer of complications.

I step under the hot water, groaning with pleasure as it rolls down my back, and my thoughts circle back to Sofia. She's a complication, too. I thought I would be able to neatly shelve her away post-wedding, but it's clear that won't be the case now. She'll remain in my house and my thoughts for longer than I feel comfortable with, and I don't know how to reconcile that.

It would be easier if I were a man like Rossi. But while I'm not above giving Sofia as good as she gives me, even pushing her to face her own desires like that night that I bent her over the couch, I draw the line at forcing her to sleep with me. That holds no appeal for me. I'm a violent man—but never with women, and to tell the truth, it's part of what I feel separates us from the Bratva. I would never harm a woman.

Still, Sofia is driving me fucking insane.

Just the thought of her is making me hard. I can feel my cock thickening as I stand under the water, rising stubbornly just at the memory of her warm body under my hands two nights ago, her small cry when I slid into her for the first time, the way she tightened around me, her virgin pussy clenching around my cock like she wanted me in her as deeply as possible. She might have told me to get it over with, but her body had said otherwise.

Fuck. My cock throbs, pre-cum pearling from the tip as my balls tighten with need, and I groan, unable to stop myself from wrapping my hand around my thick length and stroking slowly. It's just my luck that when I was forced to marry, I've been given a bride that refuses to play the part of a dutiful wife. There are so many pleasures I could introduce her to. So many things I could teach her. I think of how soft her lips felt under mine, how they parted as her cheeks flushed when I thrust into her, and how good they would feel wrapped around my cock.

My whole life, I've said I despised sleeping with virgins, that they were clingy and no good in bed, that my rule to never sleep with the same woman twice meant that to me, a virgin meant nothing more than a bad lay. But Sofia is *mine*.

I could train her to my pleasure. Teach her to suck my cock the way I like, to take it deep in her throat, to look up at me with those pretty dark eyes as her lips purse and redden around my shaft from the strain of taking all of me. And I've never been a selfish lover. I'd reward her with my tongue on her pussy, licking her to as many orgasms as she could stand. I'd make her limp with pleasure before taking her in every position I can think of to teach her. Just the thought of Sofia atop me, her breasts bouncing as she rides my cock, of her upturned ass if I took her roughly from behind, is enough to bring me to the brink of orgasm.

My cock throbs in my hands, my aching balls warning me that I'm close, and the urge to stroke harder and faster hits. I could be finished in a matter of seconds and have some relief. But for whatever reason, I slow down, savoring the sensation of skin on skin as I picture all the ways I could take my new bride, all the things I could make her do if only she'd give in.

I could break her to my will, I think, groaning as my palm rubs over the slick head of my cock. *I could make her accept that she wants me. Make her be my wife in all ways.*

I let the fantasy overtake me for a moment, even as I know that I won't do it. It's too much of a distraction when I have a war to stave off, an organization to run, and the Bratva to bring to heel. A desire to remain emotionally unattached isn't the only reason I've avoided sleeping with the same woman more than once.

It's also to keep myself from losing direction, from being so immersed in pleasure that I forget what it takes to keep all I've earned for myself. And up until now, there's never been a woman who could threaten that.

Standing in the luxurious shower, my hips thrusting into my fist as I work myself to the edge of climax again, it's clear that's changed. I've lost count of how many times I've pleasured myself now thinking about Sofia, how many times her pretty face and full lips and perfect figure have been what flashes in front of my eyes as I climax. Whether I ever touch her again or not, she's become something close to an obsession. Something that threatens to destroy the careful control and discipline that I've built up over so many years.

Just call someone. Just go out. Just fuck some other woman for God's sake, I think even as a flood of images fill my mind—Sofia on her knees, Sofia bent over, Sofia taking me in her mouth and moaning around my cock as I lick her pussy at the same time, choking on my length as I make her come. Sofia trying not to look at me as I took her virginity, the sweet wet heat of her clamped around me, a tightness I'd never felt before, a pleasure I hadn't imagined I could have with her. I'd been lying when I said that it was bad—I'd never felt anything like that orgasm. All I'd wanted was to rip that fucking condom off and feel her pussy clenched around my bare cock, filling her with my seed until there was nothing left for me to give her.

"Fuck! Fuck—oh god, fucking hell—" I groan as my cock erupts in my fist, cum spraying over the wall of the shower as my balls tighten to the point of pain, my muscled thighs rigid with the effort of it. It feels as if it'll never stop, and I jerk harder, imagining all of that cum painting Sofia's breasts, her face, her lips, her swallowing it, burying it deep inside of her, how good it would feel—

I'm panting by the time my cock stops pulsating, leaning against the side of the shower with the water still pouring over me. I know what I need to do, just as I've known since the night I pinned Sofia up against my front door and realized the kind of desire she arouses in me.

I need to find some other woman, maybe more than one, hell—as many as I can bring back to this hotel room, and fuck Sofia out of my head. I need to take this all out on as many willing bodies as I can manage until I remember that no woman holds this kind of sway over me, and exactly why I've remained single all my life.

But even as I catch my breath, I know I won't. I won't fuck anyone tonight, and probably not tomorrow either. I won't go out. I'll order room service, and I'll drink as much as I can out of the minibar. Then I'll probably jerk off again, maybe even twice, thinking about Sofia. Thinking about everything I want from her but refuse to take.

I remember Rossi in the hospital room, calling me weak. I'll never believe that wanting peace over war makes me a weak leader. But just now, with my cock deflating against my thigh after weeks of only self-pleasure interrupted by just that one night with my now-wife, I'm not sure that I don't have a weakness after all.

If I'm weak in any way, it's because of Sofia, and only her. And there's one thing that I've been taught all my life.

A man in my position can have no weakness.

SOFIA

4

I don't know what to do with myself all day. I take a shower after Luca has left, lingering in there for as long as I can until my skin turns pink and my fingertips wrinkle, trying to push our argument and everything he'd said out of my mind. I try to focus on the good things—the luxurious herbal scent of the shampoo I'd brought into Luca's bathroom from mine, the vanilla honey shower gel, the dual showerheads that make it feel as if I'm in the fanciest hotel I've ever stayed in. I'd thought my bathroom was ridiculous, but Luca's is even more so. The tiles are heated, the bathtub massive, the shower just as big. I try to focus on that pleasure, enjoying washing the lingering smell and feel of the hospital off of me until I feel refreshed physically, at least.

And then, not an hour after he'd left, I wander into the living room to find an iPad left for me on the coffee table just as he'd said, with a sticky note attached to it that has a passcode written in bold letters. *Someone already dropped this off. Is there anything he wants done that doesn't happen immediately?*

I type in the passcode to find the internet access and text messaging is disabled and only a single app for documents, with everything Luca must have asked Carmen to send over downloaded.

A quick glance shows that they contain family trees, names of high-ranking members and wives and children, the mistresses of the men who were brought to events instead of their wives, everything I could possibly need to know about the family in order to politely converse at events and nothing else. Nothing interesting, no private information, no business dealings. Just the most tepid details for me to recite if need be, like Luca's pretty little puppet.

Just looking at it makes me burn with resentment. *Luca's gone back on everything he promised,* I think bitterly. He'd promised to leave me a virgin, and here I am, deflowered and insulted on top of it. He'd promised to give me my own apartment, and now not only am I stuck in his penthouse for an indeterminate amount of time, but I'm forced to share a *bed* with him. He'd promised me we'd hardly have to see each other after the wedding, and now nothing could be further from the truth.

Now he's handed me homework.

I'm not fucking doing it. Rebellion rises up in my gut, hot and bitter, and I toss the iPad aside on the couch. *Luca can go fuck himself.* I don't want to learn the names of the men in his organization, all of whom have controlled my life since I was a child without my even knowing it. I wonder how many of those men were the ones in suits who used to come to our apartment; if any of them were the ones who came to take my mother away for questioning, who bruised her face and threatened her.

I hate them. I hate every last fucking one of them. *I wouldn't care if they all died,* I think, and as awful as the thought is, I let myself bask in it for a minute, because it feels good to be angry. It feels good to be petty, to let myself think the worst thoughts I could conjure. After all, those men get to do whatever they want, without consequence.

And the women, like Caterina, like me, like our mothers, pay the price.

It should have been Rossi who died in that blast, not Giulia. It should have been any of the men. *Even Luca.*

The thought surprises me. I don't mean it, I know that, but it feels good to let myself think it, just for a moment. I'm so angry that it feels l like I was boiling over with it.

I glance over at the discarded iPad. If I'm going to do what Luca instructed me to—and just thinking of it in those terms makes me even angrier—then what *will I* do with the day? I have the penthouse to myself, and I might as well make the best of it.

In the end, I decide to spend the afternoon on the rooftop, by the pool. Rebelliously, I go behind the wet bar and proceed to do the one thing I haven't done before—drink. There's every imaginable kind of top-shelf liquor and mixers in the stainless-steel, glass-doored refrigerator behind the bar, and I dig out a bottle of tequila and watermelon margarita mix. If Luca is going to leave me here and insist that I can't go anywhere on my own, I'm going to make him pay for it.

Even if that just means drinking up as much of his expensive booze as I can and ordering out the priciest food I can imagine. Carmen usually checks in sometime in the late afternoon to find out what I might want for dinner since Luca and I have yet to eat together. Apparently, it's been assumed that I can't cook, and even though I *can*, I'm happy to let Luca foot the bill for me to eat without having to prepare it myself.

With a watermelon margarita on the rocks in hand, complete with a sugar rim, I stretch out on one of the lounge chairs poolside, closing my eyes and soaking in the sun. Late spring in New York is rarely this warm, but we've had several hot days these past weeks, and I'm not going to complain. At least out here, on the rooftop, I feel like I can breathe just a little better. Luca's penthouse is undeniably *his*, all of it carefully curated to ooze power and masculinity, and it makes me feel as if I'm suffocating.

Having my own room, with my own things that he'd given me the night before the wedding, had made it slightly more tolerable. And now, even that space has been taken away. Sure, I can spend time there during the day, it's only at night that I have to sleep in his room. But it's not the same. It no longer feels like my escape, a place where I can sleep in peace and feel almost safe again.

The thought of spending every night beside Luca makes my

stomach clench with anxiety. How many nights will pass before he gets tired of sleeping next to a warm body that he can't fuck? How long before he brings a woman home? I'm surprised it hasn't happened already. Where would he do it? In a guest room? In *my* room?

It's not even really mine, I remind myself. I tip my glass back, drinking the margarita fast enough to give me brain freeze and make me wince. Still, I get up to make another almost immediately. I want to stop thinking about Luca. I want him out of my head, even if I have to get blackout drunk to do it.

But I can't. I drink three more margaritas on the rooftop as the afternoon passes, getting into the cool water of the pool and back out again to stretch out in the sun like a cat, trying to think of anything other than my cold, confusing husband. But it's impossible. Every time I look to my left, my ridiculously massive ring glints in the sunlight. Every time I look around, I'm reminded that none of this is mine, it's all his, and I only have it at all because of the vows I took forty-eight or so hours ago.

There's nothing else to think about because everything I had before is gone. My education, my career, my travel plans, my hopes. I don't know what my future will be like. It hinges on Luca's uncertain dealings with the Bratva and their willingness to back down. And if they don't?

Who knows what will happen then.

I'm supposed to be safe. Marrying Luca was supposed to keep me safe. But I still feel as uncertain and afraid as I did that night that Mikhail dragged me out of the nightclub.

After a while, when I can feel my skin starting to get a little too pink and I've exhausted my ability to drink another margarita, I wobble back down to the penthouse and put in my order for dinner with Carmen. Still seething, I order the most expensive four rolls from a nearby sushi restaurant that I can find on their menu and then go in search of more alcohol.

I'd expected Luca to come back at some point. After all, he'd said that the funeral wasn't until tomorrow. But as the evening wears on and the clock goes from eight to nine, nine to ten, then I start to wonder if he's coming back at all tonight. I ate my dinner in the movie room, lounging in one of the recliners with my sushi arrayed out on the pull-out tray, a gin and tonic sitting next to it. I'm barely paying attention to the movie, some bloody slasher flick that fits my mood, my thoughts still consumed with Luca as I pick at my sushi.

If he's not coming home, there's a reason for it. And I can only think of one reason that makes sense to me at the moment.

He's with another woman. Maybe more than one. He didn't want to deal with the drama of bringing someone back to the penthouse with his wife there, so he's probably gotten a hotel room somewhere to do exactly what he said he would—fuck someone who will do what he wants and be good at it. Someone who can please him. Maybe several someones.

Maybe my husband is having a fucking orgy right now in some luxurious Manhattan hotel suite.

To my horror, I feel tears burning at the back of my eyelids. There's no reason for that. I shouldn't be upset; if anything, I should be *grateful* that Luca is with some other woman and not bothering me.

But I don't feel that way. I feel hurt, which is stupid. I don't want Luca in my bed, so I shouldn't care if he's in someone else's.

I don't want him. Right? *Right?*

I think about our wedding night, trying to remind myself of exactly what it is that I don't want. But I suddenly can't seem to remember how scared and upset I was to find out that Rossi was forcing him to take my virginity. I can't seem to remember why I'd told him to get it over with. All I can remember is the way his fingers had felt grazing over my spine as he'd undone the back of my dress, how gorgeous his naked body had been. I'd never seen a naked man in person before, but I'm certain that his cock was the most perfectly made that it could be. Long and thick and straight, nearly pressing up against his belly, he'd been so hard.

Because of *me*. He'd wanted *me*. No matter how much he tries to deny it.

I rarely thought about sex before Luca. I'd only ever gotten myself off a couple times when I'd been so curious I couldn't resist. I'd been too busy with other things to really make physical pleasure, with myself or anyone else, a priority. But now, alone in the movie room, I forget about the fact that I'm supposed to despise my husband. I forget that there might be cameras, that anyone might see. The memory of Luca stalking towards our bridal bed, his face dark and determined, his body rippling with muscle, his cock rock-hard from the sight of me naked atop it, is making me wet despite myself. I can feel it, how hot and slick I am at my core, the thin cloth of my lounge shorts clinging to me.

It's easy to slide the fabric aside, pushing the tray away so that I have more room, my legs spreading slightly apart as I tease myself just a little, sliding one finger up the crease of my pussy. I remember Luca calling it that the night he bent me over the couch, telling me how wet I was for him, how much I wanted him.

And I had. But I'd told myself it was because Luca was there touching me, saying those dirty things to me, forcing my body to respond. That was why I'd been so wet, why I'd wanted to kiss him back, why I'd wanted so badly to come when he'd played with me that night on the couch.

He's not here now, though. He's not making me slide my finger between my folds, dragging the tip of it through the arousal gathered there up to my clit, making a small circle around that hardened nub until I gasp and my hips arch up. He's not making me think about the way his cock had felt filling me for the first time, the first and only time a man has been inside of me, that close to me, and the way I'd regretted just for a moment telling him to get it over with.

He's not making me think about the way he'd kissed me when he lost control, the way he'd shuddered against me, the way it had felt when he'd thrust that last time. I'd known he was orgasming, that only the thin condom kept him from filling me up with his cum, that *I'd* done that. I'd made him lose control, even with all my inexperience, all my protests.

Maybe that's why. He got off because he knew you didn't want it.

That's the worst possibility, of course. But I don't think that's the case. I don't think Luca likes forcing me because he wouldn't have made me sleep with him on our wedding night. Since then, he's gone to great pains to make me think that he doesn't want to again.

But I'm not sure I believe it.

I know that all of this is the product of my feverish mind, muddled with all the alcohol I've drunk today and overcome with a sudden rush of desire for a man I know I don't really want. Even still, I let myself imagine for just a moment what he might do if I gave in. If I said I wanted him.

Would he do the things Ana used to gleefully tell me about after her best dates? Things I hadn't imagined doing before now? Would he go down on me, lick me where my fingers are stroking right now, circle my clit with his tongue like I am with my finger, keep going until I cried out and came? How would he fuck me if I let him?

I can hardly imagine it. Part of me feels detached, unable to believe that I'm masturbating in the middle of this room right now, my thin shorts pushed aside and my bare pussy on display for anyone who might walk in. But I can't seem to stop. I push two fingers inside myself, trying to pretend that it's Luca's cock, trying to decide if that arouses me, but it can't possibly feel as big as he had. Still, my thumb rubbing over my clit makes my hips buck up into my hand, my breathing coming faster and faster as I try to imagine his mouth on me instead, his head buried between my thighs.

"Oh god—" I moan aloud, my thighs tensing as I realize out of the blue that I'm about to come. It feels stronger than any time I've done this before, the pressure building until I'm desperate for it, almost as good as when Luca teased me to the edge that night that he came all over my ass, his hot seed dripping down the curve of my cheek, over my thigh—

"Fuck!" I squeal with surprise, unable to believe that last thought pushed me over the edge as my whole body starts to shudder, pleasure sweeping over me. I moan and writhe in the seat, feeling the wet heat that spreads over my fingers onto my hand, my clit pulsing under my thumb.

And then, as the waves of my orgasm recede and the room comes back into focus, I realize exactly what I just did.

"Oh my god." I yank my shorts back into place, my cheeks flushing red. There's no place in this apartment that doesn't have cameras except for the bathroom, I'm sure of it. Luca's mentioned to me several times how much security there is here. What if one of his guards saw me? What if *Luca* looks back at the footage and sees me?

My heart is pounding, from the orgasm or the fear of getting caught, I'm not sure. He'll never let me live it down if he sees it, that's for sure. And if he finds out that one of his guards saw it—

Will he punish them? Will he punish *me*? I swallow hard, ignoring the small shiver of arousal that creeps down my spine at the thought.

Without another thought, I grab my drink, picking up my takeout trays of sushi and flinging them into the trash. My appetite is completely gone, my entire body numb now with the realization of what I just did, and I'm horrified with myself.

I just masturbated for the first time in a year or more, probably, and I did it thinking about *Luca*. My husband. The man who forced me to give up my virginity. The man who cut into my thigh afterward when I didn't bleed. The man who could have come up with that idea in the first place and kept me from having to sleep with him at all.

I feel sick all over again.

The drink is gone by the time I make it to the bedroom, and I set the glass on the dresser, not caring if Luca sees it later. My head feels dizzy with alcohol, my skin flushed and itchy, and I can't remember the last time I was this drunk. Maybe never.

I manage to make it into the shower and stand under the hot spray of water until I lose track of time, leaning against the wall. I try to push the thought of what I just did out of my head, convince myself that Luca won't find out, won't care, won't do anything if he does.

Even though I know that's not true.

I feel worn down and exhausted by the day, by everything preceding it. At some point, I get out of the shower and half-heartedly dry off, stumbling into the bedroom. I feel my stomach twist with trepidation and nausea as I climb into the massive bed, sitting awkwardly in the middle for a minute.

Which side is Luca's? Which side will he want me to sleep on? Does it matter?

The thought seems so ludicrous I want to burst out laughing. I almost do, a squeak of it escaping from my lips as I sit in the middle of the dark grey duvet in the unfamiliar bedroom, in a bed that's not mine.

Finally, I just pick a side. I crawl under the comforter, remembering the first night I woke up here in this bed, before I knew about any of this—before I knew that Luca would be my husband, before I knew that everything I'd dreamed about was gone.

I wonder what it will be like when he inevitably comes back when he's in bed next to me. I reach out and place my hand on the cool spot on the other side, where the sheet is smooth and undisturbed, the pillows neatly stacked. At some point, there will be a person here. My husband.

I'd never shared a bed with anyone before my wedding night. Now I'll share one every night with a man I should loathe, but who I clearly have far more complicated feelings about.

And I don't have the slightest idea what to do about that.

LUCA

5

When I wake up in the morning, the first thing I do is take two aspirin for the throbbing headache that threatens to split my skull, courtesy of too much whiskey the night before.

The second is to call the number that I know will put me in touch with Viktor's right-hand man, Levin. There's no number to speak to Viktor Andreyev directly, but this is almost as good. And I need Viktor to know I'm serious.

"Yes?" The thick, deeply accented voice comes over the line after one ring. "Who is this?"

"Luca Romano. Don't hang up," I say sharply. "You'll want to listen to this."

"I doubt it. But please, continue."

"I need to meet with Viktor."

There's a snort on the other end of the line. "And why should the *Ussuri* meet with you? Tell me, please, why you are so worth his time, *underboss*."

"Well, for one," I say coolly, "I'm no longer the underboss. As of yesterday, I have taken over Rossi's place as don. I would have thought Viktor's eyes and ears would have heard that already."

There's a momentary silence on the other line. I'm sure someone will bleed tonight for not finding that information out sooner. But that's not my problem.

"And Rossi?" Levin's voice is guarded now.

"In the hospital. He'll live, but he's angry. He wants war for his wife's death. As I'm sure Viktor expects that he might."

"And you don't?"

"No," I say evenly. "I don't. So I wish to speak to Viktor and see what we can do. I don't want there to be more bloodshed if it can be avoided."

"Bold words from a man who recently painted a hotel room red with our men."

"You stole something that belonged to me."

"Viktor would say she ought to have belonged to *him*."

That startles me, but I'm careful not to let Levin hear it in my voice, or falter in the slightest. If I'm going to achieve what I want, I have to be certain that the Russians sense no weakness.

Not even Sofia. *Especially* not Sofia.

"I'm sure if Viktor and I speak, we can work this out. I don't wish for anyone else to die. We can stop this now, if we can come to terms. I also want him to agree not to take further measures against us today. Giulia Rossi's funeral is this afternoon, and I think it's not too much to ask to allow us to lay her to rest without the fear of further attacks on our women and children. We men can fight another day if need be."

There's a long pause, and I almost wonder if Levin's hung up. Finally, his voice comes over the line again, crackling slightly with static.

"I'll relay the message. But no promises."

And then the phone goes dead.

Well, better than nothing, I suppose. If Viktor insists on war, it'll be difficult to stop. I need to nip this in the bud before he can take any additional steps, or Rossi can recover enough to do anything to make matters worse.

An hour later, I'm freshly showered and dressed in the suit that

Carmen sent over; I pick at the tray of breakfast that room service sent up as I check my emails on my phone. It occurs to me that I could have one of the guards connect me with Sofia to see how she's doing. I could even just check in with them and make sure that she's alright. But I push the urge away.

If there had been even a hint of danger last night, I would have been alerted. And I don't know how she'll react to my absence last night or what she'll say to me today. All of my focus needs to be on negotiating with Viktor and ending this threat.

I steel myself for the day ahead of me as I settle into the car to be driven to the funeral home. Since I received the news of Giulia Rossi's death, I've had a slow-simmering anger building in my gut that's been difficult to hold back.

I knew Giulia since I was a child, of course. My father didn't try to keep his family apart from the mafia dealings the way Giovanni did. Then again, my father married a good Italian woman, the daughter of the former Los Angeles underboss just before he passed away. My mother didn't love the life, but she'd been born into it and raised knowing what her place was. We had many dinners over at the Rossi's grand mansion; occasionally, they even deigned to come to our smaller brownstone.

Giovanni Ferretti was at those dinners often, of course, but always without his Russian wife and half-Russian daughter. It was an unspoken rule—he'd gotten away with marrying her, but she would always be kept as out of sight as possible.

Sofia's father failed to prepare her for an inevitable future as a mafia wife in so many ways because he was an unusual man. Even before his marriage, he'd been almost monk-like, refusing to take part in the sex, drinking, and gambling that most of us enjoy. He'd had as much wealth as any of us and plenty of power as Rossi's third, but he'd kept to himself, preferring books and music at home over late nights out and picking up women.

I hadn't seen any of that personally, of course, but I'd heard my father talking about it. Rossi had mentioned it more than a few times in my adulthood after both Sofia's father and mine were gone. Rossi had lamented sending him on the trip that took him to Moscow and introduced him to Irina Solovyova.

There are plenty of rumors about Irina, all of which I've heard at one point or another. Some say Giovanni saved her from a marriage she didn't want. Others whisper that Sofia wasn't Giovanni's at all, that Irina was already pregnant, and the man whose baby it was planned to kill them both.

Others have circulated, too, of course. It's my opinion that none of it is true. Giovanni was just a stupid man besotted by a beautiful woman who broke every unspoken rule that we have to bring her back to the States after a hasty wedding.

The story of Giovanni and Irina, while a romance to some, was taught to me as a lesson. This life is our bride for men of our rank, and any other woman, wife or no, will never be more than a mistress. Money, power, and the continuation of all that has been built before us and all that will come after should be our great loves—the love of another person—a wife, a child—doesn't factor into the kind of life we should expect to live. That is for other, lesser men.

Giovanni loved his wife and his daughter. But in the end, it earned them nothing. He's long dead, followed by my father, and his wife is dead too, lost to cancer that appeared as if from nowhere shortly after. Sofia is trapped in a marriage with me, a marriage she doesn't want—and to be honest, I'm feeling more than a little trapped, too.

My thoughts circle back to Giulia, Vitto Rossi's lovely wife. Even in her older age, she was still elegant, the kind of woman often called *handsome* by others in her later years. She was kind to my mother after my father was killed. She tried to do what she could for me after my mother committed suicide.

But by then, there wasn't much she *could* do. I was in my late teens, and Rossi had firmly taken me under his wing, preparing me for the position I would soon fill, protecting me from the rumblings all around us. There were plenty of older men who thought *they* should have been chosen to step into my father's place instead of his barely-legal son being elevated. But Rossi was the don, and no one would argue with him to his face.

Behind his back, though, there has always been dissent about whether or not I deserve what I've been given. There are plenty who think I don't—that I haven't earned it, which at first was true.

I'll be damned, though, if I haven't done all I could in the years since to earn my place at the head of the table. I've tortured, maimed, and killed for Rossi, ran his businesses, and handled his deals. I like to think that the teenage boy who became the youngest underboss to ever grace the Manhattan seat is long gone.

I became a man in this life under Rossi's tutelage. And I feel as much rage as he does that the only woman who gave a damn about me after my mother's death, who tried to mother me in her place when she could, is dead because of the Bratva.

Because of Sofia. That small voice still won't go away, the one that reminds me constantly that Sofia is the reason for all of this. The reason for Bratva's persistence. The reason why I'm married now. The reason why the hotel was attacked.

And I can't figure out why she's so goddamned important to anyone. A little half-Russian, half-Italian orphan violinist. The daughter of a former underboss, sure. But there are plenty of underbosses with daughters. I haven't seen the Bratva bombing hotels to get to them.

Deep down, I'd love to cut a bloody swath through the Bratva and get vengeance for Giulia just as much as Rossi would. And yet, I'm trying to broker peace. For my wife's sake. For all the other wives, mothers, and children who don't want to lose their husbands, fathers, and sons. Who doesn't want to die as collateral damage to a life they didn't choose.

The car pulls up in front of the funeral home, and I can see people already filing in. Franco is at the door when I walk up, and I frown, glancing over at him.

"I thought you'd be with Caterina."

"She can manage on her own. I was waiting for you. We should talk about what comes next."

"There will be time for that later. You should be with your fiancée. Be a good future husband to her."

Franco snorts. "You're one to talk," he says, his voice too light for the occasion. But he turns and retreats inside anyway.

He's right, of course. I'm hardly one to talk. I'm far from a good husband to Sofia, and I have no real intentions of ever becoming one. Still, Caterina is a good woman and a good potential wife—almost *my* wife, if not for the promise that had bound me to Sofia.

She's lucky she didn't wind up married to me. I'd thought Franco would be a better husband for her, for all his philandering ways. But it seems like he isn't quite living up to the job.

I'll talk to him, I think absently, as I hover at the door. *I'll impress upon him the necessity of making your wife feel cared for, even if you aren't faithful. Even if you don't love her.*

Even just thinking it makes me feel like a hypocrite. I might be faithful to Sofia at the moment, but words like *love* or *caring* certainly wouldn't describe our relationship. In fact, what I feel for her is toeing the line of obsession. A dangerous distraction. A lust like nothing I've ever felt.

Definitely not love.

This is the last place that I want to allow thoughts of Sofia to creep in, though, and I force myself to focus on the here and now, striding into the funeral home to find Franco and Caterina. They're both standing near the front of the viewing room, Caterina in a black knee-length dress with a sweater over it against the chill of the building and a short, netted veil pinned over her eyes to her upswept hair. Her eyes are red-rimmed, and her face is pale, but she's remarkably composed, standing tall with her shoulders back and not leaning on Franco.

Maybe she's sensing that he's not going to be a husband that she *can* lean on, but I personally think it's just that Caterina takes after her mother. Guilia was a strong woman, and I feel another flash of resentment that she's lying cold in a coffin instead of still alive and vibrant.

I thought I'd grown used to death, but maybe we never get used to the senseless ones. The deaths that are too soon. The ones close to us.

"You should talk to Sofia," I say quietly to Caterina, in between talking to the other mourners and family members stopping by to comfort her. "She knows something about losing a parent."

Caterina smiles thinly. "So do you."

"I'm not the best at comforting." I give her a small half-smile, reaching down to squeeze her hand briefly. "But tell me if Franco isn't doing his part, and I'll get him in line."

"He's doing his best." Caterina's voice sounds small and far away.

I know that probably isn't the case. I glance over to see Franco talking to the capo from Newark, his attention already diverted away from his future wife. "He hasn't had much responsibility until now other than being my friend and backing me up. But he'll come around. He'll grow into the role."

"He's a boy," she says quietly. "But I'd rather that than some of the men I could have been given to as a wife. At least Franco won't beat me or treat me like a broodmare. And I never expected a particularly loving or faithful husband. One that's kind is enough."

"Franco is that, I suppose." At least, I've never known him to be maliciously cruel. Teasingly cruel, maybe, but never with the intent to hurt anyone. And he's never been called on to do the things I've had to do for Rossi. He's been my sidekick all our lives, the Robin to my Batman. The one who's never had to be serious, who I've always tried to shield from those who would spread gossip about him or try to bully him.

Things are going to change now. And as I watch Franco move through the room with his easy, charming grace, his red hair standing out like a beacon among the sea of dark-haired men and women, I feel a slight unease forming in my stomach.

I hope that he's up to the task.

LUCA

6

It starts to rain as Giulia Rossi's casket is being lowered into the ground. The cemetery turns into a field of black umbrellas. Caterina is crying quietly, her gloved hand pressed over her mouth, and even Franco has grown solemn, his hands crossed in front of him as he stands beneath the umbrella that he's holding over them both.

Up on the hill where the road runs past, I see a long black car pull up. A moment later, two thickly built men step out, wearing jackets too warm for the weather that almost definitely are concealing guns, and I know with a tightening in my gut who it must be.

Viktor Andreyev.

I lean towards Franco. "I'll be back in a moment," I say quietly and nod towards the hill where the car is idling. Franco follows my gaze, and I see a flicker of nervousness cross his face.

"Do you want me to go with you?" His voice is low, anxious, and I shake my head.

"Stay here with Caterina. I'll be fine."

"I'm your second-in-command. I should be at your side—"

"Today, you're her husband-to-be. She just lost her mother, Franco, and Rossi is still in critical condition. Have some compassion." My tone is harsher than it's ever been with him. Still, I'm beginning to worry that the easygoing life Franco has led in my shadow, has failed to prepare him for his new position.

Maybe I should have been harder on him, the way Rossi was with me.

But there's nothing I can do about that now.

I stride up the hill, feeling a faint sheen of sweat down my back that makes my shirt cling to me uncomfortably. I haven't been face to face with Viktor since my father was killed, when he and Rossi came to a temporary peace. The memory of that, too, burns in my gut. Rossi was willing to make peace then, but not now.

Then, it was Viktor who came asking for a cease-fire, though. We killed more Russians that week than we had in decades.

The car windows are tinted too darkly to see inside, but I approach the guards surrounding the car turn to keep their eyes on me. One opens the passenger door closest to me, and a moment later, a tall, grey-suited man steps out, unfolding himself to his full height.

He looks older than I remember, although Viktor is only six or seven years older than I am—in his late thirties. He's unsmiling, his hard and clean-shaven face stony, and his ice-blue eyes are cold.

I've heard that women think he's handsome. He doesn't have a reputation for womanizing, though. His wife died last year, leaving him with two young daughters, and he has yet to remarry. I'm surprised that every high-ranking man in Russia and America hasn't been throwing their eligible daughters at him. Though maybe they have, and we just aren't aware of it. Or perhaps no one wants to marry the cold widower whose men call him *Ussuri*.

The Bear.

If I were a woman, I wouldn't be inclined to wed someone who traffics in sex slavery. The Bratva is well known for their cruel treatment of women—wives, daughters, and slaves alike. I have no reason to think that Viktor Andreyev is any different, though there were whispers that his marriage was one made out of love.

I find that laughable. Viktor is a man-made even less for love of a wife and family than I am.

"Luca Romano," Viktor speaks in a cultured Russian accent, more elegant than Levin's, or the soldiers who find themselves being tortured in our warehouses. "I heard you wished to speak with me. It's been a long time."

"Let's not pretend this is a social call. You know why I wanted to meet."

Viktor's mouth twitches with amusement. "Levin spoke to me of peace. I find that odd, considering that your don's wife was just killed. Murdered, I suppose you would call it. Although—" he pauses for effect, his cold gaze sweeping over me. "I hear, too, that you have usurped Vitto Rossi's place."

"The title was passed to me, yes." I keep my tone as even as I can, even though I can feel an unfamiliar rage starting to simmer deep in my gut. I've always been the calmest and most collected of Rossi's inner circle—that's why he so often sends me to do his dirty work. But seeing Viktor is making me want blood, despite all my protestations of wanting peace.

This man had Sofia kidnapped. I remember the bruises on her face, the fear in her eyes when she'd woken up. *He's responsible for Giulia's death.*

"And now you want to call for a cease-fire between us?" He still looks amused, and it makes me feel almost uncontrollably violent. Visions of grabbing the front of his shirt and shoving him back against his car or balling up my fist and striking the smile off of his face go through my head, but I know better. His guards would be on me in a second, and everything I'm trying to achieve would absolutely fail.

I grit my teeth, forcing myself to remain calm.

"I want peace, yes. No more explosions in hotels or shootouts in the streets. No more kidnapping and threats. Let's talk this out between us, man to man, leader to leader, and come to an agreement."

Viktor looks at me appraisingly. "And what will you give me for this peace, Luca?"

"Aren't the lives of your men enough? I wonder how they would feel if they knew how little you valued them."

M. JAMES

His expression darkens. "My men know their value to me. I ask again, what will you offer me for peace?"

"Is there something that you had in mind?"

"What if I asked you for Sofia?"

My reaction is unexpected and instantaneous; my hands clench into fists at my sides as I struggle mightily to keep my composure. I don't know what angers me more, the casual way that he spoke the suggestion, as if Sofia were a shipment of drugs to be haggled over, or the thought of what he might intend to do to her. The thought of his hands on her makes me homicidal, and for a moment, I consider embracing Rossi's desire for war. *I could wipe the city clean of these bastards.*

But not without a massive amount of blood and death on both sides. And I'm not prepared to send our men into war with the Bratva unless there's no other choice.

"Sofia is my wife now," I say coolly. "As I'm certain you know since it was our hotel that you attacked the morning after our wedding. You knew who would be there and why. But surely there are other beautiful women in this city for you to lure into your clutches and sell for a profit. I should know—I've probably fucked most of them."

Viktor chuckles, his face expressionless. "No doubt," he says dryly. "But I didn't intend to sell Sofia. I intended to marry her."

I wish that I'd been able to hide my shock. But I'm too startled by the revelation to control my face; I know that my startled reaction can be read plainly. Viktor sees it; I know he does from the pleased look that flickers across his.

"You didn't expect that."

"No," I say flatly. "Why would you want to marry her? That makes even less sense, truthfully. I can see how she would have sold for a considerable price—a beautiful, young virgin. But as a wife? You don't need a girl, Viktor. You need a woman who can mother your children."

Viktor's expression darkens. "Don't tell me what I need, Luca. Perhaps what I needed *was* that young virgin, something sweet and tight to take my mind off of the men that you've killed. Something to ease the pain of the territory you've stolen back these past years. I can only imagine how good she must have tasted—"

I let out a hiss without meaning to, my jaw clenched as I struggle not to slug him then and there.

"I see I've struck a nerve." Viktor smiles. "I suppose I shouldn't talk about your new wife that way. After all, she's a virgin no more, so it hardly matters. Still, you ask for peace but offer nothing in return. Why shouldn't I continue to try to take your territory for myself? Vitto has done such a good job brokering deals over the years. So many rich and fruitful businesses for me to step into."

"You killed Giulia Rossi," I growl, my voice deepening as my patience thins. "You're lucky we haven't already started cutting down your dogs."

Viktor's smile doesn't falter. "Casualties of war, Luca. Just like your father and Sofia's. Your mothers, too, in a way. And you want those casualties to stop. So I'll make you another suggestion since you've already taken Sofia for yourself. Give me Rossi's daughter for my wife. As you said, I need someone more able to step into the role of wife and mother, someone prepared for it. And what's more, I need the one thing my late wife wasn't able to give me."

"What's that?"

His gaze holds mine, cold and determined. "A son, of course."

"And what makes you think Caterina will provide that? Giulia only had one daughter."

"I hear it's the man who determines these things, and I have three fine brothers, all strong. And if she gives me a daughter, I'll sow her fields thoroughly until she gives me sons. I've seen her—she's a beautiful girl. Fucking her until she gives me what I need will be no issue."

"She's engaged to my underboss, Franco Bianchi," I say flatly, though I'm seething inside. "Choose a wife from your own women, Viktor. You have no need of ours."

"I've offered you a means to come to terms twice now," Viktor says coolly. "And yet you refuse. You must want war then, despite your insistence otherwise."

"Just because I'm not willing to barter Vitto's daughter doesn't mean I want war. I'm willing to deal at your table, Viktor. But we do not trade in flesh."

Viktor snorts elegantly. "Then offer me something, Luca. Or there will be no peace."

"We have a shipment of cocaine coming to the docks in a week. We'll pass it to your men instead and make up the difference with our buyer. I'll even sweeten the deal and add a handling fee." I name a figure, and Viktor laughs, a deep rolling sound that reaches down the hill and makes a few of the gathered mourners look up towards where we're standing.

"You insult me, Luca. I would have thought Vitto would teach you better than that. You steal back the woman I meant to marry, fuck her yourself, and then refuse me a bride. You don't think I have my own shipments? My own money? I want something better than your flimsy handouts. But since you clearly have nothing I want that you are willing to give, then there is nothing more for us to say."

"Wait—" I start to speak, but Viktor is already sliding back into the car, the door shutting firmly behind him. I begin to step towards it—I don't know what I mean to do exactly, yank it open? Demand that he agree?—but his guards move immediately, stepping in front of the door and blocking my path.

I know better than to try to get past them. I step back, a wave of futile helplessness crashing over me that leaves me cold and angrier than before. Viktor has left me feeling emasculated, unable to do anything about the situation, and I can feel the rage sweeping through me, tightening every muscle.

Almost everyone has dispersed by the time I reach the bottom of the hill, but Franco and Caterina are still waiting for me.

"What happened?" Caterina asks anxiously. "Who was that?"

"Viktor Andreyev," I reply tightly.

"And?" Franco looks at me, and there's a nervous eagerness about him that seems somehow off to me, though I can't quite put my finger on why. "Did you come to some kind of agreement?"

"As of right now, there have been no terms set." I look away from him at Caterina's pale face, and I feel angry all over again that I haven't been able to settle this. That the man responsible for her mother's death decided to show up now, here of all places, and I wasn't able to force him to come to an agreement. "You'll need to be married quickly," I tell them, my gaze flicking between the couple. "We'll talk to Father Donahue about moving up the wedding date. I'm sorry about the planning, Caterina. I know it will be hard without your mother and harder to rush it. I'm sure Sofia will step in to help where she can." *She better,* I think darkly, before I have a chance to stifle the thought. My patience is stretched so thin that I don't know how much of it I have left for Sofia's rebellion.

"I don't know what Viktor will do next," I continue. "But I'll continue doing what I can to keep things from escalating."

"I know you'll find a way," Caterina says softly, and I look at her, startled. "I trust you, Luca."

The words are simple, but I can hear what's behind them—that she trusts me to be a good leader, to put an end to these conflicts, to make this world that she lives in a place where she can raise the son who will inherit my seat without fearing for his life.

But right now, after my conversation with Viktor, those words make me feel worse than I ever have.

Because I'm no longer certain that I can do any of those things.

SOFIA

7

I'm in the kitchen, peeling a tangerine from the fruit bowl that's always mysteriously full—the pantry and the refrigerator are always full of food too, despite the fact that neither Luca nor I ever cook—when I hear the front door open and shut with a hard slam.

My stomach knots. I've been nauseated all day, my head aching and stomach churning from the hangover that resulted after my binge drinking yesterday, but this is something different. I'm almost certain Luca is home, and the feeling that sweeps over me is strange and unfamiliar. It feels like fear mixed with excitement. While I can certainly understand the fear, I can't come to terms with why his arrival sends a thrill through me as well, making me feel almost jittery.

It's almost as if I'm anticipating the fight we might have, the way he'll loom over me with anger, the taut, thick air between us as the tension builds. I never thought I would be someone who would get off on that sort of thing, but something about the way Luca and I clash makes me want more of it, no matter how much I tell myself I don't.

"Sofia? Sofia!"

I hear him call my name from the living room, loud and

commanding, and I walk out of the kitchen tentatively, my heart thudding in my chest. I don't know what sort of mood he's in, but I have a feeling I'm about to find out.

The lights in the living room are low, the room dim and lit mainly by the nighttime glow of the city coming in through the massive window. Luca is standing there, silhouetted by it, his suit jacket gone and his shirtsleeves rolled up. When he turns at the sound of my footsteps, I can see that he's already discarded his tie as well, the first two buttons of his shirt open. It reminds me of how he'd looked just before he left, when he told me the new terms of my living situation, and a shiver runs over my skin.

"You didn't come home last night." There's a slight quaver in my voice, and I hate it. "Where were you?"

"Does it matter?" His voice is tight and cold, and it sends another shiver through me.

"I don't know." I chew on my lower lip. "I just—I thought you'd be home."

"I thought you'd enjoy the peace." Luca's tone is deceptively calm, and I know by now that there must be something else beneath it. "Can't a husband worry about his wife's well-being?"

"You're not that kind of husband," I retort. "And you know it."

"No. I suppose I'm not." Luca hits the lights, bringing them up a fraction. "Were you a good girl while I was gone, Sofia?"

My heart stutters in my chest. *Does he know?* I haven't been a "good girl" in many ways—I didn't read a word of what was left on the iPad for me, I got blind drunk, I...

I can't even think about what I did in the movie room, or I'll blush, and then Luca will know for certain that I've done something I shouldn't.

And why shouldn't I have? I think defiantly. After all, it's my body. But it's not what I did that I feel guilty about. It's what I thought about while I was doing it. *Who* I thought about.

He takes a step towards me, and the way he moves makes me think of a prowling panther, something stalking me in the half-light of the room. "What about your lessons? Did you read what Carmen sent over?"

"I—"

"What's the name of the underboss for Miami?"

"Um—"

"Leo Esposito." Luca stops, still several inches away. "What about his wife?"

"I—"

"Bianca Esposito. They have three children." He recites it from memory, his green gaze fixed on mine. I can see something there—not desire, not quite anger. Something else, some restless emotion. "What about the underboss for Philadelphia?"

"Luca—"

"Angelo Rossi. He's young and unmarried." Luca takes two more steps towards me, and I can see the muscles working in his jaw. "Did you even look at the documents, Sofia?"

"I—no," I admit, my mouth going dry at the expression on his face. "I didn't."

"And why not?" There's that deceptive calmness as if he truly doesn't care. But I know he does. I know there's a storm brewing; I just don't know when it will hit.

There's nothing I can say. I didn't want to, and that's the only honest answer I can give. But I know that's the worst possible thing I could say to Luca. "I didn't know the password."

"It was left for you. On a note stuck to the iPad. Carmen told me."

"It must have fallen off."

Luca takes another step, closing more of the space between us, and my pulse flutters nervously in my throat. I could back up—I *should* back up, but I can't seem to make my feet move. I feel as if I'm frozen in place. "That's the first lie tonight." He holds up a finger. "You didn't read them. So what did you do while I was gone?"

"I—I went up to the pool—"

"And what did you do while you were up there?"

"I just got some sun, swam a little—" I try to swallow, but my throat feels parched. Luca seems strung tight, restless, and I know there's more bothering him than just whatever misbehaviors he's uncovered from me. My rebellions, though, might just be what pushes him over the edge.

Just the thought sends a shudder down my spine, my skin tingling to my fingertips. To my horror, I can feel that newly familiar sensation coiling in my belly, snaking its way down to my groin, and I don't understand it. This is turning me on, this game that we seem to play every time we're together, this mixture of fear and apprehension and lust that he seems to arouse in me.

Who is he turning me into?

"So you didn't get drunk on the rooftop? You didn't keep drinking all the way until you went to bed?"

"I—I don't really drink—"

"Except when you're left alone in a penthouse with unlimited alcohol, apparently." Luca takes a step back. "That's two lies." He looks down at me, his expression impassive, and some of the heat between us dissipates as he retreats. "Go upstairs, Sofia."

"But—" I look at him, confused. "Where do you want me to go?"

"You know *exactly* where I want you to go." His voice sounds almost angry now. "Don't fight with me, Sofia, or I swear by all that's holy you'll regret it. *Go upstairs.*"

I don't know what insane urge prompts me to do it—I must have a death wish. Or I'm secretly a masochist. It's the only explanation for why I, looking at Luca's stony face and cold gaze, would cross my arms over my chest and look up at him with a stubbornly lifted chin as I retort:

"I don't want to go up to your room."

"Sofia." Luca's voice holds an edge that sends another of those shivers down my spine. "You can go up on your own, and I'll join you in a moment. Or I can carry you, and I promise you will not like the mood I'm in or what happens next if you choose that path. You might not like it either way. But it's your choice."

I'm tempted to continue to defy him. But my foggy mind clears just long enough to remember what today was, what he's probably endured today, how exhausted he must be—and I feel the tiniest

M. JAMES

flicker of sympathy for him even through all my frustration, anger, and fear.

It's enough to make me concede. "Fine." I snap. "I'll go up."

"Wise choice." Luca turns away from me, crossing towards the bar. "Put on something nice. One of those little nightgowns from your closet, maybe."

My stomach clenches all over again. "You said you didn't want to have sex with me."

"I didn't say anything about that." There's the clink of ice into a glass. "Go upstairs, Sofia. I need a moment alone."

Something in his voice tells me not to push it further. I turn on my heel, fleeing towards the staircase and the momentary safety of his bedroom.

But it won't be safe for long. I didn't bring the lingerie from my closet into Luca's room—why would I? He'd made a point of sounding as if he didn't want anything to do with me sexually, and I don't want him—*I don't, I really don't*—so there's no reason. I'd planned to wear the most unattractive thing possible to bed for as long as I was forced to share one with him—the biggest t-shirts I could find, the frumpiest granny panties I could manage.

Unfortunately, I don't actually own anything like that. My usual nightwear at my old apartment was a tank top and my usual cotton boyshorts, or a *slightly* oversized t-shirt. Nothing that screamed *unsexy*. In fact, I'd venture to guess that many men would probably find what I usually wear to bed cute, if not erotic.

But I don't want Luca to think I'm cute. Or erotic. I want—

I don't know what I want.

I'm still mulling it over when the bedroom door opens, and he walks in, a half-finished glass of whiskey in his hand. "You disobeyed me," he says coldly, his gaze sweeping over my still-clothed body.

"I thought it was a suggestion," I retort defiantly. "You said to put on something nice. I happen to think this *is* nice."

There's a warning glint in Luca's eye as he looks at me appraisingly, tossing back the rest of the whiskey. Without another word, he stalks towards me, coming up short with hardly a hand's space between us as he looks down. "I don't think it's very nice at all."

I don't even have a chance to breathe, much less respond, before he reaches down and grabs the neckline of my shirt. It's a white, sleeveless button-down, and when Luca yanks downwards, the buttons go flying as the shirt rips open. I hear a few clattering against the walls as they fly across the room, and Luca looks down at my cleavage in the thin, demi-cup bra beneath it.

He's breathing more heavily now, and if I looked down, I imagine I'd see that he's hard already. The thought sends another dart of electricity over my skin, the memory of him on our wedding night coming back too vividly—the muscled ripple of his abs, the thick hard column of his erection. I try to breathe, but I can't because Luca's eyes are fixed on mine, and there's something so dark in them that I can't begin to imagine what will happen next.

I have a feeling I'm about to find out, though.

"Tell me," Luca says, his voice deeper than usual, almost a growl. "What else did you do while I was gone?"

A flush starts to spread over my skin. *He knows. He must know, somehow*—I try to imagine myself coming clean, telling him what I'd done. I try to form the words to tell my husband that I played with myself, out in the open, where anyone who walked in could have seen, where someone watching on cameras *might* have seen. I imagine Luca asking me what I was thinking about, questioning me further, and I can't even picture myself beginning to explain that. It was already so far beyond the realm of anything I'd ever done, and to actually admit it out loud—

I can't.

"Nothing," I whisper in a small voice, and I see Luca's eyes glint darkly.

"Lie number three," he murmurs.

He reaches out, his fingers running down my chest and between my breasts, and I suck in my breath sharply at his touch. It's the most gentle he's ever been, his fingertips skating over my skin and trailing over the upper curve of my breast, and I'm so distracted by it that I don't even notice him undoing his belt.

Until, with one swift motion, he wraps that free arm around my waist and heaves me back onto the bed.

Before I can move, Luca is on the bed, hovering over me as he grabs my wrists and yanks them above my head. The memory of that first night in the apartment comes back to me in a rush—him pinning my hands over my head against the door, kissing me for the first time, his mouth hot and urgent against mine—

There's the pressure of something against my wrists, something pulling tight, and I realize with a mixed rush of arousal and fear that Luca has tied my hands together with the belt. His headboard is leather, so he can't tie me to it—but I still can't do much, even if I brought my hands back over my head. And Luca is too close to me for that, his knees on either side of my hips as he maneuvers me into place, his face hovering over mine.

For a moment, with a feeling of queasy terror in the pit of my stomach, I remember the hotel room I'd woken up in. But I'd been *bound* to that bed, tied up with something like a zip-tie, not a leather belt. Not my *husband's* leather belt, and even as conflicted as I am about Luca, I can't deny that this is different.

My body certainly isn't.

I hate him. I'm sure of it. I could list off so many reasons why. The forced marriage, taking my virginity, all the ways he's gone back on his word, the homework he gave me today, the way he seemingly wants to push me aside until it's convenient for him to deal with me. The way he treats me like an annoyance, a burden—except in moments like these.

When I see my husband let go of his carefully honed control, these moments should be the most terrifying. And in some ways, they are.

But I'm also completely, undeniably turned on. I can feel it, how hot and wet and needy I am, my pussy aching—and just the thought of that word makes me flush all over again.

"I know what you did, Sofia." Luca's voice slides over me like silk, surrounding me like thick smoke, dark and seductive. "I saw the security tape. Don't you think I watched it before I let you know I was home? Don't you think I wanted to know what my wife was up to while I was gone?"

He reaches for the button of my jeans, and I try to squirm away from him. My shirt is still hanging open, my breasts covered by my bra, and Luca frowns as he looks at my cleavage.

"This won't do," he says, pressing a finger between my breasts. "You've been a naughty girl, Sofia. A slut. Spreading your legs where anyone might have seen, touching yourself, making yourself come. My guards watch those tapes if they think something might have happened that I need to be told about. Sometimes they even watch the cameras. Is that why you did it?"

He reaches into the drawer next to the bed, and I hear the sound of something being pulled out, though I don't dare turn my head to look. My blood chills as I look up at him in the dim light of the bedroom as his hand moves into view, and I see a knife—the same knife, probably, that cut my thigh on our wedding night.

"Were you hoping my guards were watching? Were you hoping one of them was jerking off, seeing your pussy on display? Was that your way of getting back at me?"

"No!" The horror in my tone is real, and for a minute, I forget everything except convincing him that's absolutely not the case. "No, Luca, I never even thought—"

"You didn't think anyone was watching?" The knife lowers, and I squirm under him, all of my arousal fleeing in cold horror. *He can't possibly be* this *angry, not after everything he's done to save me, no, he can't—*

The knife presses above my breast, and I realize dimly that Luca is cutting through my bra straps. Dizzily, it becomes clear to me that he never intended to hurt me at all—my hands are bound; this is just his way of stripping me naked...as dramatically as possible. I can almost *feel* the blood rushing back to my skin, turning it pink and then red as he cuts away the rest of my bra and then my shirt, tossing the scraps aside to the floor. I'm so relieved that for a moment, I don't even think about the fact that I'm naked—until Luca tosses the knife back in the drawer. I take in the sight of him kneeling over me, pinning my hips down to the bed, his eyes greedily running over my bare breasts.

I reflexively move to cover myself, my wrists jerking at the belt holding them together before I remember that I'm bound. Something about it sends a fresh quiver through me, and I try to squeeze my thighs together without Luca noticing, that ache returning.

"Oh, you don't like this?" My husband smiles cruelly down at me, his lips curving in a cold grin. "But I thought you liked being exposed, after what I saw on that tape. I watched it twice, just to be sure I hadn't missed anything. I saw the way you exposed yourself, running your fingers up and down. I saw how wet you were." His eyes never leave mine for a second as he slides downwards, his hands going back to the waist of my jeans.

"No, Luca, please—"

He yanks the zipper down, grabbing both my jeans and the edge of my cotton panties before dragging them down my hips. I squeeze my thighs together for a different reason now, not wanting him to see me like this, completely naked and tied up on his bed.

Except—my body is saying something completely different. There's a look in Luca's eyes that I've seen before—the night before our wedding when he bent me over the couch. A hungry, feral look, something primal in his gaze that tells me that no matter what I say, he's made up his mind what he's going to do next, and nothing is going to stop him. And that makes me wet.

So wet, in fact, that I'm afraid he'll be able to see the evidence of it on my inner thighs before he even touches me—if he plans to touch me at all.

For all I know, he just plans to strip me naked and taunt me.

"Three lies," he says as he tosses the rest of my clothing to the floor to join the shreds of my bra and shirt. "Three chances, Sofia, to come clean to me about what you did while I was gone. Three strikes." He reaches up, his hand just below my breasts, and he runs his palm down my flat, quivering stomach, stopping just above my pussy.

"Whose pussy is this, Sofia?"

"What?" I squeak. The question is so far beyond anything I've ever imagined being asked that for a second, I think he must be joking. He must be making fun of me.

His eyes meet mine, and I realize that he's not joking. He's deadly serious.

I swallow hard, licking my dry lips. "I—I don't—"

"You don't know?" Luca grabs my knees, pulling my legs apart as he kneels between them. "I should have guessed, after that little show you put on. It's time for a lesson, then."

"No!" I squeal, trying to squirm away from him. "You said you wouldn't have sex with me again, you said—"

"I know what I said!" Luca's voice booms over me, cold and commanding. "I'm not going to fuck you, Sofia. You haven't *earned* my cock in that disobedient little pussy of yours. I fucked you on our wedding night because I thought I had no other choice. But after the way you've behaved, I don't see why I should ever fuck you again."

I stare up at him, my mind a confused tangle of emotions. That's exactly what I'm supposed to *want* to hear. I should be glad to hear him say that. So why is my immediate reaction to feel hurt at his rejection? To be *upset* that he's not going to fuck me?

No one has ever confused, infuriated, upset, or turned me on as much as Luca does. And I'm fucking married to the man. I'm his *wife*, legally bound to him forever unless he agrees to let me go.

It's a nightmare.

His hand rests on my lower abdomen, right above where I can feel myself aching, *craving* touch. Craving pleasure. Craving the kind of orgasm I gave myself last night, the orgasm I know I'm now about to pay for in spades.

"I'm going to teach you a lesson," he murmurs, and I hear that dark, smoky sound in his voice again, the rasp that seems to pierce me right to my core. His hand slides downwards until he's cupping me between my legs, his palm pressed against me and the heel of his hand resting on the mound of my pussy. "And it's not going to stop until you've paid for all the lies you've told me, Sofia. Until you tell me that you understand."

"What—" I gasp as I feel his middle finger thrust inside of me

M. JAMES

suddenly. I twist wildly on the bed, and Luca surges forward, grabbing my wrists with his other hand as he looms over me, my pussy still clutched in his palm.

"You're going to be still, Sofia, and take your lesson. Or do I need to find some way to tie you down completely? Strap your wrists down to the bed, spread your legs open and tie your ankles so that you can't move?" He smiles darkly down at me. "I think I might like that. You, spread-eagled on my bed while you take your punishment."

I swallow hard, my mouth as dry as my aching core is wet. "No," I whisper, feeling as if I can't breathe. "No, I'll be still."

"Good." Luca leans back, a satisfied smile on his face, his finger still buried inside of me. And then, as he looks down at my naked, trembling body, he starts to move it.

It's torture. He doesn't touch my clit, which is practically throbbing at this point, pulsing with the desperate need for any kind of friction. He doesn't add another finger, which would give me the fullness I so desperately crave, that feeling I was introduced to on our wedding night when he thrust inside of me for the first time. He just kneels between my legs, slowly moving that one finger in and out of my soaking wet channel as it flutters and clenches around him desperately, wanting more that he refuses to give.

It slowly dawns on me that this is what he means by punishment. He's not going to spank me, or beat me, or hurt me in any way. He's just going to tease me for as long as he wants, and I would bet any amount of his money that he's not going to let me come. He'll do this for as long as it amuses him, and then he'll leave me wet and needy, craving something I shouldn't want and won't be able to have.

Luca smiles down at me. "I see that it's starting to dawn on you. You're a smart girl, Sofia. Which makes me wonder why you would do such a stupid thing? If you weren't showing off for my guards, then why? What could possibly have made you so aroused that you would do something so shameless?"

He thrusts a second finger into me, and I gasp, a whimper escaping my lips as I feel my pussy clamping down on his fingers, trying to pull him deeper inside of me despite myself. I can't stop myself from looking down, and the sight of his hand pressed between my legs sends another quiver of pleasure through me, threatening to push me closer to the edge. I wriggle despite myself, grinding against his palm. I see the ridge of his cock pressing against his trousers, thick and hard and as desperate to be set free as I am for more friction, more touch, more *anything*.

What would he do if I begged him to fuck me? The thought occurs to me as the flush of heat spreads through me, my arousal rising by degrees as Luca keeps slowly fingering me. Would he pull out his cock and thrust it into me, giving me some relief? Would he fuck me until we both came? Or would he just laugh at me and refuse, continuing to tease me until I go crazy?

The latter. Definitely that. My begging would only please him more, give him even more satisfaction from this sick game that he's playing, and I clamp my lips tightly shut, glaring up at him. *I won't beg. I won't even* moan. *Two can play this game.*

Except—as the minutes drag on, I'm not sure that I can. The pace of his fingers increases slightly, and Luca smiles as I whimper helplessly again, unable to keep myself from making any sound at all. My hips arch upwards despite myself, and Luca laughs, a dark chuckle coming from deep in his throat.

"You're *so* very wet for someone who swears they don't want me," he taunts. "I saw how wet you were on that security tape, too, Sofia. Your pretty little pussy was so drenched I could have seen it from a mile away. And the *sound* you made when you played with yourself." He licks his lips, looking down at me. "How did it feel when you touched your clit? Did it feel like this?"

He pulls his hand back, his fingers still inside of me as he suddenly presses his thumb against my aching clit, and I let out a yelp of pleasure before I can stop myself, a sound that fades into a long moan as he starts to rub. "Oh yes. That sound." His expression darkens. "What were you thinking about, Sofia, that made you so wet?"

I shake my head. I won't say it. He can't make me, he *can't*. But I can feel the pleasure of his touch tightening my entire body, pushing me closer and closer to a climax, one that I'm certain he's going to deny me.

"Oh—oh, fuck, I'm—" I start to gasp and moan before I can stop myself, feeling the orgasm begin to unfurl through me, and the moment the words spill from my lips, Luca yanks his hand away.

"My pussy," he murmurs, his voice so deep and rough that it sends a bolt of lust through me like nothing I've ever felt before. "*Mine.*"

My body clenches tightly, suddenly empty, protesting the loss of sensation of his fingers inside of me. *Mine.* The word sounds so firm, so final, that for a minute I have the urge to say yes, of course it's his, *I'm* his, if only he'll let me come. If only he'll slide his fingers inside of me, his tongue, his cock, anything he'll give me. I can feel myself squirming on the bed, thighs clenching together with desperate need, my hands balled into fists with frustration.

I'm not his. I'm determined not to be.

But I'm not the same girl I was before, either.

SOFIA

8

"Mine," Luca murmurs again, and I see his hand go to his trousers, his palm rubbing over the thick ridge that I can see straining against the black fabric. "That's for the first lie, Sofia."

I whimper, staring up at him in confusion. What could possibly come next?

"I've wondered what that sweet pussy might taste like," he murmurs, stroking a finger down my inner thigh. His fingertip brushes over the healing cut there, and I shudder. "Do you want me to eat you, Sofia? Do you want me to lick my pussy?"

Oh god. I can't even form words. Luca starts to unbutton his shirt as I stare up at him, revealing his muscled chest button by button, the smooth tanned skin there making my mouth go dry all over again with desire. He's the most handsome man I've ever seen, chiseled like a movie star, every perfect inch of him made for women to lust after. I don't want to be one of those women, just another in the long line that's passed through his bed, but it's impossible to deny how I feel right now. How, if I lost the last shred of control I'm clinging to, I'd beg for him inside of me again.

He slides down the bed as his shirt falls open, his hands on my

M. JAMES

inner thighs as he spreads me wider, and I feel his warm breath on my skin as he breathes in deeply. My face flushes red as I realize that he's breathing in my scent, that in a moment, he's going to *taste* me. No one has ever done that—before Luca, I'd only ever been kissed before, and not well. I never even imagined letting a man put his mouth on me there. But suddenly, Luca's lips are brushing across me, and not only is he not turned off by it, I swear I hear him groan as his tongue flicks out to drag along the crease, not quite delving deeper yet.

He pulls back slightly, his hands sliding inwards, and then to my horror, he spreads me open with his fingers, displaying me lewdly right in front of his eyes. *He can see* all *of me,* I realize, my skin burning as Luca takes in the sight of my pussy spread open for him like a feast.

I'm so distracted by it that I can't stop my reaction when he licks me for the first time, his tongue running from my entrance up to my clit in a long stroke that makes me cry out, a sound that turns to a breathless gasp as the new sensation washes over me. I've never felt anything like it before, never even *imagined* it. I writhe helplessly under his touch as his tongue circles my clit, lapping at the small, aching bud until I'm whimpering with a pleasure I never thought existed. I can feel myself starting to slip away, my determination not to give in, not to let Luca know how good it feels, fading into nothingness as his tongue licks and teases me to the edge of orgasm again.

"Oh—oh, god!" I shriek as he flutters it around my clit, his fingers teasing my entrance. Luca jerks back immediately, sitting up between my thighs with a satisfied smirk on his face as I writhe helplessly on the bed, my hips arching upwards for a mouth that's no longer there.

"Please—oh god, please—" I bite my lower lip hard, trying to stop myself from begging for more. Every inch of my body feels electrified, brought to the peak twice now and then denied. I look at the gorgeous man kneeling between my legs with the kind of desperation I'd never thought I would ever feel for anything sexual in my life.

"Do you want to come?" He strokes my inner thigh, and I squeeze his hand between my legs. "So needy. So wet. Tell me what you imagined when you touched yourself, Sofia. Tell me what turned you on so much that you had to make my pussy come without me there."

"Luca—" I gasp his name as he pulls his hand back, reaching for his zipper and drawing it down slowly. "Luca, please, I can't take any more."

"Then just tell me." He taps his fingers on my mound, and I whimper. "Did you like my mouth on you? Did you like feeling my tongue while I ate you out?"

I bite my lip hard, refusing to answer. To tell him *yes, oh my god, yes, it felt so fucking good,* which is exactly what's running through my head right now.

"That was for the second lie." Luca smiles. "And this is for the third."

He pulls his cock out then, and I can feel my eyes widen when I see it in his hand. He's impossibly hard, thick, and more erect than even on our wedding night, and I can tell that what he's doing to me is turning him on, too. I can see the fluid shimmering at the tip, and Luca reaches up, spreading it around with his thumb as he strokes himself once, very slowly, his hand resting at the base and squeezing.

"You said you wouldn't—" I can't finish the sentence. If he decided to thrust every inch of himself into me right now, I wouldn't be able to say no. I want relief, an orgasm, and I'd take anything that would give it to me. My body is trembling with it, wound taut, but deep down, I'm terrified of how I'll respond if he does, how much I'll give him if Luca decides to fuck me right now. *Please don't,* I think desperately, and then in the same moment, *oh god, please, yes.*

I'll lose it if he does. I'll come screaming around his cock, and he'll know then exactly how much I want him, what I was thinking about when I lost control and touched myself.

But if we ever have sex again, I want him to lose control too, like he did for a moment on our wedding night. And the Luca kneeling between my legs right now is entirely in control. Every inch of him is tense and rigid with it, perfectly disciplined. It's me that's losing it, squirming on the bed with desperate need.

"I'm not going to fuck you," Luca repeats. "But you'll wish that I would by the time I'm done."

He moves forward, his thick length gripped in his fist, pushing my legs even farther apart to make room so that I'm completely spread-eagled. I can feel my pussy spread open for him, my clit lewdly on display, the cool air of the room brushing over my soaked flesh as Luca's hips push forward—and the head of his cock presses against my clit.

I scream. All of the need bubbles up inside of me as I feel the velvet head pushing against my aching, wet, over-sensitive skin, and my hips arch up, grinding against him, wanting more.

"Be still!" Luca's voice fills the room, commanding, ordering, and I freeze, my heart pounding so hard in my chest that I think surely he can see it. "Don't fucking move," he warns. "Or I'll do this to you every night. I'll tie you up in bed and leave you wet and begging every morning, and you'll stay there until I come home."

He'd do it. At that moment, I absolutely believe that he would. And so, against every instinct I have, I lie perfectly still as the gorgeous man between my legs looks down at my exposed pussy, rubbing the head of his cock against my clit as he groans with pleasure.

I'm completely gone. He's so fucking handsome, his black button-down shirt hanging open to reveal his muscled chest, his forearm flexing as he strokes his shaft, rubbing the tip against me in small circles. His eyes are dark and full of emotions I can't name—lust, anger, frustration—all of which I can feel emanating off him in waves. This is a man with wealth, with power, with a thousand men and more at his command, and right now, I'm completely under his control, too.

But no matter how much he might say I'm here for punishment, he wants me just as much. I can see the evidence of that right in front of my eyes, thick and hard and throbbing as Luca's gaze rakes over my naked, quivering body again and again as he rubs me to the edge of orgasm for the third time, this time using his cock like a sex toy until I'm moaning helplessly, wishing more than anything that this will be the one where he lets me come.

But of course, right as I start to tense, gasping, Luca pulls back, his hand still firmly on his cock as he moves backward.

I almost burst into tears with frustration, my eyes burning as I stare up at him. "Please," I whisper. "I need to come. Please."

The words slip past my lips before I can stop them. Luca's hand doesn't move, not stroking, just holding his cock, pointing it at me like a weapon.

"Whose pussy is that?" His voice is hoarse, the way it was on our wedding night.

"Yours," I whimper. I know what he wants to hear, and I'd say anything now if he'd let me orgasm. Almost anything—

"Can you come without my permission?"

I stare up at him, confused. Is this real? Is my husband really telling me I can't—

"Can you—"

"No!" I moan. "No, I can't. I'm sorry, Luca, please—"

"What were you thinking about when you touched yourself?"

I shake my head mutely. I won't say it, I won't—

Luca leans forward, pushing the head of his cock against my clit again and holding it there. I can feel the heat of it, the slick wetness, my arousal and his mixed together. "I'll leave you like this all night," he says darkly. "Tell me, Sofia. What were you—"

"You!" I almost scream the word, my body shuddering and aching all over, the pleasure crossing over into something that's nearly pain. "I was thinking about you, on our wedding night, and, and—"

"And what?" His cock pushes against my clit harder, and I squeal with pleasure.

"You coming on my ass, oh my god Luca, please—"

He laughs, his face twisting in a smirk as he pulls back again, moving backward until he's too far away to touch me with any part of his body. "Go ahead," he says, almost contemptuously. "Make yourself come if you can."

I'm too far gone to be embarrassed, too far gone to think twice. Before he can take it back, I manage to get my hands down from over my head, my wrists still bound together, and shove my hands between my thighs, my fingers plunging into my pussy as I rub my clit madly, fingers slipping against my soaked skin.

I come in seconds. Almost as soon as my fingers are in my pussy it starts to spasm. When I touch my clit I arch upwards with a moan that's practically a scream, writhing on the bed and grinding against my hands as I orgasm for what feels like forever, the pent-up need spilling out of me as I come and come and come.

And Luca watches the entire time. When I finally go limp on the bed, staring up at him in a daze, he laughs. And then he leans forward, yanking the belt free of my wrists.

"Go clean yourself up."

I look at him, confused. He's still rock-hard, his hand still gripping his cock, but he makes no move to do anything more. I'd expected him to jerk off on me the way he had the night before our wedding, but he looks annoyed now, glaring at me.

"Fucking go, Sofia. Clean up."

"Aren't you—aren't you going to—" my gaze flicks down to his erection. My pussy throbs traitorously as if I hadn't just had one of the biggest orgasms of my entire life, as if I *want* Luca to fuck me.

At this point, I don't have the slightest fucking idea what I want.

"Of course," Luca says. "But not with you. Go clean up while I finish myself off."

"I—" I swallow hard, managing to slide off of the bed. My legs feel as if they won't hold me up, and as I take a tentative step back, Luca turns to lean back against the pillows, his hand starting to slide up and down his cock in slow, firm strokes. His shaft is glistening, and I realize with fresh embarrassment that it's my wetness he's using to get himself off, left from him rubbing against me.

"Go!" he snaps, and I retreat quickly, rushing into the bathroom as hot tears gather in my eyes for some reason I can't entirely explain.

I hope he'll be done by the time I'm finished. I turn on the shower, so I won't have to hear his groans, tears sliding down my cheeks as I step under the water. I don't know why I'm so upset, why I feel as if I'm choking with the tangled rush of emotions rising up in me, why I feel rejected that Luca is in the bedroom jerking off without me, that he doesn't even want me there.

I'm not supposed to want him. *You hate him*, I remind myself, and somewhere deep in my head, I'm sure I still do. But right now, I don't feel that. All I can think about is that my husband is in our bedroom pleasuring himself, and he doesn't even want to look at me while he does it.

I walk back into the bedroom, a towel wrapped tightly around myself, just in time to see Luca tossing a wad of tissues into the wastebasket next to the bed. My gaze follows him, and he smirks at me as he stands up, still completely nude, his cock now softened as he strides towards the dresser.

"I told you," he says as casually as if nothing unusual happened this past hour, as if he didn't just torture me with pleasure until I lost my mind, "that you would have to earn this, Sofia, if you want it." He turns towards me, stepping into a pair of black silk pajama pants. "You said you didn't want me. But you were lying." He strides towards me, reaching beneath my chin and tilting it up as I clutch the towel against my breasts. "You acted as if you hated it when I bent you over the couch when I came all over your ass. Like I'd violated you. But you were lying then, too, weren't you? Don't bother lying again," he adds, as my cheeks flush red. "You admitted it earlier. If you want my cock again, Sofia, if you want my cum all over you, then you're going to have to earn it. Just like you'll have to earn your place here, as my wife."

My mouth drops open, and Luca laughs. "Don't look so shocked. I'm tired of your rebellion, Sofia, when all I've done is try to keep you alive, try to keep you safe. I rescued you from the Bratva, rescued you from Rossi, married you and fucked you and offered you money and luxury and everything you could possibly want here. And you still act like a spoiled child, like I'm imprisoning you, torturing you. Keeping you against your will, when all I'm doing is keeping you alive."

He jerks his hand away from my chin, stepping back, and the contemptuous glare is on his face again. "I have responsibilities. People are relying on me and pressures that you couldn't possibly imagine. A woman has died, Sofia, a woman who cared about me, who treated me like her son, and you're playing games. So if you want me, then grow up. Take your place as my wife. Learn a lesson from Caterina, and accept the hand you were dealt in this life. But until then, I'll do with you as I please. And I'll take my pleasure where and how I please, too."

I can feel the tears welling up in my eyes again. "You fucked someone else last night, didn't you?" I whisper. "That's why you didn't come home. You wanted to sleep with another woman, but you didn't want to bring her here. So you went to some hotel, and—"

"That's none of your business." Luca turns away, climbing into bed.

"Just tell me!" I swallow hard, trying not to shriek at him. "I just want to know—I have a right to know—"

His upper lip curls. "You have no rights, Sofia, other than what I give you. If I choose to fuck a dozen women, it's not your business. If I choose not to, that's not your problem either." He reaches over, turning off the bedside light, and casting the entire room in darkness as he slides down, rolling onto his side.

"I'm tired. I'm going to sleep. I suggest you do the same."

The sudden coldness feels like a shock to my system, even though by now, I know it shouldn't. Luca has been this way since the night I woke up in this very bed—cold then hot, and then cold again. *He doesn't love you*, I remind myself as I choke back the tears and go to my own side of the bed, thankfully very far away from him. *He never will. What he just did to you was a game. A way to exert his power over you, and nothing more. He doesn't want you.*

It shouldn't hurt. None of it should. But as those thoughts run through my head, circling back on themselves over and over again as Luca's light snores punctuate the silence, I can feel the tears dripping down my cheeks.

My freedom from this place can't come soon enough.

SOFIA

9

Luca is already gone when I wake up, and I'm grateful for that, at least. I don't know how I would face him this morning, after what happened last night.

I feel achy and sore when I climb out of bed, and I take another hot shower, trying to wash away the memory of it along with all of the physical soreness. But both of them linger, and even though I go through the motions of my new morning routine—washing my face, stretching, getting dressed, going down to the kitchen to find breakfast—I can't shake the confusion.

So I try to work it out as I open up a yogurt and smear almond butter on toast—I still can't figure out the espresso machine, so I've given up on coffee for now. I try to think about Luca, about my feelings for him.

He rescued me. Okay, one point for him. He saved me from the Bratva.

He forced me to marry him. In his defense, though, Rossi would have killed me otherwise. I can't give him credit for forcing me against my will, but I can't deny that he saved my life.

He was an asshole about it, though.

I mentally subtract his one point, swirling my spoon around my yogurt. What else?

He took back his promise to give me my own apartment. He took back his promise to leave me alone after the wedding.

But he hadn't chosen that. He hadn't wanted us to be attacked the morning after. Luca might be a cold man, an asshole in so many ways, even brutal in others. Still, I believed him last night in his anger and hurt over Giulia's death. He wouldn't have wanted that. I don't think he really even wants me here in his penthouse still.

He threw himself over me during the explosion. He protected me.

Okay, a point for that. What else?

The front door. The couch. The wedding suite. Last night, in his bed. All times when I swore I didn't want him, that I wanted nothing more than to get *away* from him, and yet I responded to him every time anyway, my body is drawn to his like a moth to a flame.

And I'm equally likely to get burned.

I give up on the mental math. There's no way to make it make sense. Luca is a man I would never have chosen in the real world, a man I would have been too afraid of to ever get close to. The kind of man who exudes power and charisma, who I would never have been brave enough to look at, let alone speak to.

And now I'm married to him. I wear his ring, I took vows, and last night he did things to my body that I never even knew could feel that good. And if I gave in, if I went to bed with him without a fight—

You have to earn it.

His words echo in my head, and resentful anger replaces every other emotion in a hot rush that leaves me feeling dizzy. How dare he treat me like a child? How dare he tell me that I have to earn something I didn't even want, something—

A knock at the door cuts off my train of thought, and I yelp, almost dropping my yogurt in surprise. I toss it in the trash as I walk out, only half-eaten, but my appetite is long gone.

When I open the door, Caterina is standing there.

She looks elegant as always but pale, her face bare of makeup. She must have eyelash extensions because they still look long and fringed despite her red eyes, but there's not a speck of makeup otherwise on her skin. It doesn't matter—she still looks flawless, and I feel a small flicker of envy.

And then I remember what she's lost, and I immediately feel guilty.

"Can I come in?" she asks quietly, and I back up, letting her step through the doorway.

"Of course. Are you okay?" I ask and then mentally kick myself. *Of course she's not fucking okay.*

Caterina smiles thinly. "I just needed someone to talk to. Franco is busy, of course, and—well, Luca said you might be someone who could listen. On account of—" she takes a deep breath. "You having lost a parent, too."

"Both of them, actually." A sort of calm settles over me, and I feel a little more like myself. This, I can help with. This, I understand—being a friend, grief, loss. It's simpler to handle than my strange marriage or my confusing feelings about my husband. Caterina's presence helps push the thoughts of Luca away, and I shut the door behind her, glancing over at her sympathetically. "Do you want something to drink? I can't figure out the coffeemaker, but I can still make tea, or—"

"Tea would be lovely." Caterina follows me to the kitchen, sinking into a chair as I poke around for a mug and tea leaves. Luca has one of those fancy strainers, the kind you put leaves in that sits in the water, but the rest is easy enough. Thankfully there's a microwave. Even though it looks as expensive as everything else and is built into the wall, I can heat up a mug of water, even if I can't figure out much else in here.

"I have—peppermint, vanilla, Earl Grey, and—rooibos." I stumble over the last word, and Caterina laughs, the sound breaking off abruptly as if she's surprised herself.

"Earl Grey, please," she says politely. "Just black, no cream or anything."

"I can do that." I hope I'm telling the truth as I fill the mug with water from the pitcher in the fridge and pop it into the microwave. "So Luca told you to come to see me?"

"He said you would understand. I didn't want to bother you, but—"

"It's fine," I assure her quickly. "I don't have anything else to do, really. Luca wants me to memorize all the names of all these people in the organization that I might meet at a dinner or something one day, but—" I glance over at Caterina's pale, drawn face and trail off. "That doesn't matter, though. I'm glad you came over, that's all."

"It was just—" Caterina bites her lower lip. "It was so unexpected. Out of nowhere. I was just in your *room* with her before it happened, and then we came down and got our breakfast while we waited for you and Luca. We were complaining about the *eggs*, oh my god—" she puts a hand to her mouth, choking back a sob. "The last thing I ever said to my mother was that the scrambled eggs were dry, and I just—"

She starts to cry, and I abandon the tea, crossing the room as quickly as possible to pull up a chair and sit down in front of her, reaching for her hands to squeeze them in mine.

"I know," I whisper. "My mother didn't die out of nowhere. She was sick for a while. But my father did. I was waiting for him to come home when my mother told me he was dead. I remember how pale she was, how she was barely staying upright—she looked like she wanted to dissolve with grief, I know that now—but she kept it together long enough to tell me. I didn't want to believe it."

Caterina swallows hard. "I didn't want to either," she whispers. "They told me at the hospital—I passed out from all the smoke, and I woke up in a hospital bed. I was *fine*, not a scratch on me, just a sore throat, and then the nurse came in with Franco, and she told me—" she chokes back another sob. "I told them they must be wrong, they must have mixed her up with someone else, but—"

I sit with her for what feels like a long time, each minute stretching into another as she cries quietly, composed, and elegant even in her grief. I know that feeling too—I've never been as elegant as Caterina, but I know the feeling of needing to hold something back, that if you let all the aching sadness in your chest go, you'll fall apart. You'll shatter and cry, and cry until you scream until you can't breathe, and you're afraid to let that happen.

It always happens, eventually. It'll happen to Caterina too, but when she's alone, when she's sure that she's safe, and she can break down with no one to see her crumble.

For now, she cries quietly, her hands wrapped around mine until her knuckles turn white, and I let her cling to me. When the sobs slowly fade, I get up and bring her a box of tissue and turn the microwave back on to reheat the water that's grown cold, and Caterina smiles up at me gratefully.

"Thank you," she says softly. "I don't have very many friends. People tend to shy away from me; they're too afraid of my father. And I can't—I know it sounds strange, but I can't cry like that in front of Franco. I just can't."

"It doesn't sound strange at all," I reassure her. "I don't think you love him, do you?"

Caterina shakes her head. "No. I don't," she admits. "I don't even really feel that I *should*—I don't think my mother loved my father, not in the way we're told to think about love. She loved the security he gave her and the family—she loved *me*, and she wouldn't have had me without him. But she didn't love him. I always knew my husband would be picked for me. I'm lucky he's young and handsome." She shrugs. "He doesn't love me either. But I didn't expect love. I did expect—" she hesitates. "Respect."

I look at her curiously. "You don't feel like Franco respects you?"

"I don't know." Caterina bites her lip. "I shouldn't say that."

"I won't tell anyone." I laugh a little, shaking my head. "Who would I tell, anyway? Luca? Not likely."

Caterina smiles at that. "I guess not. Things aren't good between you, are they?"

I shake my head. "We're here to talk about you," I insist. I'm not ready to share what's gone on between Luca and me—I don't even know what there would be *to* share. Certainly not the lust-filled encounters we've had over the past weeks. Not his agreement to protect my virginity that her father forced him to break. So what, then? It's not exactly like we've been having real conversations about anything. Every time we try to talk, we end up fighting.

Does that mean something? I don't know. If it were a normal relationship, I'd say yes, of course. I'd tell Ana that if she had a boyfriend that she just seemed to fight with or end up in bed with.

But nothing about my relationship with Luca is normal.

Caterina hesitates, and I can tell that she wants to ask more about Luca, but she doesn't, to my relief. "I thought Franco would be more attentive," she says quietly, turning the conversation back to him. "It sounds egotistical, I know, but I'm the daughter of the former don. He's—well, he has a checkered past in the family. There were questions a long time ago about who his father was. It was all cleared up, but I thought—I don't know, I thought he'd be *grateful* that my father chose him for me. Instead, he acts now almost like I was owed to him. Especially since Luca was made don and Franco is underboss—he's more arrogant than ever."

"You don't think he appreciates you?"

"I don't know. I thought he would. But I felt so alone at the funeral yesterday."

"I'm sorry I wasn't there," I say quietly. "I wanted to be. But Luca said it was more dangerous for me to go."

"He was probably right." Caterina wipes at her face, smiling tiredly at me. "It's not your fault, Sofia. None of this is."

It feels like it is. I can't help but think that all of this is because of me, somehow, even though I don't know why. I never thought I was anyone special. But ever since that night at the club, everything seems to be spiraling more and more out of control.

"And now—" She takes a deep breath. "Viktor showed up at the funeral. Not like *at* it—" she adds quickly, seeing the look on my face. "But Luca went to go speak with him. He was trying to come to some kind of terms with him, settle things down. But it didn't work. I'm not sure why, exactly, but he said that my wedding date will have to be moved up."

"What?" I blink at her, startled. "After what just happened, though—how can he expect you to be married sooner? You just lost your mother."

"He was apologetic about it. But clearly, it's important—I could tell that he wasn't going to be argued with. So—my wedding is in a week. And now—"

"You don't have your mother to help you plan it." I can only imagine what she must be feeling. My mother has been gone for a long time now, but I missed her terribly in the week leading up to my wedding, as rushed as it was. I didn't even have a hand in planning it. Caterina would have been planning with Giulia this whole time. Giulia was probably thrilled to be finally helping her daughter with her wedding. And now it's all gone—in a flash.

"Yeah." Caterina chews on her lower lip. "I don't even know how to move forward. I don't know how to pretend to be happy about any of it when she isn't there—" She pauses, shaking her head. "I'm supposed to go tomorrow to shop for dresses again. We went once already. And now I just want to get the dress that my mother liked best. Even if it wasn't my favorite."

"I'll go with you." I squeeze her hand. "You shouldn't have to do any of this alone."

"Luca isn't going to let you! He wouldn't even let you leave for the funeral—"

"I'll figure it out," I promise, standing up to get the steeped tea for her. When I hand it over, Caterina takes it gratefully, wrapping her hands around the cup as if she's cold, even though the penthouse is always warm. "I'll talk to him."

Truthfully, I don't think I could convince Luca to let me do anything. Especially not after last night.

But I know I have to at least try.

* * *

True to what I'd feared, Luca almost laughs in my face when I ask him to let me leave the penthouse with Caterina. "Not a chance," he says flatly. "Everything I'm doing to keep you safe, and you want to go wedding dress shopping? I'm not even sure I believe that. I told you that you're staying here, and I meant it."

After all that coldness, I don't expect a knock on the door the next day. But right about ten a.m., as I'm finishing up the bowl of yogurt and granola I managed to throw together, I'm startled by exactly that.

I open the door to see a tall redhead in a black wrap dress standing there, smiling brightly.

"Hi!" she says cheerfully. "I'm Annie. I work for Kleinfeld's. My assistant and I are here for Caterina Rossi's appointment?"

I stare at her, slightly dumbfounded. Caterina isn't here, obviously, and I blink at her with confusion for about ten seconds until I hear the *ding* of the elevator door opening down the hall. A moment later, Caterina appears behind her.

"I have my assistant here too, and the dresses, if I can bring them in?" Annie's smile doesn't falter for a second as I step aside, still a little dazed, and the blonde assistant and Caterina follow her in, along with a garment rack frothing with silk and satin and lace.

I pull Caterina aside immediately, of course, as Annie and her assistant are setting up. It takes all of five seconds of talking to her to figure out what's happened.

Luca called her after our conversation and arranged for the final dress appointment to be at the penthouse instead of the salon. Which, of course, he could have told me that he was going to do—but he didn't. He opted to let me think that he didn't care instead and let this happen out of nowhere.

As always, it leaves me confused as to how to feel. I was so angry and frustrated with him for refusing to let me go—and then he turns around and does something like this, something kind for Caterina, something that makes it possible for me to be there for her despite the limitations. And yet, I'm still mad at him for refusing to let me leave the apartment at all.

I wish I'd never met him, I think as I sink onto the couch, watching Caterina talk to the assistant quietly, touching each of the dresses as she looks at them. *I wish none of this had ever happened.*

But even as I think it, I'm not entirely sure that it's true anymore. Without Luca and our forced marriage, I'd be graduating in a few weeks, getting ready to go to Paris and then London. I'd be on my way to leaving Manhattan forever, becoming an accomplished member of an orchestra, starting a new life far away from the memories here.

When I imagine that now, though, it feels like a dream. Like a life that belonged to someone else. And the thought of never seeing Luca again makes me feel almost like I'm losing something.

Like a drug that I don't want to admit I'm getting addicted to.

"I'll try this one on," Caterina says, jolting me out of my thoughts. "What do you think, Sofia? Is it nice?"

I glance over at the cascade of lace that she's holding up and force a smile. I'm supposed to be supporting her today, not lost in my own thoughts. "It's gorgeous," I tell her, which is easy to say. Anything would look good on her.

She tries on a few dresses, changing in the downstairs bathroom and then coming out for me to see. They're all beautiful—the first is a fitted white lace dress with a v-neckline and elbow-length sleeves, another is a strapless lace bodice with a floaty tulle skirt, and the third is a sleek mermaid made of heavy, plain white satin.

And then she comes out in the fourth. It's simple, made of heavy off-white satin, an off-the-shoulder neckline, and a fitted bodice that flares out into a full skirt. There's nothing fairy-tale or princess-y about it. It's an elegant, gorgeous dress, one that makes Caterina look like a queen. Her tanned skin glows against the soft candle white of the satin, the dress clinging to the lines of her body in a way that's beautiful without being too sexy, and when the assistant pins a veil to her hair, sweeping the tulle around her, I feel the prickle of tears at the corner of my eyes.

"This is the one my mother loved," Caterina says quietly. "I thought I wanted something more ornate. But now that I've put it on again—" she hesitates, looking in the mirror that the assistant set up for her. "I think it's perfect." She glances back at me, biting her lip. "What do you think, Sofia?"

My chest tightens, and it takes me a moment to be able to speak. We don't know each other that well—it's only through circumstance that we know each other at all, and I want to say the right thing. This is an important moment in her life, one that she should be sharing with her mother, or a sister, or a close friend—anyone closer to her than I am. But I'm all she has.

"I think it's perfect, too." It's true—I can't imagine a more perfect dress. The others were gorgeous, but this suits Caterina as if it were made for her. "And it'll feel like she's there with you, at least a little bit."

"That's what I was thinking, too." Caterina bites her lip, crossing over to the couch and sinking onto it next to me while still in the dress. She reaches out for my hands, grasping them in both of hers as she smiles through the tears that are starting to run down her face. "Thank you so much, Sofia. I can't tell you how much it means to me that you were with me today. It feels like I have a friend."

My chest tightens with emotion as she squeezes my hands. Like that moment at our engagement party when I caught a flash of what my life could be like with Luca if we actually loved each other, that moment where we were joking and teasing one another, I see a glimpse of what my life could be like if I were actually a part of this family. If I accepted my place as Luca's wife, I worked to be a good one, support him, and love him. Caterina would be my friend, married to Luca's underboss. I can see the dinners we would host, the parties we'd go to together, the events we'd help organize. I can't imagine a day when Ana isn't my best friend, but I can see the place in my life that Caterina would occupy too, and the place I would have in hers.

And it wouldn't be bad. It would probably even be *good*, a happy, fulfilling life in many ways.

But in order to have that, I'd have to let go of all of the ideas I've always had about what my life would be. I'd have to come to terms with my feelings about what Rossi and his thugs did to my mother, the fact that Luca is now occupying the spot that Rossi used to, and the way I've been dragged into all of this.

I don't know if I can do that. I don't know if I can find a place here when I resent how it all began so much. When I don't even understand my feelings for my own husband. When I'm alternately unsure if he's someone I could fall for or someone who I should be terrified of.

But I do know one thing I *can* do.

I squeeze Caterina's hands back, looking at her with a smile on my face. "You do have a friend in me," I tell her firmly.

And that, I know I mean. More than anything I've said in a long time now.

LUCA

10

For the next week, I manage to avoid Sofia as much as possible. Besides the conversation where she ambushed me asking me to let her go shopping with Caterina, which led to my penthouse being turned into a bridal salon for the day, we barely speak. I leave as early as I can for the office, and by the time I come home late at night, she's already asleep.

Which suits me, because I don't know what to say to her—*especially* after what happened between us the night I saw the security tape.

I'm not sure what came over me when I watched it. I hadn't intentionally been spying on her. Still, I'd wanted to make sure that nothing out of the ordinary had happened while I was gone. I hadn't expected to see *that*. I'd been concerned about her inviting a friend over without my consent, or trying to leave, or—

To be completely honest, I'm not entirely sure what I'd worried about that had led me to check the footage. The meeting with Viktor had left me on edge, feeling thrust into a situation beyond my control, one where I'm constantly one step behind. I'd wanted to regain some of that sense of control, somehow. And when I'd seen Sofia reclining in that chair, her delicate fingers holding her shorts to one side while the fingers of her other hand plunged into the pussy that I hadn't been able to stop thinking about—something snapped inside of me.

I've never done anything like what I did to her with another woman. I've always been dominant in the bedroom, the one in charge and calling the shots, but it's always been easy. Women are too awed by me, too desperate for a night with me, too hopeful that they'll be the ones to seduce me out of my avowed bachelorhood to be particularly challenging or creative in bed. They do whatever I ask them, whenever I ask for it. I've never met a single woman who challenged me in the bedroom or who would dare to talk back to me once the clothes start coming off—or even before then, really.

I've never met a woman I needed to master. A woman that I couldn't get out of my head. One who drove me to the brink of control over and over again.

Until Sofia.

The sight and sound of her making herself come drove me wild when I saw it. The thought of her touching herself, giving herself pleasure when she insists on denying me, fighting me, rebelling against me at every turn, had made me feel slightly unhinged. I'd been rock-hard the entire time I watched it, glad that I'd opted to view it alone instead of with the guards.

I'd also made a point of asking if anyone else had reviewed the footage. I was grateful they hadn't—I'd have had to fire them on the spot. In fact, I'm not sure what else I would have done if I'd thought any other man had gotten to see my beautiful wife spread-eagled in the penthouse and fingering herself.

I hadn't intended to punish her at first. Everything that had happened after that, once I'd gone into the penthouse and found her, had been unplanned. But then she'd failed to do the one thing I'd asked of her.

Lied to me.

Denied everything I asked about.

And I'd lost control.

I'd spent that entire night in my hotel room, unable to stop fantasizing about her. Trying to force her out of my system by thinking of every possible thing I could want to do to Sofia's beautiful, perfect body while pleasuring myself over and over again.

It hadn't worked.

And she's driving me insane.

She's a burden. A distraction. Another responsibility in a sea of other responsibilities is a person depending on me to keep her safe when so many others are. And yet, she fights me at every turn. Lies to me. Pretends to hate me when I know she's as conflicted as I am.

I'd only been able to think of one way to regain some control. And the entire time, it had felt like the most natural thing in the world to dominate her. To demand her body's submission, to torture and punish her with pleasure, to tease her to the brink of madness, so that she could feel what I do every time I think of her. To tell her that her body is mine, to give or withhold pleasure as I please.

And she'd loved it. It had been obvious. The problem was—I had too.

It had taken every ounce of control I had not to fuck her then and there. I wanted it, craved it, needed it desperately. But that night wasn't supposed to be about losing control. It was supposed to be about winning it back. It was supposed to be about exerting my power over her so that I can finally get her out of my head.

So I hadn't fucked her. I'd done the opposite. I'd mocked her, taunted her with her obvious desire, and then kicked her out of the room so that I could jerk off into my lonely hand again, when I probably could have fucked her all night long if I'd tried. She'd been so aroused she'd have probably done anything I wanted.

Sometimes I feel as if she's making me lose my mind.

She's been so careful to avoid me that I have no idea what's going on in her head. And I shouldn't be concerned with that. I have an empire to run and a war to try to stop in its tracks.

Since my meeting with Viktor, there's been a tentative peace despite his threats. I've doubled the security everywhere—on my office, Franco's home, his family's home, the Rossi residence where Caterina is staying. The quiet is almost more alarming than the attacks because it makes me worry that he might be planning something big. I can't possibly add more security to my own penthouse, but I'll be leaving a personal bodyguard with Sofia this weekend.

Which brings my thoughts full circle to the thing irritating me the most right now—the upcoming weekend. Despite the tension and danger hovering over us, Franco is insistent that he can't *not* have a bachelor party. And I get it—he'll only ever be married once, and there's nothing Franco loves more than a good party. But the last thing on *my* mind right now is getting wildly drunk somewhere.

"It'll be good for you to get away from Sofia. Away from all of this." Franco is in my office now, leaning forward as he makes his argument for fucking off away from Manhattan for a weekend once more. "You look like you're about to explode, Luca. This much stress isn't good for your health. Isn't that what you used to tell Rossi all the time? To relax once in a while?"

"He didn't have a war on his hands when I said that," I growl, looking up at him. "You're really willing to leave your fiancée here while we go off to party—where was it you said you wanted to go again? Cabo?"

"Tijuana," Franco says with a smirk. "You can get away with a hell of a lot more there. And yes, I am. We'll leave plenty of security with her. Come on, Luca, I know I'm not expected to be faithful once I'm married, but when do you really think I'll have a chance to go out of the country and fuck three hookers of questionable legal age at once while high on cocaine after I'm a family man? Caterina is going to want me to stay home and put a baby in her."

"Truly the worst possible task," I retort dryly. "Jesus, Franco, your fiancée is one of the most beautiful women in Manhattan. Heiress to a fortune. Almost certainly a virgin. And you're complaining about having to fuck her?"

"Not complaining," Franco says cheerily. "But virgin pussy gets boring fast. You can only fuck it for the first time once, after all. What if she turns out to be a cold fish in bed?"

"She's still rich." I let out a sigh, leaning back in my chair. "Franco, you realize that things aren't going to be the way they used to anymore, right? It's not just us being married men now. It's everything. It's the danger around every corner, my new position, *your* new position. We spent our twenties fucking everything in sight and showing up to the job still half-high or hungover and making it work. We lived like princes, but now we're kings. And we've got to do the job right."

"No, Luca." Franco frowns. "*You're* the king. I'm still your lackey. And I'm asking your majesty for one more weekend like the ones we used to have before I have to stand up and take vows to marry a woman who, I'll admit, is way out of my league."

"Well, at least you admit that." I sigh. "Fine. I'll arrange to make sure Caterina is well-protected while we're gone."

It's on the tip of my tongue to tell him what Viktor asked me—that he'd requested I give Caterina to him instead of honoring her engagement to Franco. Right now, I'm irritated enough with him that I can't help but think it would serve him right if I did exactly that and bought peace with Caterina's hand in marriage.

But a promise has been made, and I'll honor it. Not to mention the fact that I can't imagine handing Caterina, who has always been sweet and kind and amenable in every interaction I've ever had with her, over to a man like Viktor. I've stretched my morals considerably thin over the years, and I expect I'll stretch them further still. But that's a step too far, I think.

The best way to ensure that Caterina is safe is to have her stay with Sofia and have both security contingents watch over them, along with the bodyguard I plan to leave. But I'll have to let Sofia know what's going on, which means doing the thing I've been avoiding all week.

Talking to my wife.

With that in mind, I head home early enough that there's little chance Sofia will already be in bed. I send Carmen a message, asking her to have dinner sent to the penthouse—whatever sushi Sofia had ordered from the night that I left her there alone for the night.

When I get there, she's definitely not asleep. But she is standing next to the dining table with her arms crossed, a suspicious look on her face.

"What's going on?" Sofia nods towards the takeout trays of sushi. "This is out of character for you."

"I can't want to have dinner with my wife?"

"Luca." She purses her lips, which makes my cock throb instantly. *Those lips would look so good pursed around my—*

"Luca!" Sofia stares at me. "What is going on with you? We've never had dinner together, not even once. Not even when I *tried* to--"

"I just had Carmen send some takeout. We need to talk—"

She rolls her eyes. "This is from the same place I ordered from the night that—" her voice trails off, and she swallows hard. A faint pink blush creeps up her neck. I have a sudden, immediate fantasy of bending her over the table, shoving the denim miniskirt that she has on up over her hips, and fucking her until she screams right next to the sushi.

"This is some kind of joke, right?" Sofia glares at me. "What are you going to do to me this time?"

If you only knew the things I'd like to. I clear my throat, shoving the thought aside. I don't have time for our usual games, time to get sucked into the back and forth that arises whenever we're together. I don't have time to remind Sofia that she's not the one in charge here, to remind her that for all her attitudes and protestations, she wants me as much as I want her.

However delicious that would be.

"It's not a joke," I say flatly. "Clearly, you like their food. And since you didn't have a chance to finish yours the other night—" I shrug, smirking at her. "We need to talk. So sit down, and we'll discuss it."

The suspicious look doesn't leave her face for even a second, but she slowly sits, watching me carefully. Without a word, she takes the lids off of the trays, picking up a pair of chopsticks and parceling pieces out onto the two china plates on the table—ridiculously fancy for something like this, and even I know that.

"Do you want a drink?" I haven't sat down yet, hovering behind my chair.

Sofia looks at me, the suspicion on her face intensifying, and I let out a long-suffering sigh.

"I'm not trying to trap you, Sofia, or make an allusion to your little bender the other night. I'm just asking if you would like a drink with your dinner. I'm going to have one. Not every conversation we have has to be this difficult."

She mutters something under her breath that sounds remarkably like *you could have fooled me.* The thought springs into my head that I could easily come up with an excuse to punish her for that kind of insolence, the way I did the other night—and I feel my cock throb again, tightening uncomfortably in my pants.

Stop. There won't be any punishment tonight, any games. Tonight, for once, I need to be as straightforward with her as possible. It's the only way I'll be able to go along with this ridiculous jaunt of Franco's and feel safe leaving the women here.

"I'll have a glass of white wine," Sofia says quietly. "Thank you."

There's a moment's peace in the silence that descends over the dining room as I go to get our drinks, broken only by the tap of chopsticks against trays and plates, the slide of china over wood. It's a glimpse into what things could be like for us if our marriage worked out. If we could stop fighting with each other and live together like a normal couple. We would have more ordinary, domestic nights like this, with Sofia arranging our dinner while I poured drinks, and while we ate, we would talk about—

About what, exactly? I know almost nothing about my wife. I know that she's an accomplished violinist. She loves books, especially classics, from what I saw Ana bring over from the old apartment. I know now that she prefers white wine with her seafood, but that's hardly a revelation.

I know the gasp she makes when I kiss her and the taste of her mouth, the way she looks when she's lost in pleasure, and the sound of her orgasm, but I don't know what she likes for breakfast. I don't know what kind of music she prefers to listen to or if she likes the theater. I don't know what her favorite genre of movie is or her favorite color. I told her once that I didn't have one, but of course, that isn't true.

Sofia pushes my plate towards me as I set both glasses down and take a seat, toying with her chopsticks as she looks over at me apprehensively. She's not wearing any makeup tonight, so far as I can tell—I don't think she expected me to be home until after she was asleep, like usual. She looks beautiful without it, a sprinkling of freckles visible over the bridge of her nose that makes me think, suddenly, about leaning forward and kissing her there.

Where the fuck did that come from? I've never had a thought like that in my life. But for a moment, I can't deny that I had the urge to lean in and kiss my wife, right on her perfect, freckled nose.

Sofia eyes me. "Okay. What's so important that you rushed home and brought sushi in order to con me into a conversation?"

"*I* didn't bring the sushi," I point out. "I had Carmen order it."

"Naturally." Sofia rolls her eyes. "Just tell me what it is, Luca."

"It's about Caterina."

She looks slightly alarmed at that. "We didn't leave the penthouse. The entire wedding dress appointment was here, and—"

"Sofia," I speak calmly, my voice even and measured. "You're not in trouble, okay? Let's just try to have a normal conversation for once."

She leans back, biting her lower lip in a way that once again makes me want to kiss her. "Okay," she says finally.

"Good." I set my chopsticks down, turning a little to face her. "Franco is insisting that he, I, and some of our other friends go away this weekend for a bachelor party. I don't think it's a good idea, but he's very firm that he needs this last hurrah before his time as a single man ends."

"Okay—where are you going?" Sofia frowns, and I can see from her expression exactly what she thinks of Franco's insistence. Ironically, it's the first thing I can recall us agreeing on. "Isn't that a bad idea with everything that's happened?"

"For once, we're in agreement." I let out a sigh. "But he's my oldest friend, and he's basically made it clear that *he* thinks we need this. And I think—" I pause, wondering how much to share with her. But for better or worse, we're married now. And if there's *ever* a possibility of Sofia being a functioning part of my life instead of something I have to constantly worry about, I have to be able to share some measure of what I'm thinking with her.

"Franco has led a very privileged life since we've been friends," I begin slowly, and Sofia snorts.

"You're *all* privileged." She sets her chopsticks down too, looking at me as if I've grown two heads. "Do you really think you're not?"

"Do you think *you're* not?" I retort, glaring at her. *Goddamn it, how does this woman get under my skin so easily?* "For fuck's sake, Sofia, you've been on a free ride since you turned eighteen. An automatic deposit from Rossi's accounts went into yours every month like clockwork, paid your tuition in full every semester. No rent, no utilities, no grocery bill. You've never had to live like a normal person. You never would have, for as long as the money held up. And now you never will since you're *my* wife."

"I think that's fair since my father *died* because of him!" Sofia's teeth are gritted as she speaks, her posture ramrod straight. I can feel the tension rising in the air, just like it always does.

"Your father died because of himself," I say flatly. "Because of his mistakes. Not because of Rossi. And *my* father died because of yours. Because of their friendship. Yet here I am, carrying out their promises."

The room is very quiet for a moment. Neither of us moves or speaks.

"I'm sorry," Sofia says finally, and I can feel the tension rush out of the room like air from a balloon. "You're right. There are still things that I don't know. And I have been privileged, too. So tell me what you're talking about, Luca."

It takes me a moment to be able to gather my thoughts. I hadn't expected her to give in like that, to concede. It makes me look at her with fresh eyes and wonder briefly if I've underestimated her.

If maybe I just haven't bothered to give her—*us*—a chance because I'm so fixated on never having anything to lose.

If maybe, just maybe, Sofia Ferretti is stronger than I think.

"When I say Franco has led a privileged life, I mean that I've sheltered him from a lot of the realities of *this* life—life in the mafia," I explain. "I protected him from the bullies that spread lies about him when we were younger, and I just never stopped protecting him. When there were jobs for us to do for Rossi, when there were men who needed to be made to talk, men who needed to be killed, unsavory things, I protected him from the worst of it. I've always done the dirtiest work because I wanted to keep my friend from having to battle the demons that follow you after." I pause, then, realizing that I've said more than I meant to. *Revealed* more of myself than I meant to.

Sofia is absolutely silent. Her hands have fallen into her lap, and she's watching me with those liquid dark eyes, her face so smooth that I can't see what she's thinking.

"But I can't do that any longer. I'm no longer the underboss. I'm the *don* now. Franco is my underboss, and if we're going to continue this legacy, if we're going to push back the Bratva and keep this territory safe, I need him to step up and do the things that I once did for Rossi—for *me*."

"And you think giving him one last weekend of freedom to do as he likes will enable him to do that once you come back home?"

Sofia speaks softly, but her words cut right to the heart of it, with a precision that startles me. I hadn't expected her to be so acute, but once again, it makes me wonder if the circumstances of our meeting—of our marriage—have led me to vastly underestimate her.

My wife isn't stupid. I've always known that deep down—after all, she was a student at Juilliard, a brilliant violinist. I've seen the books in her room; they're not all fluff without substance. There are classics in there, philosophy, books that I probably have in my own library. And yet, I've been treating her like a child.

Maybe that's why she resents you.

Abruptly, I pull my thoughts back into focus. I don't have time to spend reevaluating my marriage just now. That can come later—maybe. If this first serious conversation that we've had isn't just some kind of fluke.

I've bared more of myself in these last fifteen minutes than I have in a long time—maybe ever. It feels uncomfortable, and I straighten up stiffly in my chair, my voice cooling and turning more formal as I continue.

"Yes. That's what I hope. But to make this work, I need something from you, Sofia."

She blinks at me. "From me?"

"Yes. If Viktor catches wind that Franco and I are away—and I can hardly keep him from finding out if he's intent on it—then he'll likely see it as an opportune time to strike. If I'm trying to protect both you and Caterina separately, it spreads the resources thinner. So what I want is for Caterina to stay here while we're gone. And I need you to not fight me on this. I need you to be a gracious host and have her here for the weekend, and I'll double the security here. I'm also going to have a personal bodyguard here for each of you."

"Oh." Sofia laughs suddenly, and it strikes me how rarely I've heard that sound from her. "That's all. Of course, Luca. You do realize Caterina and I are—well, we're basically friends at this point. I'll make it into a bachelorette party for her. It won't be as exciting as we would do if we could go out, but I'll do my best."

The ease of it catches me off guard. "You don't want anything in return?"

Sofia hesitates. "Well—"

Of course. "What? What can I do that you don't already have?"

Sofia stiffens, and I can tell that I've hit a nerve. "I was just going to ask if Ana can come, too. It's not a party if there are only two people," she adds hurriedly. "I can't see how it would hurt anything to have her here."

It's on the tip of my tongue to say no. Although she's proved herself to be a good friend so far, I don't entirely trust Anastasia. And I can't help but think that it's almost a taunt in Viktor's direction to have Sofia's Russian friend here.

Thinking of it like that, though, makes me want to agree. And Sofia's right that it probably won't hurt. As far as I know, no one is after Anastasia. And I don't think she has any real value to Viktor, beyond the ordinary value of a beautiful girl to him.

"Fine," I concede. "Anastasia can stay as well."

Sofia's eyes widen. "I didn't expect you to say yes! Thank you, Luca."

I can hear the sincerity in her voice, and it warms me a little. I'm hesitant to trust the thaw between us, though.

"Is there anything else?"

"No," she says quickly. "Of course not. I'm just happy to see Ana again. I haven't seen her since the wedding—I don't even know if she knows I'm okay."

"Of course she does. I reached out and let her know you were safe." I look at Sofia quizzically. "You don't think I would really have let your friend wonder if you were alive or dead?"

"I—"

"I can be cold, Sofia, but I'm not a monster." I let out a long sigh, rubbing a hand across my forehead. "And I know there's something else you want. So just tell me."

She's quiet for a long moment, and I'm not entirely sure that she's actually going to tell me. I'm on the verge of letting it go and just returning to our food when she finally looks up and blurts out:

"I want to go back to sleeping in my own room."

The immediacy with which I want to say no startles me. Not because I want to refuse—but because my first unconscious thought is that the bed would feel empty without her.

When did I get used to having someone next to me?

"I don't know if that's a good idea—"

"It's been a week, Luca. Nothing has happened. You're doubling the security and giving us personal guards. You just said that yourself. Do you really think that me sleeping in your room versus my own is going to change anything?"

"If someone comes after you, I'll be there."

"How would they even get in? I can't get *out*; there's so much security." She looks at me, and I can see how much she wants me to agree. For once, we're having a normal argument, not a blistering fight. Though my instinct is to tell her no, of course not, she'll continue to do as I've said and stay where I've told her to. I know that there's no real reason beyond my own stubbornness.

And the fact that apparently, I like having her in my bed even if it's only to sleep.

I don't want to relent. But I find myself nodding anyway. "Alright. But if there's the slightest hint of danger, we'll return to the arrangement we have now."

A smile spreads across Sofia's face, and I don't think she could look any happier if I'd told her she could move out entirely. She looks thrilled. And of course, if she's happy, that's one less burden for me to deal with.

So why does the thought of spending tonight without her sleeping next to me make me feel as if I've lost something?

LUCA

11

The Dominican Republic, where we finally settled on as a place to disappear for the weekend for Franco's party, is as hot as New York was still chilly.

We arrive on Friday night, barely a day after my conversation with Sofia over dinner. I left with assurances that Caterina would be at the penthouse within an hour and Ana a little later when her classes were over and that no one else would be there for the weekend. I also left so many men on security detail that an entire floor of apartments in the building is now temporarily devoted to housing them while they take turns watching the cameras inside and out and patrolling the halls.

As promised, I also left two bodyguards—Gio and Raoul-both former fighters and bodybuilders turned professional security who have worked for the family for years. If anyone can keep the women safe, I'm certain it's them—and this way, there will be security *inside* the penthouse as well as out.

All of that, coupled with the remarkably peaceful way that Sofia and I left things after our last conversation, should have me feeling good. But instead, as the private jet taxis to the hangar and Franco downs the last of his drink, I still feel as on edge as ever.

This is the last place I want to be. I want to be home, working on a

M. JAMES

plan to drive the Bratva back for good. I want to figure out what Viktor will accept in order to agree to peace that isn't a wife and doesn't come with a human price. And I want—

I want to be in bed with Sofia. It's been over a week now since that night, and it didn't get her out of my system the way I'd hoped. It didn't make me feel any more in control of my lust for her.

And I haven't been inside a woman since our wedding night. It's the longest I've gone without sex since I lost my virginity at fifteen, and I feel as if I'm going slightly mad. I've never been so sexually frustrated in my entire life.

"We're here!" Franco lifts his empty glass, his freckled face slightly flushed as he grins at me. "I'm ready to get high and fuck as many women as I can fit into a hotel bed all at once. Last single weekend, boys!"

There's a general cheer, and I join in as well as I can. There are four others here with us—other friends since we were in high school together. Tony, Berto, Adrian, and Max have all been part of Franco's and my inner circle for more years than I like to count now. They all have positions within the family. Tony is the capo in Chicago. Berto and Adrian are both made men who've had my back on many jobs, and Max is the consigliere in Newark. All of them understand the life, the highs and lows, and the responsibilities that come with these positions.

And all of them felt this trip was ill-timed. But the reservations they expressed seem to be falling away with the promise of warm sun, water, drugs, and beautiful women willing to do anything they ask. Money talks here, and there will be plenty of debaucheries this weekend, I have no doubt.

How much of it I'll be participating in, I'm not sure. There was a time when I'd have been as thrilled as anyone else on this jet about a weekend of no-holds-barred frivolity, in a place where no one will question the legality of any of it so long as we have money to hand over—which none of us have any shortage of. But at this particular moment, it doesn't seem to hold the same appeal that it used to.

Am I just getting fucking old?

The hotel is tucked several yards away from the beach, rented out in its entirety for our weekend. Just as I'd requested, there's already a handful of gorgeous, bronzed models waiting in the living room when we walk in, draped over furniture in bikinis.

Franco's eyes nearly pop out of his head. "Who wants to make me a drink?" he yells out, waving his hands above his head. "Last weekend of freedom, ladies!"

"He sounds like a broken record," Tony says with a laugh, heading to the bar as well. Tony has been married for several years, with a toddler-aged son, but I'm sure he'll avail himself of everything that the weekend has to offer too. Fidelity isn't a virtue any of us were raised to appreciate. Still, he's less blatant about it than Franco is, glancing appreciatively over at a dark-haired model who raises one perfect eyebrow and crooks a finger at him.

"Maybe this wasn't such a bad idea," he says with a grin, crossing the room towards the girl, who reaches up to grab the front of his shirt and pull him down towards her.

It doesn't take long for everyone to change into swim trunks, the girls all getting up to make drinks as we open the wide doors that lead out to the pool. The sun is beating down already, but it feels good after the mercurial weather of Manhattan in the late spring. I feel myself relax a little as I take the tequila and ginger that a tall blonde girl in an electric green bikini hands me and sit down on the edge of a lounge chair, breathing in the scent of the orange slice on the side of the glass and the salty air blowing in from the beach.

I wonder if Sofia would like it here. The thought startles me because it's the first time anything like that has ever occurred to me. I've never considered taking a woman with me on vacation. These getaways are meant to be exactly what they are to every other man here, a place to escape and lose ourselves in pleasure for a few days, shake off the stresses of home.

I've never known any man I'm acquainted with to take his wife on vacation. Mistresses, sometimes, but usually because they'll be alright with however many other women wind up in that bed, too. Wives go on vacation with other wives or their children.

Romancing one's spouse isn't exactly something mafia men are known for.

But despite the fact that I'm surrounded by the most beautiful women money could possibly buy, a cold drink in hand, and the promise of as much sex as I can have if I want it, all I can think of is what Sofia might look like in a bikini, standing at the edge of the pool with a glass of wine in hand and her dark hair fluttering in the breeze that occasionally springs up.

I can feel my cock twitch in my swim trunks, hardening just at the thought of a bikini top stretched over her full breasts, the way they would sway as she walked towards me—

Fuck. I'm long past what's acceptable for any man in terms of sexual frustration. I've got to get laid tonight and put all of this behind me. I haven't fucked another woman since the day I pulled Sofia out of that hotel room, and enough is enough.

I'm a man with wealth and power, the don of the Italian mafia, one of the most powerful men in the world. I can have anyone and anything I want.

So it's time I make that a reality.

Pushing Sofia firmly out of my head, I glance over at the tanned blonde, who couldn't be more different from Sofia if I'd planned it. She's at least five inches taller, thin as a rail with almost non-existent breasts, the ties of her green bikini clinging precariously to sharp hipbones. Her eyes are almost as bright green as the bathing suit. She smiles seductively at me when she sees me looking at her, walking towards me with a lazy, swinging gait that makes her seem curvier than she is.

"Hey, handsome," she purrs, coming to stand in front of me. I can smell the scent of coconut oil and sunscreen coming off of her skin. She's so close that I could lean forward and lick her if I wanted to, her pussy inches from my face, and I can see from the flawless skin on either side of her bikini that she's waxed smooth.

All of these women will be, though. They're all the highest-priced escorts that could be bought. All of them are in perfect physical shape, groomed to perfection for our pleasure, and paid to do literally anything that the men here tonight ask of them. And none of them will be shy about it.

I loop one arm around her waist, pulling her down into my lap. Her blonde hair swings into my face, scented with something that smells like caramel, and my cock reacts instantly to the feeling of her warm skin pressing against my bare chest, hardening almost to the point of pain and digging into her ass cheek as she squirms in my lap.

"Ohh," she moans faintly, and I feel my balls tighten as she bends her head into the crook of my neck, wriggling against my hard-on without the slightest subtlety.

Well, at least I can still get it up, I think dryly. But it's purely a physical reaction. Before, I wouldn't still be sitting on this lounge chair. I'd have already headed inside, looking for the nearest bed to fling her on top of for an afternoon quickie before coming back out to the pool to see who I'd want to fuck next, once my cock had a chance to recover. And it's never taken all that long when there are this many gorgeous women available for the choosing.

Or I'd be in the pool, with her discreetly on my lap while I slid her bikini aside and pushed myself inside of her, letting her squirm atop me for a long, pleasurable session of teasing until I pushed her underwater to swallow my cum. As it gets darker, the guys will be doing exactly that—we've never had a full-on orgy in front of each other. Still, we're not averse to getting some discreet head while the others pretend not to know what's going on. I'm not sure that Berto isn't starting already, with the dark-skinned beauty he has straddling him in the pool.

But even though those brief fantasies make my cock thicken even more, pulsing against the blonde's warm pussy through the thin material of her bikini as she grinds down on my lap a little more, they seem like just that. Fantasies. Nothing that I'm actually going to follow through on—even though I've done it a hundred times before.

No matter how I try to force myself to feel otherwise, the woman I want squirming against me right now, practically begging for my cock, is Sofia.

Quite simply, after seeing her panting and writhing on the bed while I buried my fingers inside of her, after tasting how sweet she was and feeling her pulse against the head of my cock while I rubbed her to the edge of an orgasm, a woman paid to pretend that she wants me isn't going to cut it. And neither, I think, is some woman picked up from a bar who only wants me because of my status and wealth.

Sofia wants, more than anything, to *not* desire me. And yet, a week ago, she was in my bed, frantically fingering herself to an orgasm in front of me, grinding against her bound hands even as she flushed with embarrassment.

She'd do anything to not feel the way she does about me. She doesn't want my money or my power. She barely even wants my protection.

But she can't help herself.

And as I sit out in the Dominican sunshine, watching Berto climb out of the pool and head inside with the woman he's undoubtedly about to fuck, Franco two lounge chairs away with three models surrounding him and one horny blonde on my lap, I'm pretty sure that I'm no better off than Sofia is.

For better or for worse, we seem to be addicted to driving each other insane.

And I have no fucking idea what to do about it.

SOFIA

12

The "party" for Caterina isn't anything like what we would have done under normal circumstances. Especially with Ana along—I can only imagine the kind of places she would have dragged us to. But Luca asked me to make a list of things I'd want to have for it, and I'd done exactly that. Still a little caught off guard by how nice he's been.

That night at the dinner table was the first time we've ever argued and not ended up with one of us storming off or making out violently. It didn't end with me bent over a couch or tied up in bed while he showed me who, exactly, is in control.

It ended, shockingly, with him conceding something to me. Something I'd wanted since the morning we came back from the hospital and hadn't thought I'd get back—being able to stay in my own room.

But it hadn't made me as happy as I'd thought it would. I'd felt almost lonely last night, without Luca's soft snores in the dark or the scent of his cologne on the covers, or the heat of his body warming the sheets even from all the way on the other side of his massive California king. The fact that he'd given in hadn't felt like a victory. It had felt like—

Like he hadn't really wanted me in there at all. Like he'd only ever forced it to make me do something that he knew I didn't want.

And now that he's gone back on it, it feels as if *he* doesn't want *me*.

It's stupid. I know it's stupid. I got what I wanted, and yet I'm still as confused and unhappy as ever. So instead of focusing on that, I think about how I'm going to have two more full days without Luca here, days to hopefully clear my head, and even better—days that I'll get to spend with my friends. It won't feel lonely in the penthouse with Caterina and Ana here. And hopefully, we'll be able to cheer Caterina up, at least a little.

She shows up about an hour after Luca leaves, striped weekender bag in hand, and the first smile I've seen on her face since before the explosion. "This is really sweet of you," she says as she sets the bag down, leaning forward to give me a hug.

"Are you kidding me? This place is huge; I feel like I get lost in it every day that I'm here by myself. It'll be nice to have you and Ana here for the weekend."

"When is she getting here?"

"Probably in a few hours." I glance over as Gio, one of the two bodyguards Luca left, crosses through the room towards the kitchen. "I don't know how I'm going to get used to having them here."

"They'll blend in soon. I remember having a bodyguard around the house off and on when I was a child, after what happened to your and Luca's fathers. After a while, I didn't even notice anymore."

"I hope so." I force a smile, trying to shake off any hint of a bad mood. "Luca asked me what I'd want to have here for your party. So we have plenty of wine, cupcakes, and he left instructions with Carmen for you to order whatever you want for dinner. We're going to have a good time tonight, no matter what. We have the whole place to ourselves, and we'll be safe. There's so much security in this building I don't know if a spider could crawl by without them seeing it."

"Well, that's a good thing," Caterina says with a laugh. "I hate spiders."

Sometime around nine, Ana finally shows up. After a back-and-forth about what to do, we find ourselves on the rooftop by the pool under the stars, with Ana making frozen daiquiris at the bar and pizza boxes scattered around.

"Oh my god." Caterina practically moans as she takes a bite out of a sausage-and-cheese slice. "I can't remember the last time I had pizza. I've been extra strict about my diet for the wedding, and I just—mm." She takes another bite, folding half the piece into her mouth, and I cover my mouth with my hand to keep from laughing out loud.

"What?" She grins at me, wiping sauce away from her cheek with a napkin. "Have you never seen someone eat pizza before?"

"I've never seen *you* eat pizza before. You're always so elegant. I never thought I'd see the day when you'd stuff half a slice into your mouth in one bite."

"Well, there's no one else here besides you two to see, so I can do what I want." Caterina laughs, laying back on the lounge chair and swallowing the last bite of her pizza. "It's actually really freeing."

Just that sentence gives me a glimpse into how strict her life must have been all these years. "What about college?" I ask curiously. "Didn't you get to cut loose and have some fun then?"

Caterina snorts. "Hardly. I had to keep living with my parents, and I had a strict curfew. I was lucky they let me go at all. Nowadays, there's no stigma among the younger mafia men about a wife with an education. But I wasn't allowed to have many friends, or go out to parties, or do anything really except go to class and come home. They were too worried that I might 'slip up.'"

"And do what, exactly?" Ana walks towards us with three strawberry daiquiris and hands them out, perching on the edge of her own chair as she takes a sip.

"Sleep with someone," Caterina says flatly. "My virginity is quite the commodity. My parents made sure to protect it just as fiercely as any other part of the family business."

Ana makes a face. "Wait, so you're a virgin, too? God, I feel like a slut hanging out with you two."

"I am." Caterina laughs. "Sofia isn't anymore."

"Barely," I mutter. "But I wasn't being *made* to stay that way. I just never dated."

"At least you both got super-hot husbands to be your firsts," Ana says, leaning forward. "Are you nervous?"

"A little," Caterina admits. "Franco is like all the other younger men—and honestly, some of the older ones, too. He sleeps around constantly, from what I've heard. I don't want him to not be happy on our wedding night."

"So wait—you haven't done anything? At all?" Ana frowns. "You've kissed him, right?"

"Of course!" Caterina blushes. "I've—we've—well, we've done a little bit. I—" she chews on her lower lip, suddenly turning brighter red than I've ever seen her. "I went down on him in the limo after he proposed to me."

"I would too! Look at that fucking ring!" Ana crows, laughing. "Come on, Sofia, chime in here. Give the poor girl some advice, one virginal bride to another."

"I don't think I have very much advice to give," I admit. "I'm basically clueless."

"You and Luca—you did sleep together, right?" Caterina frowns. "We saw the bed the morning after."

Ana makes a gagging noise. "They seriously checked your fucking *sheets*? What is this, the fourteenth century?"

Caterina shrugs. "We're all disgusted by it. My mother tried to talk my father out of doing it for Sofia. But he insisted. He's very traditional." A flicker of sadness crosses her face, probably at the mention of her mother, but it's fleeting. I can tell that she's trying to stay in a good mood.

"Luca won't keep up that tradition, I'm sure." I take a sip of my drink, trying not to think about the last night I was up here on the rooftop drinking and what that led to.

"Don't be surprised if he does. He's inherited a position and everything that goes along with it. I don't know if he'll be quick to make changes, especially while my father is still alive." Caterina pauses. "But

—you *did* sleep together, right? I mean, I can understand if you faked it, but—"

"No, we did," I say quickly. "I just—"

"It wasn't good?" Ana raises an eyebrow. "Guys as hot as Luca do tend to be shit in bed. They're so gorgeous they don't even have to try. Girls fake an orgasm just in hopes of getting to date them for a while, and then they think they're gods." She rolls her eyes.

"No, I mean—"

"Did you come?" Ana leans forward, her eyes glinting with mischief. "Come on, Sofia, we're having a girls' night. Spill a little."

I think of the night a week ago, of Luca's hard cock rubbing against my clit, his tongue on me, the way I begged him to let me come until he finally relented. The way I shamelessly got myself off in front of him, not even caring any longer that he was watching.

And then the way he rejected me afterward.

I can feel myself flushing bright red, and I'm glad that it's nighttime, so at least it's less obvious, even with the lights on the rooftop. "No," I say quietly. "I didn't. It wasn't bad, I guess. I just—told him to get it over with."

"You what?" Caterina sits up. "He didn't force you, did he?"

"I mean—" I let out a sigh. "You guys know this whole thing was arranged for me from the start. I didn't want any of it. And I didn't want to sleep with him."

"You don't think he's attractive?" Caterina frowns.

"No—" *If only.* This would all be so much easier if Luca were ugly or if I just simply weren't attracted to him at all. But how could anyone *not* be? He's like something out of anyone's fantasy—muscular, dark-haired and dark-eyed, tall, dark and handsome in every sense of the word. He's gorgeous, and I can't think how any woman wouldn't want him.

"I just—I didn't choose any of this. I didn't want to marry him. We've never even been on a date."

"I didn't choose Franco either." Caterina shrugs. "But even though I'm nervous, I'm excited about our wedding night too. He's handsome.

Hopefully, he's a good lover. I don't see any reason to be upset about it. It could have been so much worse."

"Make sure he goes down on you," Ana says with a laugh. "Especially since you've already done it to him. He better give as good as he gets."

Caterina blushes red at that, but I'm still struggling with what she just said. Am I really so wrong to resist Luca when I didn't ask for this marriage? Am I being ungrateful?

"I just don't see why I should willingly sleep with him," I insist. "I did it on our wedding night because I had to. But just because this is the way it is for women who are born into and marry into the mafia doesn't mean that it's what I want for me."

"If you don't want to, then you shouldn't," Ana says firmly. "You should never feel forced."

"I—well, I mean, I—" I stumble over my words, not knowing how to explain myself.

Caterina glances over at me. "You do want to, don't you? You just feel like you shouldn't."

She's hit the nail so directly on the head that I don't even know what to say. That's it, of course, and I've known it for a while now. If I'm being honest with myself, I've lusted after Luca since the night he pinned me up against his front door.

But I feel like he's someone I shouldn't want. Shouldn't be married to. I'm afraid of what will happen if I let myself fall under his spell.

"He's not the kind of man I would have ever dated, much less married. I would have been too intimidated to even talk to him. And —he's cold. Cruel, even."

"To you?" Ana frowns. "Has he hurt you?"

"No! I mean, he's kind of a dick sometimes, but—" I try to think of how to explain it. "He feels distant. Unreachable. Like there's this whole other side to him I can't possibly understand."

"Sofia, these men are different. Men like Luca and Franco—they're conditioned to see wives and children as just another asset or liability on a balance sheet. Something to consider in terms of its value. My father was always like that. He would have taught Luca to be the same, and I'm sure Luca's father did that too."

"I don't remember my father ever treating my mother like that," I say quietly. "He loved her. I know he did."

Caterina is quiet for a moment. "I don't remember much about your father, Sofia. But I think I remember him coming over for dinner occasionally when I was younger. He would talk about a daughter, and I always asked if I could meet her, and my father would always tell me to be quiet. But yours was always kind. Soft-spoken. I can see how having him in your life would have raised you to expect more from men."

I feel tears burning behind my eyelids, and I do my best to force them back. The last thing I want to do is break down on a night that's supposed to be happy. It's meant to be Caterina's night, and it's the first time I've seen Ana in weeks. If Caterina can be cheerful after losing her mother a week ago, then I can manage not to cry over the mention of my father, who has been dead for nearly ten years now.

"Luca makes me feel confused," I admit. "I do want him. I've never felt this kind of attraction to a man before, ever. But I can't help thinking that it's just physical because he's so handsome. That I can't possibly love someone like him."

"What do you mean?" Ana asks curiously. "What is it about him?"

"He's the *don* now." I stare at her. "And before that, he was Rossi's underboss. He's killed men. Probably tortured them, done all kinds of awful things to them—and for what? So he can sell drugs, or guns, or whatever businesses he gets all this money from? How am I supposed to love a man like that? Someone who could hurt someone else just for, for—"

"It's not about the *things*," Caterina says quietly. "It's about loyalty, about trust, about not going back on your word. All of these men do terrible things, but they all have a code. And if Luca hurts someone, it's to keep them from hurting others he cares about. It's not about whatever merchandise they're moving. It's about making sure that betrayal is unacceptable. That all the men around him are loyal. And that the other mobs stick to the agreements that the leaders have made."

I frown at her. "How do you know all of this?"

"I listen." She shrugs. "My father isn't always quiet when he has meetings at the house. And I've heard him talk about Luca before. Luca is restrained when it comes to those things. He's never more violent than he needs to be. He doesn't enjoy it."

"And what about Franco?"

Caterina is quiet for a long moment. "I don't know about him—how he feels about all of that. We've never talked about it."

I remember, suddenly, what Luca said at dinner that night. That he'd always protected Franco, done the worst of the things that needed doing so that Franco wouldn't have to. *So that Franco wouldn't have to deal with the demons that came with it.*

I hadn't paid much attention to what he was saying then. But it occurs to me that it shows a side of Luca I hadn't seen before. The kind of man he is beyond our interactions.

The kind of man who would do awful things, get blood on his hands that he can't wash off, to spare his friend. The kind of man who shielded a childhood friend from gossip and then kept on protecting him.

The kind of man who is struggling now, knowing that he can't protect his friend any longer—and that maybe he protected him for too long.

"Luca mentioned to me that he's kept Franco from having to get his hands dirty too often." I glance at Caterina. "I think he's been trying to protect him from some of those realities."

"They've been joined at the hip since they were kids." Caterina rubs her hands along her thighs, letting out a long breath. "There were always rumors that Franco's father was Irish. His mother got pregnant not long after the head of the Irish mob in Boston came to visit, and with Franco's red hair—well, you can see how the gossip would start. It was proved that he wasn't illegitimate. Which was good—for him and his mother."

"Wait—what would have happened?"

"Probably the kind of thing that happens in any of these crime families," Ana mutters. "And it's never good for the woman."

"I think it's safe to assume his mother would have been killed. Franco—possibly him, as well. And it would have started a war with the Irish. Franco's father wasn't part of the inner circle. Still, he was respected enough that the Irish leader sleeping with his wife would have been seen as a terrible insult. It wouldn't have gone over well."

I stare at her, horrified. But even as I open my mouth to protest that surely, Franco's mother wouldn't have been murdered even if she'd cheated—for one thing, what if she hadn't? What if she'd been forced?—but then I realize that of course, that would have been the result. Rossi had wanted to kill *me* just because it was easier than trying to keep me alive. If it weren't for Luca, I'd be dead.

Do you see a pattern here? The small voice in my head whispers. *He's protected Franco. He's protected you. Maybe he's not as terrible as you think he is.*

"I told you that my mother and I came here after my father was killed by the Bratva," Ana says quietly. "Sofia, I know that you're struggling with the circumstances that forced you into this marriage. And I know Luca isn't the kind of man you would ever have swiped right on in the real world. But I don't think he's a bad man. I think—" she hesitates, chewing on her lower lip. "I think he might even have feelings for you."

"I agree," Caterina chimes in. "I think he's falling for you, even though he's not going to admit it. Not now, at least."

"I don't think Luca is the kind of man who has feelings for anyone," I say flatly. "You said yourself, Caterina, marriages in the mafia aren't made for love. So why would he be falling for me?"

"Maybe it's different." Caterina shrugs. "Wouldn't it be nice if it was?"

"I just want what he promised me," I insist stubbornly. "I want him to give me an apartment away from him, where we don't have to see each other. And then I can try to forget about all of this."

But even as I say it, I'm not sure I mean it. Just last night, I'd missed having Luca in bed beside me. I'd felt lonely, even though being back in my own room was exactly what I'd wanted.

"We fight all the time, almost every time we try to talk. If there are feelings, it's just lust. I know that's all it is."

"What about the morning after the attack on the hotel?" Ana asks suddenly. "You didn't know if he was okay, right? So how did you feel about that?"

I felt relieved that he wasn't dead. And confused about why he tried to save me. But I don't want to say that out loud. I don't want to admit that some part of me might want this husband that was forced on me, that I might actually want to try to make this work. That our conversation the night before last gave me a small window into what it could look like if we had a real marriage—and it wasn't terrible.

I keep getting these slight glimpses into what my life could be—the way my friendship with Caterina would grow, the way Luca and I could make the best of this situation.

But this was never meant to be a real marriage. There will always be things stopping us—the fact that we can't ever have children, the first night we spent together, the women that I'm sure will always chase Luca, and the knowledge of the kind of man he is when he's not home with me, the things he does for his job. Things that I'll benefit from because I live in this house and spend his money. I can't believe that he'll ever be faithful or that he'll ever be anything other than what he is now—a cold and brutal man who has flickers of warmth at unexpected times.

"I didn't care," I say flatly, putting as much effort as I can into making it sound as if that's true. "The only thing I was worried about is what would happen to me if he'd died."

I *know*, for a fact, as the words come out of my mouth that it's not true.

And looking at Caterina and Ana's faces, I don't think they believe me either.

SOFIA

13

By the time we all crash in one of the guest rooms, in a giant king-size bed that more than fits the three of us, we're buzzed on daiquiris and wine, full of cupcakes, and thoroughly exhausted. After a little while, the conversation had strayed away from my fraught relationship with Luca and turned back to Caterina's wedding—and more often, her upcoming wedding night. Ana had plenty of tips to share, and by the time we'd finished off two bottles of wine, we were all laughing more and more with every outlandish story she shared about her exploits with the men she'd dated.

It was nice to see Caterina laugh. The night had accomplished exactly what I'd hoped for—to take her mind off of her grief and give her a chance to cut loose and enjoy something about the wedding that had been so dramatically moved up. It also allowed us to take her mind off what Franco was probably doing at his own bachelor party. Luca hadn't told me where they were going, exactly, only that it was out of the country and that they were taking the private jet.

She'd mentioned it just once before we'd quickly changed the subject, but I'd seen the look in her eyes. She might say that she didn't love him, that she'd accepted the way he and all of these other men are, I could tell that the idea of Franco partying with a bunch of other women, probably fucking them and doing god knows what in some other country bothered her.

Luca's probably doing the same thing. I'd managed to avoid thinking about it for most of the night, but now lying in a wine-and-frosting induced stupor on the far left side of the bed, suddenly images of Luca in some faraway place with gorgeous women hanging off of him fills my head. I try to push them away, but all I can think about once the first image enters my head is Luca feeling up some supermodel, Luca bending her over a bed, Luca naked and tangled up in sheets with three or four women at once. I remember the way he'd taunted me with that exact image a few weeks ago—what feels like a million years ago now—and the thought gives me a sick feeling deep in my stomach.

I can't expect him to be celibate if I don't want him. If I keep refusing to sleep with him. But—the idea of him teasing some other woman the way he did me, of him kissing someone else with the same passion, makes me want to burst into tears. It's not even just jealousy anymore; it's a deep, aching feeling of sadness, almost as if—

Almost as if I'm starting to fall for him.

I squeeze my eyes shut, trying not to think about it. If I think about something else, I'll manage to fall asleep. I try to focus on the sound of the city outside, faintly coming through the window, or Gio and Raoul's footsteps down the hall as they make their rounds in the penthouse. True to what Caterina had said, they'd done a remarkable job of blending in all night. I'd hardly even noticed they were there after a while, but I do feel safer.

Luca has gone to such lengths to keep me safe. Is it really just because he's trying to keep a promise that was made for him? Simply because of his own ego and need to protect what's "his?" Or is there something deeper to it, the way Ana and Caterina seem to think that there might be?

Part of me wants to believe that. But what if I'm wrong? What if I let myself start to fall—and he breaks my heart?

He's still in my thoughts when I fall asleep. And I can't shake him, even in my dreams.

I'm in his bed again, naked under the black sheets, and I can feel the warmth of his body behind mine as he slides towards me, his fingers trailing over my throat as he pushes my hair out of my face. His lips run over my jaw, down the back of my neck, and the brush of them against my nape makes me shiver. He slides his hand over my hip, down between my legs so that his fingers brush over the crease of my pussy, and I shudder, arching up into his hand.

"Have you been a good girl?" he whispers. "Have you been touching my pussy without my permission?"

"No," I whimper, arching my back so that my ass is pressing against him, and I can feel that he's naked too, his thick cock hard and pulsing against me as the head brushes against the small of my back.

"You must need to come so badly then," he whispers into my ear. His fingers slip between my folds as he murmurs the words. I shiver at the groan that he makes when he feels how hot and wet I am, already drenched from the feeling of his muscular body against mine. "Do you need it, Sofia? Do you need me to make you come?"

"Please," I whisper it in a small voice as I squirm against him, and I feel him reach between us, guiding his cock so that the swollen head presses against my entrance. I'm so tight that even as wet as I am, it's an effort for him to push it inside, but it feels so good when he does. My skin feels electric with sensation as he thrusts into me an inch at a time, his fingers toying with my clit as he pushes deeper.

"Fuck, you feel so good," he groans, his hips thrusting up against me as the last inches of his cock slide into me. I can already feel the orgasm building as he starts to move, grinding against my ass and matching the rhythm with his fingers as he rubs my clit. "I'm going to come too if your pussy keeps squeezing me like that."

I clench around him just at the words, my head thrown back against his shoulder, my body moving with his as I lose myself in the pleasure of it. I can't remember why I ever said I didn't want this, why I ever tried to fight him. He feels so good, like he was made for me, his cock filling me as he teases me to the edge of an orgasm, and I don't know how I ever pretended that this wasn't something I—

A noise at the foot of the bed makes my eyes fly open, and to my horror, I see a gorgeous blonde woman in an evening gown standing there. She has on sparkling diamond earrings that glitter in the light as she watches us, and she smiles at me as if she knows a secret she's not telling.

"Doesn't it feel good?" she coos. "His cock is still the best one I've ever had. I still dream about it sometimes."

"I loved sucking it," the brunette who appears next to her out of nowhere says. "Have you sucked his cock yet? You'll have to if you don't want him to cheat on you."

"He loves girls who swallow."

"He fucked us both at once."

"Will you let him do it in the ass? If you don't, he'll find someone who will."

"He ate my pussy all night long."

Woman after woman appears around the bed, surrounding us, their voices joining together in a chorus as they describe the dirty things that they did to Luca, that he did with them. They're so loud that I want to clamp my hands over my ears, my orgasm was long gone, but Luca keeps thrusting as if he doesn't see or hear them, groaning in my ear with each stroke.

"He's so close. I can see him tensing up."

"He never came in me. I think he knew I would've tried to get pregnant."

"He always came on my face."

"I loved the taste of it."

There are so many of them. They're everywhere. "I'm so close," Luca groans, and the chant starts up again until I want to scream. I think I am screaming, but Luca doesn't care. He rolls me over onto my stomach, thrusting hard into me from behind, and I scream into the pillow over and over because I can still hear them, I can still—

There's a loud cracking sound, so loud that I sit bolt upright in bed, the dream shattering all around me. The scream wasn't from me after all. It was either Caterina or Ana, both of whom are sitting up already. Ana's hands are knotted in the blanket, and Caterina's hand is over her mouth. She looks ghostly pale.

"What—"

"Shh!" Caterina slaps a hand over my mouth. And that's when I see it—or rather, *him*.

There's a black-clothed figure in the door, with the build of a man, looking directly at the bed. And he has a gun in his hand, pointed at us.

Pointed at *me*.

"You're not getting away this time, you bitch," he growls. "I'll do the job right."

He steps into the room, the gun perfectly steady, and I feel myself go cold with fear. I can hear the blood rushing in my ears, my heartbeat deafeningly loud, and I'm terribly, viscerally aware of the fact that if that gun goes off, those beats could be my last. That I might die here in this bed—that my friends might die.

"No!" Ana shrieks and the man glares at her. "Shut up, little Russian whore. I'll deal with you next. And *you*," he grins at Caterina through the hole in his mask, the gun still pointed at me. "Viktor has plans for you."

Caterina gasps softly, and I feel myself wobbling, my vision going dark at the edges as if I'm going to pass out again. I was terrified in the hotel room after the Russians kidnapped me, but this is a new fear altogether. I can see down the barrel of the gun as the man advances towards the bed. I feel nauseated, my stomach flipping wildly as I try desperately to think of what I should do—if I should stay still, if I should run, if I should scream.

Luca saved me in the hotel room, but he won't be able to save me this time. He's too far away.

I hear footsteps on the stairs, and just as the man swings around, one of the bodyguards—I think it's Gio—bursts into the room. The man fires at him, the gunshot painfully loud in the small room, and I clap my hands over my ears as all three of us scream with terror.

Gio recoils backward, and I shriek again, realizing that he's been hit. "Oh my god!" Caterina screams, and the black-clothed man wheels to face us again, the gun less steady now.

"Shut the fuck up!" he shouts, and I see the gun waver in my direction, his finger tightening on the trigger.

This is it. This is how I'm going to die. Luca is going to come home and find my body. I'll never know if—

The sound of a shot rings through the air as I squeeze my eyes tightly shut, and I jerk backward as if hit, my body reacting to the noise.

But there's no pain, and the next thing I hear is the sound of something hitting the floor, the force of it shaking the bed. Next to me, Caterina is almost hyperventilating.

I open my eyes slowly to see Ana staring wide-eyed at the foot of the bed. Raoul is standing in the doorway next to Gio's slumped body, gun in hand and the man who had found his way into the bedroom is bleeding out onto the carpet.

I leap out of bed, my frozen muscles suddenly working again as I rush towards the two bodyguards. "Is he dead?" I ask frantically, kneeling down next to Gio. His head is lolling sideways, and I can see that his shirt is almost soaked through with blood.

Raoul kneels down next to me. "No," he says gruffly. "Not yet, at least. We need to get him to the hospital, though. I'll call the driver. We'll get him down to the garage and rush him over as fast as we can." He glances over at the body. "I'll need to deal with this."

"I'll go with him," I say quickly. "Someone should, and—"

"Sofia, you can't!" Caterina exclaims. "Luca will be furious if he finds out you've left. I can go if someone needs to—"

"That man was going to shoot me." I grit my teeth. "Gio took a bullet for me—for all three of us. The least I can do is go with him."

"Sofia—" Caterina starts to say, but Ana is already climbing out of bed.

"We'll go with you then," she says decisively. "We should all make sure he gets there safely. And you shouldn't be alone." She reaches for the pair of jeans she threw across the chair by the window, stepping into them carefully while avoiding the body on the carpet. Caterina is still motionless in the bed, and I'm a little bit amazed at how well Ana is handling this. I always knew she was fairly tough, but this is surprising even for her.

I can't believe that I haven't fallen apart either. The only reason I think I haven't is that I'm focused on Gio, who is completely unconscious by this point and still bleeding. I can hear Raoul on the phone just outside the door, and a moment later, he steps in, a towel in hand.

"Put this on his shoulder and hold it there," he says sternly. "A couple of guys will be up in a minute to help get him down to the car. I'll deal with the body. You girls need to get out of the room. It's no place for you right now."

"We're all going to the hospital," Ana says firmly. "Come on, Caterina. Get dressed."

I see Caterina start to get out of the bed, moving stiffly. "She's in no condition," Raoul says. "I'll have a couple of the guys keep an eye on her. But neither of you are going anywhere." He turns to face me. "Luca would have my head if he knew I let you out of this penthouse. Gio will be fine with the guys going with him, and if he's not, there's nothing else you could do."

Ana visibly bristles, but says nothing as she strides past Raoul and the body, squatting down next to me. "It'll be okay," she says quietly, and I don't know who she's speaking to exactly—me, Gio, or herself. But it feels good to hear it out loud, even if I don't quite believe it.

"I have to go—" I start to say, but the look on Raoul's face silences me. I know he's right—Luca would probably kill him, literally, if he let me leave. It's going to be bad enough when he gets back and finds out that someone was able to break in at all.

Deep down, I'm terrified and trying to hold it back. If someone could get to me—to us—even with so much security and two bodyguards patrolling the apartment, then it means two things.

One, someone helped the man get inside.

And two, nowhere is safe for me anymore.

I choke back the fear as the men come upstairs to help carry Gio down. Ana and I watch, trying not to look at the overturned couch or broken glass or the other body on the living room floor. I don't even know who that is—it could be one of the security team, or it could be the intruder's accomplice.

It feels terrible that I don't know. I feel shaky and nauseous, on the verge of going into shock probably, and Ana wraps a steadying arm around my waist. "It's okay," she repeats. "It's okay."

But it doesn't matter how many times she says it. Deep down, I know that nothing is okay.

And I'm not sure if it ever will be again.

LUCA

14

*I*t's easy to lose track of time here.

The party has steadily escalated as it's gotten darker. More girls are showing up and the guys getting looser and looser. Max and Berto are both snorting lines of cocaine off of models, Max off of a brunette's tits, and Berto off of a redhead's ass. Franco comes stumbling in a moment later, three girls in tow. He lurches towards the couch where I'm sitting, trying to ignore the gorgeous black-haired girl in lacy white lingerie who is trying her best to get me to fuck her.

"You're all alone, Luca," he slurs, obviously drunk. "I know who you're thinking about. And you gotta—stoppp." He trips over the last words. "Sofia—right? Well, fuck her. Fuck your wife. You gotta—get fuckin' laid, man."

He shoves all three of the girls in my direction, and they tumble towards me, giggling as they collapse onto the couch, one of them right on top of me. They're all barely clothed, tits and long hair everywhere, and I groan as I feel my balls throb painfully. I've been hard off and on most of the afternoon, and this coupled with the two naked girls on the recliner across from me tangled in a sixty-nine for our benefit isn't helping.

The problem is, I don't want to fuck any of them. I want to do exactly what Franco just slurred at me—fuck my wife. But she's in Manhattan, and I'm here, in a hotel with five guys who won't understand why I'm not joining in on the debauchery and will probably call me all kinds of half-joking names in the morning for it.

Not that I care. I'm not a thirteen-year-old boy to get my feelings hurt because someone teases me about being gay because I didn't get laid. But I'm at my limit of patience right now, so horny that I could explode, worried about what's happening back at home, angry that I want my wife—a woman forced on me that I shouldn't give a shit about—and above all else, horribly sober.

I've had a couple drinks, but I didn't want to get drunk. The thought of getting high isn't any more appealing. And despite the unfortunate fact that I've been hard as a rock for most of the day, I have no intention of fucking any of these women.

What I want to do is get back to Manhattan.

The blonde in the green bikini is kneeling between my legs, her hand massaging the ridge of my cock through my swim trunks as I try to find the will to push her away. And then, just as I'm reaching out to guide her hand off of my aching length, one of the guards comes through the door.

"Luca." His voice rings out through the room, but no one really pays attention to it other than me. The man is a real pro. He barely even looks over at the girls moaning on the recliner, even though a third has now joined, fingering herself while she watches the other two.

"Yeah?" I push the blonde away, standing up and trying to discreetly adjust myself. I can hear groans from down the hall—probably Franco—and the sounds of flesh slapping against flesh. I'm tempted to go out to the pool, but I can see the silhouette of someone else out there, Adrian, I think, getting a blowjob.

No thanks.

"You're going to want to hear about this." He jerks his head towards the door. "Let's talk."

* * *

LESS THAN AN HOUR LATER, I'm on the jet back to Manhattan.

My entire body is shaking with rage. I left without saying anything to anyone—all of the guys are too high or too busy fucking to grasp what's going on, anyway. I told my security team to explain as best they could if anyone noticed I was gone, fill them in on what had happened in the morning, and let them know that I'd send the jet back for them.

But all I can think about is getting home.

Home to Sofia.

I'd been assured she was safe, but I'm not sure that I'll be able to believe it until I see her. *I'm going to kill whoever did this with my bare hands,* I think, my teeth gritted with anger as I look out the window of the jet, wishing that I could somehow get there faster. Everything feels thrown into sharp relief, including the fact that I very easily could have never seen her again.

It makes all of my arguments for why I shouldn't get closer to her, why I shouldn't sleep with her, why I should try to push her as far away as possible, seem flimsier by the minute. I can't even begin to untangle my feelings right now, but by far, the one that appears the strongest is the relief that she's still alive.

For now.

The entire flight back, all I can think about is murder, plain and simple. *I'm going to kill whoever let that man get past them.*

I'm going to kill Viktor.

I'm going to kill them all.

But once I'm in the car headed back to the penthouse, my thoughts switch to Sofia. I feel desperate to see her, touch her, and make sure with my own two hands that she's alive.

"Where is she?" are my first words when I step into the apartment. Raoul is cleaning up the living room, and he looks up as I walk in.

"She's in your room," he says calmly. "The other two girls are asleep in the guest rooms. It took a little while to calm everyone down, but Caterina and Ana are asleep, I think. I don't know about Sofia, but she was awake the last time I checked on her."

"And Gio?"

"He's in critical condition, but he should live."

I nod tersely, and Raoul starts to explain more, but I wave a hand at him, already heading for the stairs. "You can debrief me later. Right now, I want to see my wife."

"Of course, sir."

I take the stairs two and then three at a time, going straight for the guest room that I'd given to Sofia as hers. And then I halt, realizing what Raoul had said.

She's in your room.

Even though I'd told Sofia she could go back to her room, she's in mine instead, after what must have been one of the most terrifying nights of her life.

In my bed.

The feeling that overtakes me is something like insanity, a madness that I can't stop as my last frail thread of control snaps. I stride towards the bedroom door, throwing it open without a second thought as I walk into the room and see Sofia huddled against a mountain of pillows, a blanket over her legs.

"Luca."

My name whispered on her lips, sounds like a prayer. Like she's asking for me. Asking me to save her, like I've done a dozen times already.

Like I'd do a hundred times again.

I'm at her side in a flash, grabbing her by the arms, hauling her up to her knees as I bend down to kiss her. I need her lips on mine, her body against mine, around me, enveloping me. I feel as if I can't breathe, as if I'll die if I don't have her now, without any more arguments.

Without any more second thoughts.

She moans against my mouth, her arms wrapping around my neck, and her reaction goes through me like a shock. I'd expected her to push me away, maybe even to be angry with me for leaving her here at all, to tell me to go fuck myself.

That if I can't keep her safe like I'd promised, then there's no reason for her to be here at all.

But instead, she melts into me, her mouth parting as my tongue slides over her lower lip, plunging into her mouth the way I want to sink into her body. I bury my hands into the silk of her dark hair, feeling it run through my fingers and tangle around them as I groan into her mouth, so hard that I feel as if my cock might break. My entire body is throbbing with need for her, my pulse in my throat as I lift her up and lay her back against the pillows, stretching out over her as I kiss her again and again, until I can feel certain that she's really here.

That she's alive.

Sofia moans, arching up against me as her fingers trail through my hair, scratching over my scalp, down to my jaw. She runs her fingertips over the stubble there, caressing me like she's never done before, her hands moving down to the buttons of my shirt. She pulls at them, yanking and tugging until the shirt is hanging open and loose, her palms sliding over the smooth, muscled expanse of my chest as she pants against my mouth, her body soft and warm in my hands.

And then she goes very still underneath me, pulling back from the kiss to look up at me with those wide, dark eyes.

"You came back," she whispers. "I didn't know—"

I stare down at her. "Of course I came back." My voice sounds unfamiliar to me, deep and husky, rough with a need that I've never felt before. "I was on the jet the second they told me."

"I—you were with your friends—I thought—" she swallows hard, licking her lips. "I thought you'd be busy with some other woman—"

Fuck. My heart pounds in my chest, and I tangle my hand in her hair, tilting her head back so that her eyes meet mine and she can't look away. "I tried. There were plenty of women there, plenty of chances. I was going to. I wanted to fuck you out of my system, to forget how you—how *this* makes me feel. But I couldn't. I couldn't fucking do it." The words rush out of my mouth before I can stop them, and I surge forward, pressing myself against her as I hold her tightly in my grasp. "Do you feel how fucking hard you make me? That's how I've been for days, weeks, thinking about you. I can hardly think about anyone else. Every time I touch myself, it's you in my thoughts. Every time I go to sleep, I see you. Every time I come home, I see you in my bed, and all I want is to be inside of you."

Sofia is staring up at me, speechless, but I can't stop. Everything I've been bottling up comes pouring out, like a drunken confession, except I'm not intoxicated on anything except her.

"You're like a drug. An obsession. And it only gets worse every time. All I can think about is you—the sounds you make when I touch you, how you feel…how you taste. I can't fucking get you out of my head. Sofia—"

She looks up at me, her hands sliding down either side of my face, and I can feel her body arching upwards towards mine, drawn to me like a moth to a flame.

And right now, I don't care if we both get burned.

Her hands slide over my shoulders, pushing my shirt off, throwing it to the floor. I watch her face as she slides her hands over my arms, touching, squeezing, sliding down my chest, and I shudder with pleasure at her touch. I don't know if it feels so fucking good because it's been weeks since I've been with anyone else—with anyone at all, other than our wedding night—or just because I want her so badly that I can hardly stand it, but nothing has ever felt this good.

I don't think anything could stop me right now—not if a hundred Bratva came down on this house, or a thousand. I'm completely lost in her—in her touch, her scent, the taste of her mouth as I kiss her again and again, groaning with the pleasure of it as I feel her legs wrap around my waist, and I know that she wants me just as badly.

She's only wearing a thin tank top and a pair of soft pajama pants. I slide my hand up beneath the fabric of her shirt, up the flat smoothness of her belly, to the full curve of her breast, her nipple stiffening under my touch as I cup her breast in my hand, my cock throbbing as I squeeze her there, desperate to be inside of her.

But now that we're here, I don't want to rush, even as my body strains towards hers with a need I've never known before. I want to savor her, to touch every inch.

I grab a fistful of the tank top, resisting the urge to tear it, dragging it up over her head instead so that I can see all of her lovely pale skin, her breasts swaying softly as she raises her arms for me to pull it off. If I'd thought she was beautiful before, intoxicating before, it's nothing compared to her willing and pliable under my hands, her face soft and open as she reaches up to pull me down for a kiss again.

Even as my lips brush over hers, I'm already fumbling with the waist of her pajamas, pulling them down over her hips as my hand slides between her legs. The whimper that she makes when I trace my fingers through the wetness there, the sound that turns into a moan, almost makes me come undone.

I've never been as turned on in my life as I am when I see her naked on the bed underneath me, arching upwards for my touch, her soft pink lips parted and gasping as she leans up for me to kiss her again.

"I want you," I whisper roughly, tangling my hand in her hair as I pull her mouth up to mine. "Say yes, Sofia. Please. Say yes."

SOFIA

Say yes.
I don't know what happened.

I was convinced Luca wasn't coming back. That no one would bother him with the news of the intruder, that I'd be here with Caterina and Ana until Sunday night or Monday rolled around, and Luca would come strolling in only to find out that all hell had broken loose while he was gone.

But that's not what happened at all.

Instead, he came rushing home. Rushing to *me*. And the look on his face when he burst through the bedroom door was like nothing I'd ever seen before.

It wasn't the look of a man who was pissed that someone had broken into his home or threatened his possessions.

It was frantic. Terrified. *Lost.*

And it hadn't changed until he'd fallen into bed with me, his mouth devouring mine like a starving man, his hands grasping at me as if he's not entirely sure that I'm real.

I can't help but respond to it. My heart is pounding in my chest, the sudden, desperate need to touch and be touched, to know that I'm alive, to *feel* washing over me in waves that feel as if they might drown me, but I don't want to come up to the surface.

I want to sink with him.

Luca's kisses sear my lips, his tongue sliding into my mouth with a possessive hunger that makes me feel electrified as we strip away each other's clothing. The sight of him shirtless makes my heart race all over again, and I run my hands over him as he slides between my legs. He's the most gorgeous man I've ever seen, and I want to touch all of him, every muscular inch.

His fingers slide against the wet folds of my pussy, making me gasp and moan as they slip between, teasing me with the light touch, and I hear him groan, his cock throbbing against my leg.

"I want you," he whispers, his voice a hoarse growl that sends a bolt of lust through me. I never thought I could make any man sound like that—hungry, desperate—but Luca sounds as if he's barely holding back, clinging to a shred of control that I could make him lose in an instant.

Just like our wedding night. I remember the way he surged against me, the way that he lost himself for just a few minutes, and I want that again.

Just for a little while, I want to not think about whether we should or shouldn't.

To not worry about what's right or wrong.

I just want my husband. Just for tonight.

We can figure the rest out in the morning.

"Yes," I whisper, my hands running through his thick dark hair, down to the rasp of black stubble on his jaw, my body trembling with desire. "Yes, yes, yes."

"Oh god." He groans, kissing me again, his mouth fierce and hard against mine as he presses me down into the mattress, his hands roving hungrily down the curve of my waist and over my hips. "I want to taste you, Sofia, I want to make you come so hard—"

I gasp as Luca's lips trail to my throat, nipping at the soft flesh there, sucking lightly and then harder as his hand squeezes my breast, his thumb rolling over my nipple. I know he's leaving a mark on my throat, but I don't care. It feels so good, sensitizing every part of me as the fingers of his other hand slip inside of me, moving in slow strokes as I grind into his palm.

He keeps going, his mouth trailing down to my collarbone, setting his teeth lightly into my flesh there before continuing down. He kisses between my breasts, licking first one nipple and then another, until I'm squirming under him and arching my hips, wanting more. It feels so good, it *all* feels so good, but I want to come. I've had enough teasing, enough of touching myself and wondering what it would be like for Luca to do it.

"I want you to make me come," I beg. "Please, Luca, I want to know what it feels like—"

He looks down at me, his eyes glittering darkly. "Right now?" His fingers speed up inside of me, curling as he presses the pad of his thumb against my clit, rolling it underneath as he begins to thrust faster. "Do you want me to make you come right fucking now, Sofia?"

"Yes! Oh god, yes, please—" I half sob the words, writhing in his grip as he fingers me harder, rubbing my clit with his thumb until I feel like I'm going to go mad.

"Then come for me, Sofia." His voice rolls over me, smooth like silk, thick like smoke, intoxicating like wine. "I want my pussy to come."

And just like that, I'm thrown back to that night, overcome with pleasure as he teased me to the brink again and again, desperate for it. I think of him fingering me over the couch, of his hot cum on my ass. I hear a sound coming from my lips that I've never heard before as the orgasm hits me, my entire body arching off of the bed as I come harder than I ever have in my life, almost screaming with pleasure as I buck against his hand.

He drives his fingers into me hard, his thumb still rubbing my clit, and the waves crash over me until I feel like I can't breathe, like I might die. I'm still quivering when Luca pulls his fingers out of me and slides down the bed, pushing my thighs open wide so that he can see my fluttering, clenching pussy, my body crying out for more.

"Don't stop—" I pant, my hips rising off of the bed as Luca runs his hands up my inner thighs.

"Oh, don't worry," he promises, his voice dark and deep as he looks up at me, his green eyes glittering. "I won't."

And then I feel his mouth.

"Luca!" I almost shriek his name at the pleasure of it, his tongue sliding over my still-pulsing clit, almost too sensitive. His tongue is soft and hot, and I flush pink as I realize how wet I am. He moans as he drags his tongue from my entrance to my clit over and over again, sucking my folds into his mouth as he devours me, kissing my pussy the way he kisses my mouth.

He's going to make me come again, I know it. I'd heard Ana talk about men who had made her come more than once—they were usually the guys she went on a second date with—but I hadn't thought it could happen to *me*. It took long enough for me to make myself come once.

But not Luca. He already has me on edge again, my body quivering as I throw my head back, fingers clawing at the duvet as I grind shamelessly against his face, past caring what he thinks of me. From the way he groans, the sound of it vibrating against my already oversensitive flesh, it's turning him on too.

He thrusts two fingers into my soaked channel again, thrusting in hard, firm strokes that make me crave his cock, and I arch against his mouth, whimpering and moaning. "Please fuck me," I hear myself beg, my thighs splaying wider as I try to push myself over the edge, desperate for it. "Please, Luca, I need—"

That stops him for just a moment, and his eyes roll upwards, looking at me from where his mouth is buried between my thighs. "You want me to fuck you?" He licks me pointedly, letting me watch as he drags his tongue upwards and swirls it around my clit, making me moan helplessly again. "Do you want my cock?"

"Yes, please—"

"Then come one more time for me, and I'll fuck you hard."

His tongue flutters over my clit, his lips pressing against my soaked flesh as he sucks it into his mouth, and I feel as if I'm dissolving.

I'm coming apart at the seams, lost in a whirlwind of pleasure that's like nothing I've ever felt. I arch and writhe and moan and scream, the orgasm endless as Luca thrusts his fingers into me again and again, sucking at my clit, driving me into what feels like an endless pulsing orgasm that, when it finally starts to recede, leaves me limp and gasping. I look up at him dizzily, and I know that when this is over, I'm never going to be able to resist again. I'd do anything to feel this.

If I'd known sex could be this good, I'd never have stayed a virgin that long.

But somewhere deep down, I suspect that it's just Luca. Or worse still—that it's just him and I. Together.

I realize in a daze that he's naked, his jeans undone and tossed away, and he kneels between my legs, his cock thick and hard and so close to me. He's stroking it slowly, his green gaze fixed on my body, raking over me hungrily. "Tell me again, Sofia," he rasps, his voice almost a growl. "Tell me you want my cock."

"Yes, please, I want—"

"Say it." His face is nothing but naked hunger, his entire body rigid with desire. "Tell me."

I'm past caring what I say. I need him. I need him inside of me.

"I want your cock, Luca, please—please fuck me, oh god please—" The words tumble from my mouth in a rush as I reach up for him, wanting to pull him down to me, and as the last *please* slips from my lips, Luca groans, his body coming down atop me as his mouth claims mine in a searing kiss.

He thrusts inside of me in one long, hard stroke, his cock filling me completely as he sinks to the hilt, his hips settling atop mine. I feel him shudder, a ripple of pleasure going down his spine, and I run my hands down his back as he kisses me again, unmoving as he savors the taste of my lips.

And then Luca pulls back, his eyes dark with lust as he looks down at me.

"I can't go slow, Sofia," he groans, his voice hoarse. "I need—"

"I don't care."

I wrap my arms around his neck, dragging him down for another kiss, and he starts to thrust.

Every stroke is hard and fast, and I can feel his need, his hunger, everything that he's tried to hold back since that night that he pinned me up against his door and kissed me for the first time. And it feels so fucking good. I want more of it, I want all of him, and I arch upwards, pressing my breasts against his muscled chest as I kiss him back, my hips meeting his every thrust, my legs wrapping around his as I cling to him, the pleasure rising up in me too. I want to come again, want to come with him. I hear his groans intensifying, his thrusts harder and harder as he fucks me with the kind of wild abandon that I know now is exactly what I wanted.

"Yes," I hear myself whispering between kisses. "Yes, oh god, Luca, that feels so good—"

"So fucking good," he groans, shuddering as he thrusts again. "You're so fucking tight, oh fuck, Sofia, you were made for me—*fuck*." He breaks the kiss, his eyes locked onto mine as he grinds against me. I can feel the head of his cock pressing against a sensitive spot deep inside of me, pushing me to the edge as his hips roll atop mine. "I'm going to come, Sofia, fuck, I can't—*Sofia*—"

He groans my name, his mouth slanting over mine as he kisses me so hard that it's almost painful. I feel myself clenching down around him, shuddering with pleasure as he thrusts once more, forcefully, and then he starts to shudder.

"*I'm coming*," he growls, the words ground out between his teeth as he presses his mouth to my shoulder. I feel myself falling over the edge too for the third time, my body spasming around him as I come hard on his cock, tangling my arms and legs around him as he pushes me back against the pillows, and I can feel his cock throbbing inside of me as he erupts, the hot rush of his cum filling me as I moan helplessly, so overcome by pleasure that I couldn't have stopped it if I tried.

His mouth presses against my shoulder, his hips still moving against me, and I realize that he's still hard. "I can't stop," he mumbles. "Fuck, Sofia. You're like a goddamn drug, I swear—"

He pulls back slightly, looking at me with dazed eyes. He looks as if he's never experienced anything like this before. I think of all the women who must have laid in this very bed, who had him inside of them like this, and I feel a fit of burning jealousy that threatens to consume me.

But looking up at Luca's face, I know without him saying a word that it's never been like this. Whatever he's feeling with me, he's never felt before.

I take his face between my hands, his stubble scratching my palms, and I look up into my husband's eyes as I wrap my legs around his, my hips moving to meet his slow thrusts.

"Don't stop."

LUCA

16

I feel like I'm in a haze. It feels better than being high, better than any sex I've ever had in my life, better than anything I ever imagined. I just came harder than I think I ever have before. However, I'm still rock hard, moaning with pleasure at the feeling of Sofia's tight pussy fluttering around me from her orgasm. I can still taste her on my lips, the scent of her surrounding me, and I don't want to stop. I *can't* stop, and I keep thrusting inside of her, pushing myself up to look down at her as I rock my hips slowly, savoring the feeling of her wet, velvet heat sliding along the length of my cock again and again.

I can't let her go. It's half the reason I don't want to stop fucking her, because I feel that somehow if I stop, if I pull out of her, if I go to sleep —when I wake up, she won't be here anymore. She'll be in her own room, or she'll be gone, lost forever. It's a ridiculous, delirious thought, but I've stopped trying to make sense of it since the moment I stepped on the plane back home.

This is all I wanted.

I don't want it to end.

Don't stop.

I lose track of how long it goes on. I want to do more than just fuck her like this, in missionary, but I don't want to slip out of her long enough to change positions. I keep thrusting, long and slow, kissing her over and over again until, at last, she tightens around me and cries out again. I feel my cock start to throb as I spill my cum into her again for the second time, shuddering as I wrap my arms around her and bring her with me as I roll onto my side, her leg wrapping over mine.

We fall asleep after that for a little while, my half-hard cock still inside of her. Sofia's head is tucked under mine, her face pressed against my chest, and I can feel the warmth of her breath against my skin.

I've never done this before. I've had women sleep over a handful of times, when I was too worn out to bother calling them an Uber, but I've never held a woman in my arms after sex, never fallen asleep with someone else's body pressed against mine. I never thought I would want to. I like my space, my giant bed, the ability to sprawl out, the king in his castle.

I hadn't thought I'd ever find a woman who I'd want to be the queen of it, too.

When I wake up again, Sofia stirring against my chest, the clock reads five in the morning. At some point, she'd rolled over, nestled against me so that I'm spooning her. As her back arches slightly, and her ass pushes back against my groin, I feel my already partially erect cock harden completely, my balls aching as I grind against her without thinking.

Sofia moans, her head falling back against my shoulder. "Again?" she asks sleepily, her voice light and teasing even half-asleep, and my cock throbs.

"Yes," I growl and reach down to angle myself between her legs, moaning as the head of my cock slips easily inside of her. She's so wet, her body hot and eager for me, and I thrust up into her with one stroke, seating myself to the hilt as I wrap an arm around her waist and pull her against me.

"Oh god, this feels so good," Sofia whimpers, and I feel a rush of lust as I remember that she's never done any of this before, that everything we do together will be new for her. No one has ever made her come with his tongue like I did last night. No one has ever fucked her like this. It drives me wild, my balls tight and painful with the need to come as I slide one arm underneath her head so that I can drape it over her shoulder, playing with her nipple as I slide the other hand between her legs and start to rub her clit, pinching it lightly with every thrust.

The feeling of her squirming in my arms, arching against me as I play with her, exploring her body as my cock sinks into her again and again, is better than anything I'd imagined—and I'd imagined quite a bit. This time I go more slowly, both of us still lazy with sleep as I push her towards a climax, holding my own back until I feel her back arch deeply, her mouth falling open as her hair spills over my chest, her head pressing into my shoulder as she grinds into my hand and moans loudly, her pussy fluttering around me as she comes.

"Fuck—" I groan against her shoulder as I thrust up, my cock throbbing as a flood of cum erupts from me, filling her for the—oh fuck, I don't even know. I've lost track of how many times we've fucked now.

We fall asleep again like that, and when we wake up, I roll her onto her back. She whimpers a little when I enter her, and I can tell that she's sore. "Do you want me to stop?" I ask gently, and Sofia shakes her head, wrapping her arms around my neck.

"No," she whispers, and I groan as I sink into her again, my body already tensing in anticipation of another orgasm.

It's nine o'clock before I finally relent and sit up, hitting the switch to open the blinds and flood the room with light. "We need to get up. We should check on Caterina and Ana, and I need to talk to Raoul—"

Sofia sits up slowly, wrapping her arms around herself as the sunlight fills the room. I can see the reality of last night settling over her again, and my stomach clenches. I can easily imagine things going back to the way they were before in the harsh light of day. I can easily imagine her willingness last night being a fluke.

I'm not letting her go. She's mine, now more than ever. My wife.

But if she doesn't want me, there's nothing I can do short of forcing her. And if I couldn't do that before—

I definitely can't now that I've known what it's like to have her willing, to have her give herself completely to me without reservation, the thing I'd dreamed of since I'd held her, a spitting, clawing hellcat bent on escape, that first night.

I clear my throat. "If you want to shower first—"

"What was that?" Sofia turns to face me, pulling the sheet up to cover her breasts as she looks at me with those wide, dark eyes. "Last night. You—what was that?"

My first instinct is to go cold, to tell her that it was nothing. That I was angry that someone had dared to try to hurt what was mine. That I took advantage of her, that I used her vulnerability to get what I wanted.

I could shut all of this down with a few well-placed words. I could put a divide between us that would never be able to be crossed again and save us both the pain of trying to make this work.

Because really, how is it ever going to work in the end? I'm not a man who was made to love. Not someone who can give her what she really needs, what she *deserves* from a husband.

But she's stuck with me.

You could at least try.

I decide to go for the truth. Just this once.

"I don't know," I tell her honestly. "One of the members of the security team came to tell me what had happened. And when he said that someone had broken in, that you'd almost been killed—" I run a hand through my hair, feeling it stick up. "Something snapped inside of me. All I could think about was getting back home. Home—"

"Home to me," Sofia says quietly. "That's what you said last night. Right before—"

"If you're regretting it, you can tell me." I can hear my voice hardening. "I'm not going to go back on what I said, even after this incident. You can stay in your old room. I won't touch you again if –"

"I don't regret it."

It takes a second for that to sink in. I turn towards her fully, the sheet pooling around my hips and sliding down my thigh. I see Sofia's eyes flick downwards, her throat contract as she swallows, and my cock throbs traitorously at the thought of what it would feel like to have her throat squeeze around me like that, to have her swallow my cum—

"You don't?"

"No." She lifts her chin, and I can see a little of that old stubbornness shining through.

And it makes me hard as hell. *Fuck, how does she turn me on so fucking much?*

"I didn't just sleep with you last night because I was feeling vulnerable," Sofia says, crossing her arms over her chest. "I wanted to know what it would be like."

"Oh." I'm not sure why that stings a little. God knows I've fucked enough women out of sheer curiosity. "Glad I could be of service."

"That's not what I meant." She chews on her lower lip, flushing a little. "I mean—I wanted to know what it would be like if we…if we actually tried."

"Tried what?"

"This." Sofia waves her hand in the space between our bodies. "Us." She takes a deep, shaky breath. "Look, I know you probably just wanted to get laid last night. And I know that you didn't ask for this marriage any more than I did. I realized that last night, talking to Caterina—you got dragged into this too. And you're probably just as resentful of it as I am. But maybe—"

She looks up at me, and I can see how nervous she is. It occurs to me that I could make this easier on her, but I don't even know what to say. Last night I hadn't thought past my uncontrollable desire to consider what might happen in the morning.

In the cold light of day, Sofia is as beautiful as she ever was. And I want her as much as I ever have. But I know that marriage—a real marriage—is so much more than that. "I don't want to be the kind of husband Rossi was," I say, the words forming slowly. "I didn't want to be a husband at all, for exactly that reason. I didn't want to have a wife that I ignored, that I handed over the duties of house and family to while I continued to live the same way I always had. I wanted to be a bachelor because I didn't want the guilt of being an absent husband."

I take a deep breath. "I never gave much thought to marriage because I never thought it would happen. I never thought *we* would happen—that particular debt was never supposed to come due."

Sofia looks at me cautiously. "And now? If you were going to be a husband—what kind would you want to be?"

I consider that question. I don't know where this conversation is going, but after last night, she deserves an honest answer at least. "Fair," I say finally. "Loyal."

"Kind?" Sofia smiles a little, her mouth twitching at the corners.

I let my gaze sweep over her body, allowing her to see the lust in my gaze. "Sometimes."

She shivers, but the faint smile doesn't leave her lips. "When you say loyal, do you mean—"

I reach for her then. I can't help myself. I run my fingers through her messy hair, trailing the tips down her delicate jawline. "I meant what I said last night, Sofia. All of yesterday, the guys were harassing me to fuck someone. As many girls as I could, honestly. And I won't lie to you—I tried to make myself do it. To fuck you out of my system, like I said."

"But?" Her cheek tilts into my hand, her dark eyes never leaving mine.

"I couldn't do it. All of those women—they were just like every other woman who's ever been in my bed. Gorgeous, perfectly fit, willing to do anything I asked."

"Luca—" Sofia winces. "Maybe I don't need all the details."

"Fair." I chuckle. "The point is, Sofia, I only wanted you. The night before the funeral, when I left you here alone and stayed in a hotel? I wasn't with another woman. I let you think that because I wanted there to be distance between us. But I spent the entire time thinking about you. Wanting you. Fantasizing about you." I shake my head, my hand sliding down her jaw until her chin is resting in my hand. "I went a little crazy when I came home and saw that video. I wanted you so fucking bad, and to see you—"

"It's okay." She laughs a little, tugging her face out of my grasp. "If you couldn't tell, I liked what you did to me."

Fuck. My cock throbs under the sheet, rising just at the mention of that night. "Is that so?"

"I've liked everything you've done to me so far," Sofia says softly. "Even if I didn't want to admit it."

"Does that mean—" I hesitate. "Sofia, I told you before we were married that I wouldn't force you. I meant that then and I mean it now. Especially after last night, I don't want you if you're unwilling. But I *do* want you in my bed. Now, tonight, tomorrow night. Every night after that."

"For as long as we both shall live." Sofia chews on her lower lip again, a sad expression sliding over her face. "I don't know what to do, Luca. You say you'd be a fair husband. A loyal one, even, which is a hell of a lot more than I think any other woman in this organization can expect. Caterina doesn't expect fidelity from Franco. But if you're thinking I would, then you're right. I know I've married into the mafia, but—I'm not a mafia wife." She looks up at me, her chin tilting up defiantly. "I can't go to bed with you knowing that you might have fucked some other woman a few hours before. Or sit at home, miserable because you're out late and I don't know what—or who—you're doing. I'd rather not have you at all than only have a part of you."

She pauses, letting out a slow breath. "I know that my parents' marriage wasn't ideal in a lot of ways. But I'll never believe that my father was faithful to my mother. That he loved her. I've struggled so hard with trying to understand why he gave me to you. Why he *trusted* you enough because I *know* he loved me. So tell me, Luca. Why should *I* trust you? Why should I believe that my father didn't make a mistake?"

Her eyes are misting over slightly, and I feel my chest tighten at the expression on her face. "Sofia, I don't know what to promise you. I promised you my protection, and I meant that."

"And last night, I was attacked. Almost killed." Sofia wraps her arms around herself again, and that look of misery that I know so well returns. "So much for protection."

"I shouldn't have left you here alone. That was a mistake." I reach out to touch her face, but she pulls back, and I can see her walls going up. Shutting me out. Remembering why she's fought so hard to keep away from me.

I don't want that to happen. I feel as if I'm fighting for something I don't understand, a future that I can't see. All I know is that the thought of losing her makes me feel as if I'm standing at the edge of a cliff, too far above the bottom to see what will happen if I fall.

"I'm going to find out how this happened. I'll talk to Viktor again." I hesitate. "Sofia, I don't know how to do this. I can promise that I'll do everything in my power to keep you safe. I can promise that I'll never harm you, never lay a hand on you. I can promise you that I'll take you to bed like I did last night every time you desire, for the rest of your life. I'll even promise you fidelity if you want it." I laugh shortly. "God knows I've been faithful anyway, despite my best efforts. But Sofia, I don't know if I can promise you anything else."

"Not love." She looks at me shrewdly. "Not the kind of marriage I saw, growing up."

"That love got your father killed. It almost got your mother murdered, too. It put you here, married to a man who can't be what you want, who can't love you, who—" I pause, shaking my head. "Sofia, I'm wrong for you in every way. You deserved better than this. But here we are."

Sofia takes a deep breath. "Okay," she says softly. "Let's try this, for now. Just trying to exist together, as a couple. I'll sleep in here with you. We'll try to talk more and argue less. We'll try to understand each other. And we'll see how that goes."

Some of the tension leaves me as I listen to her. I might not be able to make peace with the Bratva so easily, but it seems as if here, in this bedroom, I've made a tentative peace with my wife.

It's not everything. But I think it might be enough.

For now.

SOFIA

17

I leave Luca's room, not knowing what to think.

I never expected any of what happened last night. Just like I'd told him, I'd expected him not to come home. To leave me here, afraid and vulnerable, until he was done with his weekend away. I hadn't expected him to come rushing home.

But it's not just that. It's everything that happened afterward.

And I'm afraid—just as afraid as I was last night when that man stood in the doorway with a gun pointed at my face—but in a different way.

If I trust Luca, he has the potential to break my heart. He's told me over and over again that he's wrong for me. That he can't love me. That he was never meant to be a husband. And yet we keep slipping closer to just that—to living as man and wife in reality, and not just on paper.

If I *don't* trust him, I'm going to live a lonely life. One without pleasure, without happiness, without touch. Even if I could somehow escape him, eventually, I know that I'll never be entirely free of him. I'll always be looking over my shoulder, waiting for him to come after me, to reclaim what's his. After that, I could never be in another relationship and put someone else that I might love in danger.

And after last night—I'm not sure if anyone else could ever quite measure up.

I'd known sex could be pleasurable, of course. Fun. Exciting. I'd heard Ana talk about it often enough. I might have been a virgin, but I wasn't an idiot. I knew sex could run the gamut from disappointing to mind-blowing.

None of that late-night gossip had prepared me for the reality of last night, though. Somehow Luca had taken the pleasure I'd felt that night he'd teased me to the point of begging and doubled it, tripled it. I'm sore and raw and aching, and part of me still wants to fall back into bed with him right now, just to feel it all over again.

Something happened between us that was more than just ordinary sex. It was desperate, hungry, passionate. The kind of sex that I'd thought only existed in fiction.

But it had been real. And it was addictive.

You're like a goddamn drug. I can hear Luca's voice rasping in my ear, and I know exactly what he meant. I could lose myself in that kind of pleasure, forget everything other than how good it was. How it made me feel so alive, so connected to him.

I have to keep my head on straight, I tell myself as I get dressed, pulling a t-shirt over my head and quickly braiding my wet hair. Luca's gone to talk to Raoul and the rest of the security, and I need to check on Caterina and Ana. I can't afford to lose my head and fall into the trap of thinking that this is more than it is. For all that he told me he'd be faithful, Luca didn't pretend this morning that we were suddenly in love. That we were going to be happily married.

In fact, he made a point of reminding me exactly the opposite—that he *can't* love me. That he's not the kind of man I would ever have wanted to marry, and he never will be.

The problem is, I don't fully understand it now. I'd thought that Luca clung to his bachelorhood because he wanted to keep being the same playboy he'd always been, because he didn't want a wife in his space, cramping his style, putting restrictions on what he could and couldn't do. He didn't want to have to sneak around in hotel rooms or go to other women's apartments instead of bringing them here and then kicking them out.

But clearly, that's not the case. He'd had no problem agreeing to fidelity—if I believe everything he said, then he's *been* faithful since the night he brought me home, even though I never expected it.

So if he doesn't want other women, then what's the problem?

Maybe it's just me, I think as I walk downstairs. *Maybe, you're just not the kind of woman he could love. Too innocent. Too naïve. Too weak.*

He'd have been better off marrying someone like Caterina, someone who knew how to be a mafia wife and what to expect. But instead, he got me.

Caterina and Ana are sitting at the kitchen table when I walk in. There are takeout containers in front of them, and Caterina has her hands wrapped around a cup of coffee, taking a sip of it just as I walk in.

Ana raises an eyebrow at my wet hair. "You look like you're feeling better. Did you get any sleep?"

I flush pink, and Caterina sets her coffee down, looking at me suspiciously. "Sofia?"

"Luca came home last night." I sink into a chair opposite them, glancing at one of the takeout containers. "Did Carmen send this over?"

"Yeah. It's from that place a few blocks down that does really good brunch." Ana shoves it towards me. "There's some ricotta pancakes left. But let's go back to the part where you said *Luca came home?*"

"Someone alerted him about the break-in. He flew back last night."

"Is Franco here?" Caterina asks hopefully, and I wince as I look up at her. I can see her expression faltering as soon as she sees my face, and I feel my heart break a little for her. I feel guilty for the hours of pleasure I spent in bed with Luca since last night—I was fucking my husband all night after he came home in a rush to make sure I was okay. Meanwhile, her fiancé is still banging models in some other country for his bachelor weekend.

You could be married to someone like that, a tiny voice in my head whispers. *You thought you were.*

I can't argue that. For all Luca's faults—and I'm not forgetting them just because he gave me several orgasms last night—he cared enough to come back to me as soon as he'd heard what happened.

"Luca said he's sending the jet back to pick them up," I say lamely, knowing that it doesn't make up for the fact that Franco isn't here now. "He'll be back sooner than they planned, I think."

"I figured as much," Caterina says quietly.

"I'm sorry." I bite my lip. "I wanted this to be a good weekend for you."

She smiles weakly, shrugging. "This is just life. I didn't really expect more from him. I'd just—hoped, a little bit. But it's alright. I knew what kind of man he was when I agreed to marry him."

That last statement gives me pause. I *hadn't* known what kind of man Luca was when I'd agreed to marry *him*. I'd thought I did, but I'm beginning to suspect that I was wrong in some ways. And it makes me wonder if I was wrong about other things, too.

As if summoned, Luca steps into the doorway, looking over the three of us before his gaze settles on me. "Morning, ladies," he says, that deep voice sending a shiver over me. He walks behind my chair, looking at Caterina and Ana.

"I apologize for what happened last night," he says, and I can feel his hands resting on the chair behind me. "I'll be talking to and questioning the security today to try and find out how anyone managed to get up here in the first place. I'll find out how this happened, I promise." He pauses, hands gripping the back of the chair. "It wasn't my intention for any of you to be in danger. I'm sorry."

"It's not your fault," Caterina says quietly. "You did try."

"Bullshit." Ana spits out, and I'm suddenly aware of how quiet she's been this entire time. "You told Sofia you'd protect her when you married her. You *forced* her into this marriage because it was supposed to keep her alive. And yet, she almost was shot last night. Whatever is going on, you should have been here, dealing with it, instead of off getting your dick wet with your boys." She glares at him, her gaze flicking down to my neck and then back up to Luca. "And then what?

You were still so horny you had to come home and fuck Sofia, too? You're a disgrace. And a liar."

"Ana!" I exclaim, my heart suddenly pounding in my chest. Luca has been remarkably calm throughout all of this, but I don't know how he'll react to being spoken to like that. Rossi would probably have Ana killed on the spot for that kind of disrespect. While I know Luca isn't that kind of man, I don't know that he'll stand for being yelled at by a girl that I know he doesn't particularly like or entirely trust.

"No, it's fine," Luca says, his voice cool and even. "Anastasia, can I speak to you in private?"

"Luca, she didn't mean—" I start to protest, but Ana is already standing up, still glaring at him.

"I'd be happy to," she says coldly, stalking out of the kitchen.

Luca follows her out without a word, and I feel my stomach clench, turning over as I watch him walk out to the living room with her. Their voices don't carry well, but I can hear them talking in low, angry tones, and it makes me feel a little sick.

"It's fine," Caterina says, trying to console me. "Luca is probably angrier with himself than she is with him."

"I wouldn't bet on it." I bite my lip, glancing in the direction that they went.

Caterina stands up, collecting the empty containers from the table and carrying them to the trash. "Did you two really--?" she trails off, glancing at my neck. "Did you want to?"

I hesitate, feeling myself flush a little. "Yeah," I finally say quietly. It's hard for me to admit that I gave in, but I also don't want Caterina to think that Luca forced me to do anything that I didn't want to. "It just—kind of happened."

"It might be a good thing." Caterina turns on the faucet, washing her hands before facing me. "Some peace between the two of you might help Luca focus on the problem of solving the feud with the Bratva before it spins out of control." She takes a deep breath. "You've been there for me, Sofia, even though we don't know each other all that well. So I'm going to give you some advice, even though I know you might not want it. Being a mafia wife isn't just about looking the other way while your husband sleeps around, raising kids, and being a pretty face at dinners."

"Then what is it about? Because so far, that's all I've seen."

"It's about knowing when to let things go so that your husband can do what he has to. It's about accepting that the man you married has sides to him that might frighten you sometimes, might even disgust you, but that it's part of who he is. And if he's a good man, he won't like those parts of himself, either. It's up to you to help him live with it."

"What about Rossi?" I know I shouldn't, but I can't help saying it. "He seems to like those parts of himself. And he wants Luca to be the same way."

"My father isn't a good man," Caterina says evenly. "I've always known that. I love him because he *is* my father and I know no other way to be a good daughter. But he isn't good."

"And you think Luca is?"

"I think he wants to be." Caterina looks at me, her gaze unflinching. "And I think what happens next, in these coming days and weeks, will determine a lot about what kind of man he is in the future."

I don't know what to say to that. "I didn't ask for any of this," I say quietly. "I didn't ask to be his wife."

"You could have said no." Caterina shrugs. "I know that's not what you want to hear. But you didn't *have* to take the vows."

"What kind of choice was that? Marry him, or die? That's not a choice."

Caterina laughs then, and there's nothing cruel in it, but it still catches me off guard. "Yes, it was."

* * *

I CAN'T GET that conversation out of my head for the rest of the day. Luca doesn't tell me what he and Ana talked about, despite my asking him, only that he sent her home after their conversation. He has his driver take Caterina back to the Rossi house as well, assuring her that Franco should be back by the evening.

After that, he leaves me to question the rest of the security team, with Raoul there to keep an eye on me. He doesn't mention our conversation this morning or really say much at all other than to tell me he'll be back this evening and to stay in the penthouse—not to go up to the roof or outside at all. The latter annoys me a little, but I let it go. I'm not going to be a pushover, but I can't deny that things are better when Luca and I aren't fighting.

The apartment feels huge and empty without Caterina and Ana, and I don't really know what to do with myself. Exhausted and sore from last night, I decide to take a nap. I *could* go back to my room, and as I walk up the stairs, I tell myself that I'm going to. But as if my feet have a mind of their own, I find myself walking towards Luca's room.

The sheets still smell like us, like my soap and his cologne, the faint scent of our warm bodies still clinging to them, and I press my face into the pillow, feeling more lost and confused than ever. My skin tingles with the memory of what we did last night, and I don't know how to reconcile that with my conviction that I shouldn't love a man like Luca.

And then, of course, there's the problem of him believing he can't love *me*.

My dreams are a mess when I finally fall asleep, a mixture of terrifying montages of running away from men with guns, finding myself tied up, trapped, unable to flee, that turn into glimpses of me tangled up with Luca, panting and moaning as he makes me come over and over again, and then vanishing into thin air right as I call out his name.

I wake up feeling bleary and disoriented, sometime in the midafternoon. The room feels too hot, the sun shining through the window directly onto the bed, and I sit up slowly, pushing my tangled hair off of my face.

There's a long, flat box sitting just inside the door, white with a huge black bow wrapped around it and tied elaborately on top. Someone must have left it while I was sleeping, and after last night, the thought of someone coming into the bedroom while I'm sleeping makes me feel jittery and anxious. But Raoul has been watching the interior of the apartment, and I can't help but think that with Luca home, the security team won't put a foot wrong.

I hope that when he said he was "questioning" them, he meant with words and not anything more violent.

Gingerly I get out of bed, padding barefoot across the hardwood floor to the box. It feels light when I pick it up, and I set it on top of the bed, tugging at the bow until it comes undone and the sheer black ribbon falls onto the dark grey duvet.

The interior of the box is filled with metallic gold paper, and I push it apart to see a dress nestled there, with tags that read *Alexander McQueen.*

When I pick it up, I can't help but gasp. My closet is full of designer clothes now, thanks to Luca, but I've never seen anything as beautiful as this dress. It's made of red silk that feels as soft and fragile as a butterfly wing, with small white and gold chiffon flowers scattered across the knee-length, full skirt. Each petal is perfectly cut, with a small crystal at the center of each flower, and looks as if they're floating above the rippling silk. The neckline is plunging—even just looking at it, I can tell that it ends just about at my ribs, with wide, gathered straps at the shoulders.

It's a wearable piece of art, and I can't imagine where I'm actually going to wear it or why it's here. I can't even leave the apartment, let alone go out somewhere worthy of this dress. It almost makes me sad because it's so incredibly gorgeous.

There's a white and gold envelope inside the box, and I set the dress down carefully, unsure how I'll even feel brave enough to put it on. It's not that it's all that daring other than the neckline, but it's so beautiful and delicate that I'm almost afraid to touch it. Reaching for the envelope, I open it to find a card inside, with bold handwriting on thick, cream-colored stock.

Sofia,

Even though we've been husband and wife for a week now, I've never taken you out on a proper date. Since it's so overdue, I thought you should have something exceptionally beautiful for the occasion. Meet me on the rooftop at 9 pm—not a second earlier.

Your husband,

Luca

My fingers feel numb, and I almost drop the card out of sheer shock. I read it again, and then a third time, unable to quite believe what's written there.

Luca and I had a great night, sure. Hot, passionate, undoubtedly driven by the fact that I'd come so close to death. But a *date*?

I can't imagine Luca taking anyone out on a date. Well—if I think about it, I guess I can, but not *my* idea of a date. When I think of Luca dating, I think of Italian villas and helicopter rides, the kind of over-the-top romance you see on the *Bachelor*, nothing that ever lasts.

There's no part of me that can imagine Luca and I going out for a movie and dinner at some cute hipster-y bar, the kind of place that I always pictured going on dates to, in the occasional moment that I pictured it at all.

But there it is in black and white—admittedly, written in flowing script on a card that looks like a wedding invitation, instead of typed out in a text. Still—it's Luca, my husband, asking me out on a date.

I don't know if it's the passionate sex we had last night or the fact that we've managed to have two whole conversations without it devolving into a fight in almost as many days. However, I still feel a tingle of excitement instead of the dread I would have expected.

The only thing I'm even slightly sad about is that I can't just call Ana and ask her to come over. Normally, I'd have her help me get ready, but I can't even text her to tell her about it. Still, even that doesn't ignite the incandescent rage that I would have felt a couple of weeks ago. Maybe I'm just getting used to this new apartment and the restrictions that came with it, or—

Is it really so hard to understand why it's like this? I'd felt so suffocated by Luca's orders—because if I'm being real, that's what they are—but after looking down the barrel of a gun held by a man who unquestionably wanted me dead, it's hard to argue that he's been unreasonable. The Bratva threat is clearly not under control. And as for the fact that marrying him was supposed to keep me safe from all of this—

If there's one thing I do believe, it's that Luca wants this threat stopped as much as I or anyone else does. And even if our marriage didn't make Viktor stop these attacks, it did keep me safe from Rossi.

I could just be rationalizing this all away. My brain might just be scrambled from so many orgasms. But I can't deny that my stomach is fluttering with butterflies at the thought of what Luca might have planned for tonight, and it has nothing to do with fear.

It's impossible to concentrate on anything else for the rest of the day. I take a shower to freshen up from my nap and start getting ready about an hour before I'm supposed to meet Luca upstairs. I tell myself that I don't have any specific reason for the fact that I made sure that every inch of me was freshly shaved or that I chose a lacy pink thong to slip on underneath the dress, but as I stand in front of the mirror curling my hair, I know it's not totally true.

I want Luca to like what he sees if he winds up taking that dress off of me tonight.

After coloring my hair blonde for so long, it's still strange to see it back to my natural deep, rich brown, but I can't deny that it does look better on me. The pale blonde washed out my olive-toned skin, but the mahogany shade that the stylist gave me with the mixture of lighter and darker balayage that she painted in makes my skin almost glow. My dark eyes look even wider as I blend cream and gold eyeshadows over my lid to match the little flowers on the dress. The effect is only more exaggerated. I've never been a beauty expert, but once I'm finished swiping on mascara and adding a red lip to match the dress, I have to admit that I look beautiful.

Beautiful enough for someone like Luca. Beautiful enough to hold my own. If Caterina always looks like a queen, I look like a princess. Belle going on a date with the beast—right after she figured out that maybe he wasn't so bad after all.

I know that I might be slipping down a dangerous slope. One that could end with my heart broken, or worse. But I feel helpless to stop it. Now that Luca and I have started—I want to know where this goes. It feels dangerously like what I imagine chasing a high must be.

Just before nine o'clock exactly, I make my way to the stairs that lead up to the rooftop deck. I'm careful not to go up them until the clock changes over. Then I walk up them carefully in my high-heeled Louboutin sandals, gingerly touching the diamonds at my ears. It felt strange to put on diamonds to go up to the roof. Of course, I'm still wearing my mother's dainty necklace that I never take off, which always looks small and insignificant next to the glittering expensive jewelry that I have from Luca. But this isn't the kind of dress I could wear pearl studs or silver hoops with.

If there was ever a dress made for diamonds, it's this one.

I push the door leading up to the roof open, stepping out onto the deck. And then, as my eyes adjust, my mouth drops open as I take in the sight in front of me.

SOFIA

18

Half of the rooftop has always been the pool and wet bar, and the other half has a fireplace and pit with lounge seating and tiki torches. But at some point, the part of the roof dedicated to the fireplace and lounge has been transformed.

The fireplace is lit, crackling merrily, and all of the seating has been removed. Instead, there's a thick rug spread out over the wood surface of the deck, with an iron café-style table and two chairs set on it. There are candles in the center and place settings ready for the guests to sit. All around the fireplace and surrounding the edge of the deck, planter boxes full of flowers have been brought in so that there's an explosion of color. The air is full of the scent of them, the entire scene lit up by twinkling fairy lights strung all around. It looks like the pictures I've seen of outdoor Parisian cafes, except this one is just for us.

Just for Luca and me.

He's standing by the fireplace, dressed immaculately in a bespoke suit, and I can hear string music playing faintly from somewhere. He smiles as I manage, somehow, to start walking towards him despite my utter shock.

I was right, after all. This is the most ridiculous, fairytale-like, over-the-top date I could possibly have imagined. It's not dinner and a movie, for sure. But I don't care. I feel completely blown away, and when I stop in front of Luca, all I can do is stare up at him.

"You did all of this?" I manage finally, my voice a whisper. "For a —date?"

"Well, I had someone come in and do it," Luca says, the corners of his eyes crinkling in a smile. "But yes. I told them what I wanted. Do you like it? And the dress?"

"Yes—yes, of course," I manage. His green eyes are holding mine, an expression in them almost as if he's hoping for my approval—which feels insane. Why would Luca care about whether or not I like any of this? He's always seemed to be the kind of man who goes through life assuming that everyone around him is happy with everything he does. "It's beautiful. The dress is beautiful."

"Good." Luca smiles and reaches for me, pulling me into his arms. I breathe in as I feel them go around me, pulling me up against his strong, hard body, and as he bends down to kiss me, my heart races in my chest.

His lips on mine feel electric, like a million sparks dancing over my skin, and I can't help myself. I lean up, my arms sliding around his neck, all of my fears and doubts vanishing for the moment. I know they'll come back, I know that nothing can change how wrong we are for each other, but at this moment, it's impossible to stop. The smell of flowers and woodsmoke fills my nose, twinkling lights surrounding us as Luca's hands smooth over the silk of my dress, and I can feel my blood heating with desire as his tongue traces over my lower lip, urging me to open my mouth and let him kiss me more deeply.

I'm gasping by the time he pulls back, the taste of his mouth still on my lips as I look up at him in a daze.

"Dinner will be served in a minute," Luca says, taking my hand. I can feel my engagement ring pressing into his palm as he leads me towards the small table, the chairs situated so that we're sitting next to each other instead of across from one another as we take our seats. I look around and catch a glimpse of a black-suited server discreetly across the deck by the wet bar, where he must be keeping the food.

Sure enough, as soon as we sit down, the server brings two small plates and sets them in front of us, along with a bottle of red wine. "Salad with spring greens, goat cheese, prosciutto, and a mustard vinaigrette," he says in such a serious voice that I almost want to laugh, holding out the wine cork for Luca to sniff.

It's every bit a five-star restaurant experience—but on a private rooftop, all to ourselves. "This is just like the outdoor restaurants I wanted to go to in Paris," I say softly as I pick up my fork. "It's like something out of a movie or a fairy tale."

"I know," Luca says, glancing over at me. "I asked Ana what an ideal date for you would be, considering our—limitations right now. What I could possibly do without leaving the apartment. And she told me about your plans to go to Paris after graduation. Plans which, of course, our marriage ruined."

He sounds almost apologetic. I can't quite wrap my head around it as he pours the wine for us, the lights glinting off of the glass as he hands it to me. "So you tried to bring Paris to me?" It sounds ridiculous, but after all, why not? Luca has more money than God. He can do anything he wants. And for some reason, after everything, he decided he wanted to do this for me.

"Yes." Luca watches me for a moment. "I've never done this before, you know."

I blink at him, momentarily confused. "Have dinner on a rooftop?"

"No." Luca laughs. "Go on a date."

"What?" To be fair, I've only ever been on a few, but I know Luca's past. He's slept with more women than an army of men, and he's never been on a date? "How is that possible?"

"I don't date," he says simply. "I know you don't want to hear about all the women I've been with. I'm not saying this to rub that in your face. But all of those women were ones I picked up. Someone I saw at a gala, who caught my eye at a bar, who sat across from me at the theater. I never had any trouble finding women who wanted to go out with me, but I've never taken one out on a date."

"Not to dinner? Not out to drinks?" I can't wrap my head around it. "This is seriously the first date you've ever been on?"

"Yes."

Of all the things I'd thought he might say to me tonight, that hadn't been one of them. "You know this isn't exactly a normal date, right?"

"I guessed as much," Luca smirks. "But I'm not a normal man."

"I know." *Boy, do I ever.* "So I was a virgin, and you were a virgin at—dating?" I laugh then. I can't help it. "What a pair we make."

"It could be worse." Luca's mouth twitches as he pushes my wine glass towards me. "What *do* you consider a normal date?"

"Dinner somewhere that isn't too expensive. Burgers, maybe. A movie. Or depending on where the relationship is, pizza at home and watching something on tv. Or playing a board game, maybe." I shrug. "At least, that's what I've seen with Ana and her boyfriends. I've only ever been on a few dates. I'm not exactly an expert either."

"Well. Maybe we can learn together." Luca picks up his glass. "What should we toast to on our first date?"

I'm completely speechless. I lift my glass, but I can't find a single word.

"To trying," Luca says softly, touching his glass to mine, and my heart flutters in my chest in a way that it never has before.

I take a sip of the wine. It's delicious, rich and fruity, just the right amount of dry, and as I spear a bite of my salad with my fork, I consider what this could turn into. What life with a man like Luca could be if I let myself enjoy it.

It's clear that there's no easy way out of this. Even if Rossi and the Bratva both were no longer a threat, Luca has made it clear that he doesn't intend to easily let me leave. And after last night, I know that he'll be even less inclined to do that.

After last night, I'm no longer so sure that I want to leave.

The food is delicious, better than anything I've ever tasted, except for maybe the food at our wedding. But that might as well have been made of sand for how little I enjoyed it—I barely even remember what was served. I can feel myself relaxing little by little as the server brings the next course, a collection of small plates with various foods on them.

"I told them to do a tasting menu of things you might order in

Paris," Luca says, sliding one of the small plates towards me. "Quail with blueberry sauce. Duck with orange. Salmon braised with lemon. Scallops in butter."

I reach for my fork, but instead, Luca digs into the quail breast, taking a forkful of the delicate meat and holding it up to my lips. I blink at him, momentarily startled, but I obediently open my mouth, letting him slide the fork almost sensually into my mouth. "What do you think?" he asks softly, his green eyes never leaving my face.

"It's delicious," I manage. My heart is racing again, my skin tingling. He's so close to me, close enough that I can feel the warmth of his skin and smell the scent of his cologne, like fresh salt air and lemons. I want to breathe him in, to lean past the forkful of scallops that he's holding out to me and kiss him, with blueberry on my tongue and red wine on his.

Is this how it feels to fall for someone? Our fights, the humiliating night before our wedding and the way I rebelled so fiercely against everything he's done, the fear of our wedding night and my anger all feel a million miles away. I can't remember why I felt any of those things. I'm overcome by stars and twinkling lights, the rich taste of food that melts on my tongue washed down by expensive wine. Luca's bright green eyes searching my face, for all the world looking as if he's begging me to give him a chance.

I don't understand why. Why the change of heart? But it's hard to ask that when I can feel my own heart shifting, opening up to him despite myself.

By the time the dessert course arrives, I feel as if I'd do anything for him to kiss me. The server sets the marble tray in front of us, covered in strawberries, cheeses, and small pots of crème brulee and chocolate mousse. Luca picks up a strawberry, holding it up to my lips, and as he places it on my tongue, his fingertip brushes over my lower lip.

I make a small sound, and I feel his hand on my knee, sliding up under my skirt as he slides a strawberry into his own mouth, his full lips sliding over the fruit and reminding me of his mouth on me last night, kissing between my legs until I lost myself in pleasure like I'd never felt before.

A teaspoon of chocolate mousse is the next thing he feeds me. With every bite, his hand creeps up my thigh, his fingertips trailing up my soft skin until I feel breathless with desire, aching for him to touch me.

"Here," Luca says, handing me the spoon. "I want to eat my own dessert."

He winks at me, and for a wild second, I think that he's going to slide under the table and up my skirt, but instead, he just reaches for his own pot of mousse, watching me between bites as his fingers finally reach the top of my thigh, brushing over the front of my panties as I almost choke on a bite of brulee.

"Oh," he murmurs softly. "Lace. My favorite."

I can't stop the moan that slips out as his fingers slide under the edge of the thong. "You're so wet," Luca says in a low voice. "You must have wanted this so badly."

Nervously, I glance over my shoulder to make sure that the server isn't watching, biting my lip hard as Luca's fingers trail over the outer edge of my pussy.

"Don't worry, he can't see us," Luca says quietly. "As long as you don't make any noise, he won't even know what's happening."

Oh god. I know exactly what he's planning then. For a brief second, I consider telling him to stop, even though I don't have the slightest idea if he actually would. But the truth is that I don't want him to.

I feel like I'm in some kind of wild fantasy, Luca's fingers sliding upwards as I taste burnt sugar and cream on my tongue, his index finger teasing the tip of my clit as I gasp, trying to stay silent as he presses down, rubbing in small circles that grow faster and faster. And all the while, he keeps eating his dessert, as if I'm not slipping towards the edge of having an orgasm out here in the open, on the rooftop.

"Mmm," he groans as he takes another bite. "So delicious, don't you think?" He glances sideways at me, clearly expecting an answer just as he slides two fingers knuckle-deep into my pussy, curling them upwards as I stifle a moan, clenching around him as my body spasms with pleasure.

"Don't you like it?" He smiles, thrusting his fingers into me again as I swallow hard, unable to speak. If I say anything, I know I'm going to moan or scream, on the verge of such an uncontrollable pleasure that I don't know how I'll contain it when I finally do come.

"Yes," I manage to whimper somehow. "Yes, it's—it's so—oh god, it's so good—" I can hear the words tumble from my lips, breathless— just as the server walks towards us.

Oh, fuck. Surely Luca is going to stop, I think. Surely he won't keep going with someone standing right next to us. Even though his hand is hidden under the white tablecloth, I can't imagine how anyone could stand next to me and see my flushed skin and heaving chest and not know what's going on.

But surprisingly, the server seems oblivious. "Do you need anything else?"

"Maybe more wine," Luca says, his fingers still moving inside of me as he rubs my clit faster, and I realize with horror that he's intentionally pushing me towards an orgasm. "What would you suggest? Maybe a port while we finish dessert?"

"A port would be perfect, sir. I'll bring it right over."

"Luca, please—" I gasp as the server walks away. "Please—"

"Please, what?" His eyes are glittering wickedly. "Do you want to come?"

Yes. Oh god, yes. I want to come more than anything I've ever wanted in my entire life. I'm both so close and too far away to the edge.

Luca presses down on my clit, his fingers moving against that sensitive spot deep inside of me, and I stifle a cry. "You can come whenever you like," he murmurs. "But I'm not going to stop, even when he comes back."

I feel an electric rush wash over me, my heart pounding so hard that I think it must be visible beneath the thin silk of my dress, and I don't know why I'm suddenly more turned on than I've ever been in my entire life. I can feel myself on the verge of tumbling over, and just as the server returns with the bottle and two smaller glasses, Luca flutters his thumb over my clit, and I'm lost.

I don't know how I stop myself from moaning. I bite down on my lower lip hard, grinding down onto his hand as I grip the edge of my seat, pushing myself against his fingers as I feel wave after wave of pleasure rush over me. I can feel it down to the marrow of my bones, the orgasm building and crashing over me. Somehow even as I squirm on Luca's fingers, orgasming helplessly, the server doesn't miss a beat.

"Will there be anything else?"

I'm panting, red-faced, and I know that there's no way he doesn't know what's going on. And somehow, that turns me on even more.

"No," Luca says calmly, his fingers still hooked inside my pussy so that I can't even squirm away, dragging the orgasm out. "You can go, actually. Raoul will have your gratuity."

"Very good, sir."

Luca doesn't let go of me until the door closes behind the server, and we're alone on the rooftop. And then he pushes his chair back, sliding his hand out from under my skirt, and to my shock, he raises his fingers to his mouth.

Oh my god. My billionaire, mafia-don husband is sitting across from me, licking me off his fingers with the same expression on his face that I saw when he was eating dessert. I'm the furthest thing from turned off that I've ever been. If anything, I'm just as desperate for him as I was before, even though he just made me come even harder than last night.

I glance down and see that he's visibly, obviously hard, his cock pressed against the front of his suit trousers in a thick ridge that makes my mouth go dry, remembering how he'd felt inside of me last night.

As if he's reading my mind, Luca reaches down for his fly, dragging his zipper down and reaching to pull out his cock. His hand wraps around the length of it, stroking once as his eyes rake over my body.

"Take off your panties," he says, and I feel like I can't breathe.

"I—"

"Now, Sofia." There's that dark, smoky edge to his voice that I remember from last night, and there's no way on earth that I could say no to him in this moment. I never in my wildest dreams imagined myself doing anything like this. Still, as I look at the gorgeous man sitting next to me, casually stroking himself as he looks at me like I'm the most beautiful thing he's ever seen, all I want to do is exactly what he asks.

Mutely, I stand up, pushing up my skirt so that I can reach up and slide my thong off. "What should I do with it?" I whisper breathlessly, and Luca's eyes darken when he sees the scrap of lace in my hand.

"Put it on the table. Raise your skirt, and spread your legs so that I can see you."

I'm not supposed to want this. I'm a good girl. I got good grades, read Pride and Prejudice instead of trashy romance novels. I like rom-coms. This isn't supposed to turn me on. But it is. I'm completely lost in the sound of Luca's voice, sliding over my skin like the silk of the expensive dress he bought me, and without hesitating, I do as he said.

I don't just obey, either. I don't know what possesses me to slide my skirt up slowly, even seductively, spreading my thighs a little wider with every inch so that Luca has to wait the tiniest bit. I feel powerful at the look on his face, an expression of impatient lust, but he doesn't tell me to go faster. *He likes this,* I realize as I inch the flowered silk up, and when I finally slide it high enough that he can see my bare, glistening pussy, he groans aloud.

"Just stay like that for a minute," Luca murmurs, his voice raspy with desire as he starts to stroke a little faster, his hand squeezing the thick length of his cock. "Fuck, you're beautiful, Sofia."

I don't know what comes over me. But when I see the look on his face, I suddenly want to please him. And more than that—I'm turned on too, my body hot with desire. I can feel how wet I am without even touching myself, and when I reach down, sliding my fingers along my pussy, I moan aloud at the barest touch. I'm so aroused I can't help it.

"Fuck, Sofia—" Luca moans, his eyes widening, and it only makes me braver. I spread myself open with two fingers, letting him see my pussy even more, my aching clit visible as I rub one finger over it.

"That feels good," I whimper, the words slipping out before I can stop them, and Luca's jaw tightens as he squeezes his hand around his cock.

"I need you," he whispers. "Come sit in my lap, Sofia. I need my cock inside you now."

As if in a dream, I stand up, holding my skirt up with one hand as I swing my leg over him. The chair is just high enough with my heels on that my feet touch the ground. I leverage myself atop him, our lips just a breath apart as I feel him angle his cock between my thighs, the head slipping against my drenched flesh.

I'm in control, I realize suddenly. I'm the one on top, and as Luca looks at me hungrily, his free hand tangling in the loose curls of my hair, I throw all caution to the wind.

I want him. And I'm not going to fight it.

I lean forward to kiss him, my hand curving around the back of his head at the same moment that I slide down onto his lap, taking every inch of his cock into me as I moan aloud, my thighs tightening on either side of his.

And god, it feels so fucking good.

LUCA

19

I think I'm as shocked by Sofia's actions as she is. The girl who trembled in my hands when I kissed her for the first time, who blushed red when I bent her over the couch, who told me stiffly to "get it over with" on our wedding night, is nowhere to be seen. The blatant desire in her face when she obeys my instructions to lift her skirt is the most arousing thing I've ever seen, and that's what leads me to tell her to climb into my lap.

For once, I want to see what she does when she's in control. When all the choices about what we do—or don't—are up to her.

When she slides over me, her thighs gripping mine, I feel almost dizzy with lust. When she kisses me, it pushes me to the edge. And when Sofia slides downwards, impaling herself on my aching cock, I lose all control.

I'd planned to make her come again, but I know the minute I feel her velvet heat enveloping me that I don't have much time. I slide my hand between us, frantically rubbing at her clit as she grinds atop me inexpertly, her awkward rhythm making it plain that she's never done this before. But it doesn't matter. She could have sat perfectly still, and I'd be on the verge of spilling my cum into her. The rocking of her hips, the sway of her breasts in the silk dress, and the feeling of her hand on the back of my head, her lips capturing mine as she takes charge of me for the first time, are all more than enough.

"I'm going to come, Sofia," I whisper urgently, my other hand tangling in her hair. "Come with me, *fuck*, baby please—"

I can't believe what I'm saying. Dimly it occurs to me that I just called a woman a pet name for the first time in my life, that it's me begging for her orgasm, but I'm past caring. Nothing has ever felt as good as Sofia sinking down onto my cock, her pussy grinding against me as she takes all of me into her body, and as her tongue tangles with mine, I lose all control.

I groan against her mouth, grabbing both of her hips hard with an almost primal instinct as I hold her down onto my cock as I erupt inside of her, my entire length pulsing with waves of pleasure so intense my vision darkens a little at the corners. I've never been so hard, never *come* so hard, and I moan against Sofia's mouth as I crush her against my chest. I swear I can feel her heart beating against mine, and I don't want to stop. I don't want to ever let her go, to ever slide out of her, to ever stop feeling this overwhelming rush.

She feels better than anything I've ever felt in my entire life.

As Sofia slips out of my lap, I stand, quickly adjusting myself before sweeping her up into my arms. It's as if someone else has taken over my body as I carry her downstairs, her dazed eyes looking up into mine as she curls against me. "That was good," she whispers, leaning up to brush her lips over the base of my throat, and I feel a tightness in my chest that I've never felt before.

I carry her all the way to the bathroom in our master suite and set her down gently, smoothing her hair away from her face as I lean down to kiss her. Her lips part under mine, and I realize dimly that I'm doing things that I swore I never would, romancing a woman in a way that I've avoided all my life.

And not just any woman. Sofia. My wife.

But I can't seem to stop. I turn on the taps for the bath, letting the hot water pour into the whirlpool tub as I sink down onto one knee.

"Are you proposing again?" Sofia says with a laugh. "Oh wait—you never did." Her eyes glitter down at me mischievously, and I glare teasingly up at her.

"Careful, woman," I warn her. "Or you'll find yourself tied up in bed again and begging."

"Oh, that would be *terrible*," Sofia says in a mocking tone, and I can't help but laugh.

"You're going to be the death of me." I unbuckle one of her shoes and then the other, waiting for her to kick them aside before I stand up and reach for her zipper. I hear her groan as the shoes come off, a sound of pleasure that, for all the world, sounds like the one she made when she slid down onto my cock, and I feel myself throb in response.

No one has ever been able to arouse me so quickly. I feel half-mad with desire for her, doing things I never imagined doing. As the zipper comes all the way down, the dress slides off of her curves to pool on the floor, ten thousand dollars of silk and chiffon in a pile on my bathroom floor, but I don't care.

I'll buy her a dozen more. It doesn't matter.

"Pour some bubble bath in," I tell her. "I'll be back in a minute."

When I come back, I see Sofia already in the tub, bubbles foaming around her naked breasts as she piles her hair atop her head. She smiles at me, her red lipstick scrubbed off and leaving her lips stained faintly pinker than usual, her eyes skating over my chest. I took off my tie and jacket and undid the first few buttons on my way in, and the way her eyes are stripping me naked, I wish I'd taken it all off. But I have something else to do, first.

"I have a gift for you," I tell her, perching on the edge of the tub. "I meant to give it to you upstairs, but I got distracted."

Sofia's eyes widen as I hand her the slender velvet box. "Luca, you didn't have to—"

"I know." I grin at her. "But I wanted to spoil you a little. I know this hasn't been easy for you. We're trying to do this better—so…this was what I thought of to do." I pause, looking at her wide dark eyes, surrounded by her makeup still and fringed with long lashes. "I can't tell you that I love you, Sofia. But this is what I *can* do."

She bites her lower lip, and I can tell that there's something she wants to say. But instead, she just looks at the box, her eyes full of emotions I can't entirely read. Finally, she takes it out of my hand and opens it, gasping when she sees what's inside.

There's a white-gold bracelet nestled on the blue velvet, linked daisies made of yellow diamond centers and white diamond petals, each the size of my thumb and glittering under the bathroom lights.

"Luca! This is beautiful, but—"

"No buts," I say firmly, reaching to take the box out of her hand. I slip the bracelet out, taking Sofia's wrist and draping the diamond bracelet over it. Her wrist feels light and dainty in my hand, and she breathes in sharply when I clasp it.

"It's too much, Luca. I didn't do anything to deserve that—"

"You don't have to deserve beautiful things."

"But you said—"

"Forget what I said," I tell her sharply, standing up to unbutton my shirt. "Let's forget everything that happened before last night. Everything we did, everything we said. We're starting fresh. Trying something new."

I know, deep down, that this is a terrible idea. There's no forgetting the things we've said to each other, the circumstances that we married under, the horrible tangle of betrayal and blood and death that led us to stand hand in hand in St. Patrick's and say vows to each other that we didn't mean. But I can't seem to stop myself.

Stripping the rest of my clothes off, I step into the tub, sinking down into the hot water with Sofia. As I pull her against me, feeling my cock rise all over again at the touch of her warm, wet skin against mine, I can't regret the choices I'm making.

Even if I know, it's all going to come crashing down, eventually.

* * *

ABOVE ANYTHING ELSE, I know that I need to make peace with Viktor. With that in mind, I spend the next days trying to get in touch with Levin so that I can try to speak to Viktor again. The fury that I felt the night I came home to Sofia after the intruder hasn't abated—I want to kill him as much as ever.

But unlike Rossi, I know that's not an answer. Taking out Viktor isn't as easy as simply going after him or sending an assassin in the night, and I have no desire to see dozens more of my men die trying to bring him down. All I want is an end to this, a peace that will keep anyone else from dying.

Rossi thinks vengeance is worth it. I disagree.

I've been to see him once more. Somehow he'd heard about the intruder, and the satisfaction in his face when he asked me if I understood, now, why he wanted them all dead made me want to punch him. But I'm not about to hit a convalescent old man in his hospital bed, so I ignored it, just like I ignored his insistence that we go to war with the Russians as much as possible. "I'm looking for a solution," I told him over and over again, even as his aging face turned red with anger. "I've met with Viktor once. I'm going to try to do so again."

Viktor and I meet on neutral territory, near a small pond in a less well-traveled section of Central Park. Whether it's the sunlight or the stresses of the past weeks, I notice he looks slightly older than usual—the greying hair at his temples more prominent, the faint lines around his eyes a bit deeper. There's salt and pepper stubble on his chin, and it gives me a moment's pleasure to think that maybe all of this is getting to him as much as it is me.

"I hope you have something new to discuss, Luca," Viktor says darkly as I approach, my security hanging back. I can see them watching Viktor's guards with a careful eye, but I hope there won't be any conflict today. I'm not here to start a fight unless he forces my hand.

"Since there's still no peace, anything we say will be new," I tell him flatly. "Someone tried to kill my wife a few nights ago. Will you admit to it being you?"

Viktor shrugs. "How many enemies do you have, Luca?"

"As far as I know, only the Bratva. And you are the Bratva. So—only you, Viktor. But I don't wish for us to be enemies."

"I can't see how we'll ever be friends." Viktor raises one bushy eyebrow. "There's too much bad blood between Italian and Russian, mafia and Bratva. There's not enough water in the world to wash away all that we've spilled."

"No," I agree. "But we could let it wash away on its own. We could refuse to add to it." I take a deep breath. "What do you hope to achieve with this, Viktor? Surely you can't think that killing my wife is a wise move."

"Easy. Your territory to rule. Your businesses to profit from. Your women to sell." Viktor shrugs. "What is there not to want?"

"You really think that you can take all of that? This conflict has been going off and on for decades, Viktor, since our fathers had these conversations instead of you and me. Let's put it to bed, once and for all. Let us be the ones who make peace instead of war."

"You offer words and nothing else," Viktor says, anger coloring his words. "You must think of me weak to agree to such a thing."

"I've offered you money and drugs, access to a portion of our cocaine shipments," I argue impatiently. "That's not nothing, Viktor. You say it's me who keeps us from making peace, but it's you who refuses to accept reasonable terms."

"I told you what—or rather *who* I will accept as the price of peace." Viktor glares at me. "I've heard that you convinced that ballless Irish priest of yours to move up the dates of the wedding, but Caterina Rossi is still unwed. Give me the Rossi girl as my wife, and my men will not set foot in Italian territory for a hundred years. I'll put it in the fucking marriage contract."

Fucking hell. "I can't give you a wife," I growl through gritted teeth. "I don't barter and sell women the way you do. Caterina isn't mine to give to you."

Viktor laughs mockingly, but I can see the angry red creeping up his throat. "You fucking Italians," he snarls, spitting on the ground at my feet before looking up at me with icy eyes. "You think you're so much better than us Russians since you don't traffic in human flesh. But you're no different. You make slaves and whores with the drugs you sell, just as we do with the women we auction. You have as much blood on your hands from the arms you deal as any one of my men."

"It's not the same."

"It is the same, *yobanaya suka*." Viktor spits again. "You and your Italian *bliads* think you're so sophisticated, so elegant, so much more restrained. You think we Russians are nothing more than brutal dogs, to be punished or put down when we misbehave too badly. But we are not dogs. We are *volki, medvedi*. Wolves. Bears. And at least my men and I are honest with ourselves about who and what we are."

"You're making it impossible to broker peace, Viktor—"

"There will be no peace!" Viktor snarls. His ice-blue eyes glint angrily, and I can see his posture hardening, rigid with anger. The bad blood between us, generations' worth, is no longer at a simmer but at a boil. "And when you and the Irish bastard you call underboss are dead, I will take both of your wives for my own. I'll fuck them next to each other while they look at your dead bodies. I'll fuck them in the pools of your blood and then decide who I'll call wife and who I'll call mistress." He jerks his head at his guards. "*Poydem*," he growls. "Let's go. Leave this *podonok* to his own peace." His accent is thicker than ever as he speaks, and though I want to try to stop him, something warns me away from that.

But still, as I watch him go, I can feel my heart sinking. *No more blood*. I don't want to see another one of my men die. Gio is still in the hospital, struggling in critical condition. I don't want the death and destruction that I know will follow.

I can't give him Caterina, though, any more than I could or would have given him Sofia. Which puts me in an impossible position.

There's no way to know what the coming days will bring. But I know one thing for certain.

I won't let Viktor harm Sofia.

Not if it kills me.

SOFIA

20

The next few days with Luca don't feel real. They feel like some kind of fantasy, a fever dream because they're so vastly different than the ones we spent together before the intruder. I wake up one morning with a note on the pillow next to mine, telling me that he's left early for the office and that he wants me to plan "your kind of date" tonight. It's as if he watched a handful of rom-coms to figure out what women might like—the rooftop date, the bubble bath, the diamond bracelet, the note in the morning. But I can't bring myself to care. The bracelet is stupidly over the top, but I don't want to take it off. I find myself slipping it on every morning, even as out of place as it is with my plain hoops and dainty cross necklace. I catch myself running my fingers over it, thinking about Luca feeding me quail on a rooftop, his hand under my skirt, him carrying me down the stairs afterward.

I know I need to snap out of it, but I don't want to. Even Caterina catches on a little, asking me as we sit in the living room planning out details for her wedding if Luca and I are getting along better now. I tell her yes, blushing a little, and I know I ought to ask her about her and Franco, but I don't.

She's already told me what I know she's willing to share, anyway.

Franco came home from the bachelor party without so much as an apology for taking so long, brushing away her fear and trauma from the intruder by saying that he'd trusted Luca's bodyguards, and look, she was alive without a scratch on her, wasn't she? Caterina talks about it as if she should have expected him to treat it as no big deal, but I can see how disillusioned she is with her fiancé. She'd never expected a grand romance, but I know from what she's told me that she had at least hoped when she'd been matched with someone close to her own age, that it would be a better marriage than she might have had otherwise—one with mutual respect, good sex, and some laughter and fun together. The kind of marriage that a girl who snuck a blowjob to her new fiancé in the back of the limo on the return trip from the proposal and a guy who took her to an afterparty at their favorite bar post-engagement party might have. One where they could make some good memories, before age and responsibility and kids caught up to them.

But it's clear that Franco has no intention to treat his bride as anything but something owed to him, and not even as the prize that she is. It makes me angry—I don't know Franco that well, but I'd thought he seemed fun and nice enough when I'd met him briefly before and at my own wedding. Clearly, though, it was all a show for the benefit of everyone else.

Caterina seems to have accepted it, though, putting all of her energy into trying to plan the wedding as best as we can. We sprinkle as many small touches through it that her mother would have loved as we can—violets in the centerpieces since they were Giulia's favorite flower, the menu that she'd put together. Caterina has her jewelry that she plans to wear with the wedding dress they chose together. She holds herself together better than I could possibly have thought she would.

Meanwhile, Luca and I seem to be existing in some kind of relationship limbo, almost like we're playing at being together, playing house. When Caterina and I are done planning and she goes home, I start working on my date for the evening with Luca, even as I think how ridiculous it is. I'm married to the man in charge of the entire

Italian mafia. I'm trying to guess what pizza toppings he might like because I want to surprise him with what I'm choosing for our dinner together.

We can't even leave the penthouse. We're planning dates in this strange bubble we're locked inside of. Still, every time I start to argue with myself about why I should withdraw, why I should stop sleeping with him, why I should push him away, I can't help but think—*you're enjoying yourself. So why not keep doing it?*

Luca comes home to me in high-waisted jeans and a white muscle pocket tank tied up above my navel, barefoot, with the diamond bracelet he gave me looped around my wrist and my hair in a high ponytail. His hand wraps around that ponytail when I rise up on my tiptoes to kiss him, sending a thrill through me that I never imagined I'd feel with him.

Our date is pizza in the movie room and a comedy that I picked out because it's light and fun, along with popcorn and movie candy. "This is as close as we can get to a pizza and movie date," I tell Luca, laughing. "But we're married now, so I guess having you over is okay."

He smiles a genuine grin that looks almost out of place on his chiseled face and kisses me again. He keeps kissing me throughout the night, in between bites of pizza with sauce still on my lower lip, after we feed each other popcorn, when he wipes chocolate off of the corner of my mouth with his thumb. He kisses me throughout the movie, until at some point, I wind up in his lap, curled against his chest as we laugh along with the couple on screen.

It feels so weirdly normal that I don't know what to do about it. He teases me a little in the theater room, his hand on my thigh and over my shoulder, occasionally squeezing my breast. I'm hyper-aware that this is the room where he caught me on the security feed playing with myself. I half wonder if he'll try to recreate it, but instead, when the movie is over, we cuddle a little longer, and then head to bed. There's sex, of course—we've had sex at least once every night since he flew home to me, but it's slower and less wild than the rooftop date. Almost as if he's trying to perform "normal" sex on a "normal" date, Luca kisses me for a long time in bed, fingering me to orgasm while he lets me explore him. Running my hand up and down his thick, hard shaft until he slips down my body and goes down on me, licking me slowly until I come for a second time. Only then does he roll on a condom and thrust into me, fucking me long and slow in missionary until we're both close to an orgasm. Then he hooks my ankles over his shoulders, folding my legs back so that he can kiss me as he drives himself deep inside of me, making me moan helplessly against his mouth as he comes hard. I come too, my body reacting as he groans, his cock throbbing as he grinds against me, and when we collapse onto the bed afterward, he doesn't roll over to his side of the bed.

We fall asleep with Luca's arm thrown over my belly, my head pillowed against his shoulder. It's so incredibly normal that I can briefly forget who he is and who I am, why we're married, that I'm on virtual house arrest because a Russian mobster wants me dead.

And then there's Caterina's wedding.

There's no way to avoid having to leave the penthouse. She can't exactly get married in our living room—I'm pretty sure that would have stretched even Father Donahue's limits of accommodating Luca. So instead, Luca reluctantly sends me to the Rossi house to help her get ready while he meets up with Franco at the church, enough security tailing me to make the President jealous.

"Be safe," he says as we go our separate ways, kissing me hard before opening the door for me to climb into the car taking me to the Rossi house. "I don't want anything to happen to you."

"I'll be fine." I give him a little wave as the door closes, leaning back against the cool leather. I feel almost giddy at being out of the penthouse for the first time in weeks. Watching the city speed by as we drive towards the Rossi mansion makes me feel as if I can't stop smiling. Caterina raises an eyebrow at my expression when I walk through the front door and she greets me.

"You look happier than I do," she says wryly. "Come on, let's get ready."

Since I'm the only one standing up with her at the altar, Caterina told me to pick out whatever I wanted for my dress. I chose a strapless, violet-blue, floor-length gown with a band of lace at the waist that matched the flowers, sweeping my hair up into a sleek updo with my diamond studs in my ears and Luca's bracelet on my wrist—nothing overly flashy. I don't want to upstage Caterina. Even if her marriage isn't looking like it'll be what she'd hoped it would be, I want her wedding day to be as perfect as it can be.

She looks like a queen in her wedding gown, which has been altered and perfectly fitted to her so that the heavy, rich fabric skims over her figure down to the full skirt, her collarbone and shoulders standing out elegantly above the off-shoulder neckline. Her mother's ruby jewelry looks stunning on her, oval earrings surrounded by a halo of diamonds and a long drop necklace with an egg-sized ruby on a strand of diamonds. Still, looking at the gleaming red stones against her skin, I can't help but think they look like blood. It makes me shiver a little.

The last time the Bratva launched a full-scale attack, it was the morning after my wedding. Neither Caterina nor I have wanted to so much as mention the possibility, but as we walk to the car, I can see that she's paler than usual. Whether it's nerves over the wedding itself or the possibility of another attack, I don't know, and I don't want to ask. But when I hand her the bouquet outside of the church, I can see her hands shaking.

St. Patrick's is packed full, all of the guests who could possibly be invited in attendance despite the possibility of a Bratva attack. Bruno Rossi, Caterina's uncle, is walking her down the aisle in place of her father, who still hasn't been released from the hospital.

Or so we thought. But as I start my walk down the aisle on Luca's arm—the extent of the wedding party—I see Rossi at the back of the church, in a wheelchair and looking very much the worse for wear… but here.

Of course, he wouldn't miss his daughter's wedding if there was the slightest way he could be here, I tell myself. But still, seeing him again in the flesh makes me feel anxious, my fingers suddenly trembling with nerves. Luca glances over at me as if he feels me shaking.

"It's fine," he says quietly, underneath the music. "He insisted on being temporarily released from the hospital. But he's going back after the ceremony. He's not strong enough to be at the reception yet."

I realize that Luca thinks I'm worried for Rossi's well-being, when in fact, I'm worried about him being here at all—whether that will make the Bratva more likely to attack if there's something else going on. I don't trust Rossi. But deep down, I don't think the former will be the case. If there's anyone Viktor would want to attack now, it's Luca. Without him, the seat would pass to Franco—and privately, I don't have very much faith in Franco's ability to run the organization. It surprises me that Luca does.

There's none of the tension during the ceremony that there was for Luca and me. This isn't a forced marriage—for all that it *was* arranged, both Caterina and Franco are entering into it willingly. They say their vows clearly and firmly, and even though I know Caterina isn't pleased with how Franco's behaved lately, it hasn't made her falter. This is who was chosen for her, and she seems to have accepted it.

But as they say the vows to each other, I catch Luca looking at me, his face unreadable. *What is he thinking?* I wonder, the words echoing in my ears and reminding me of the day, barely over a month ago, when I'd stood where Caterina is now, shaking in my Louboutin heels as I repeated those vows knowing that I was lying, that I had no intention to keep a single one of them. And I'm sure Luca's were just as hollow.

And now? I can't help but wonder if anything has changed. Good sex doesn't make a marriage, especially between someone like me and someone as fucked up as Luca. He hasn't budged on his conviction that he can't love me, that our marriage can never be anything except, at best, a lustful companionship where we both get along.

His eyes on mine, though, watching me as Caterina and Franco repeat *to love and honor and cherish, to have and to hold, in sickness and in health, for better or for worse, 'til death do us part,* make it hard to believe that. When Caterina says *obey*, I see the smoky look in his eyes, the one that reminds me of the ways I've obeyed him, the things I've done when his voice licks over my skin, telling me to give in to his lustful demands.

But I think of other things, too. I think of twinkling lights on a rooftop, Luca telling me that he brought Paris to me. I think of feeding each other popcorn and laughing at stupid jokes in a bad comedy movie. I think of Luca at the dinner table, telling me how he's spent his whole life protecting his best friend.

Luca's new position is a lonely place. I realize that now. Franco is his best friend, but he's also Luca's right-hand man now, someone Luca has to depend on to do the right thing when Luca isn't there to do it. He can't shield Franco any longer. He has to continue a legacy that Caterina's father has built up over the years—and then pass it on to his underboss's son.

That's not really fair, is it? It's the first time I've stopped to consider that. Luca will spend his life defending a legacy that he won't pass on to anyone of his own blood. No one has really explained to me why that is —why Luca isn't allowed to have children of his own, why he's essentially keeping a place warm for Franco's eventual—hopeful—child.

It hadn't occurred to me to ask because I hadn't intended to ever sleep with Luca. I hadn't intended to even *speak* to him more than necessary, much less fall into bed with him over and over. *At least we've been using protection*, I think, remembering the box of condoms Luca had brought home with him last week since we'd apparently run through what was left of his stash.

"I now pronounce you husband and wife," Father Donahue says, breaking through my thoughts—all of which are completely inappropriate for a church—and Franco pulls his new bride into his arms, kissing her firmly. I see Caterina lean slightly into the kiss, and I hope that no matter what issues they might have, she'll be able to have some happiness in this new marriage.

There are cheers as they walk down the aisle, everyone standing as they walk hand in hand towards the doors of the church, and I see Caterina smile at her father as we all walk out into the sunshine. A health aide is with him, and as we all stand out on the steps of the church, I see him wheeled out, and Caterina turns to talk quietly with him.

"Are they taking him back to the hospital now?" I ask Luca quietly, and he nods.

"My men are doing a sweep of the hotel before the reception," he adds under his breath. "As soon as it's all clear, we'll head there."

I can tell that he's trying as hard as he can to make today as smooth for Caterina and Franco as he can, with as little reminder of the danger hanging over all our heads—the danger that took her mother—as possible. It's the same thing I've been trying to do this whole time while helping Caterina plan. For the first time, as I look up at Luca, I catch a glimpse of what it's like to be his partner in something, working together.

It's not so bad if I'm being completely honest with myself.

We're starting to head to the limos when Luca suddenly puts a hand out, stopping Caterina and me. "Hold on," he says. "Raoul just sent me something. *Stay here,*" he adds, his voice suddenly deep and commanding. "I'll be back in a minute."

Caterina looks slightly pale, reaching for Franco's hand. "I should be helping Luca," he says, and I turn towards him at that, glaring at him.

"This is your day with Caterina," I bite out, my voice harsher than I've heard it in a long time. "Worry about your new wife, for twenty-four hours, at least."

Franco stares at me, momentarily shocked into silence. "Watch your mouth," he says sharply when he's recovered. "Luca wouldn't like you talking to me like that."

"Franco!" Caterina exclaims, but he shakes her off.

"I think Luca would agree with me," I say flatly, still unsure how I'm finding the nerve to speak at all. I honestly don't know how Luca would feel about my talking to his underboss like this, but in terms of rank, I'm *pretty* sure Franco is supposed to give the boss's wife respect. As far as how I'm supposed to treat Franco, I don't really know. And to be honest, I don't really care.

Franco opens his mouth to make some retort, but the sound of Luca, Raoul, and the others coming back brings him up short.

"What's wrong?" I ask, my stomach tightening at the look on Luca's face. Whatever he went to find out about, it can't be good.

"They hit the reception hall at the hotel," Luca says, his voice dark with barely restrained anger. "Everything was destroyed, the staff held up at gunpoint. Franco, I'm sending you and Caterina back to the Rossi house with double the guards. I don't think they'll expect you to spend your wedding night there instead of a hotel or your apartment. Tomorrow, we're taking a trip to get to the bottom of this. But you and Caterina deserve your wedding night." He glances over at me. "We'll head back to the penthouse."

Caterina is so pale that her rose-colored lipstick looks like a bold pink slash on her face, the rubies standing out garishly against her skin. "Luca—I'm scared," she whispers. "The wedding—"

"I'm sorry your wedding was ruined," Luca says, and I can hear the genuine apology in his tone.

"I don't care about the reception," Caterina says, waving her hand. "The important part is done. But they're not stopping, Luca. What if—"

"They'll stop," Luca says harshly. "If I have to—" he trails off. "These aren't things you should be worrying about on your wedding day," he says more carefully. "Go with Franco. I'll make sure you're well-guarded. They'll bring food from the caterer over for you. You won't have to worry about anything tonight. I promise."

We're at the church a little longer after Caterina and Franco leave and the guests file out. I can see Luca talking quietly with Father Donahue and some of the security, and I hang back, perched on one of the pews as I wait for him to be finished.

It occurs to me how much our dynamic has changed in such a short time. If I'm being honest with myself, I like this better. Mutual respect, tentative peace—whatever this new thing is that has sprung up between Luca and me, it's better than what we had before.

It's just after dark when we get back to the penthouse. Luca lets out a long breath as the front door shuts behind him, and I see the relief etched across his face. I realize then that *he* feels safer here too, and it makes me reconsider, just a tiny bit, his genuine motives in keeping me here from the start. That maybe, just maybe, it was because he truly felt this was the safest place for me, and not just because he wanted to exert control over his bride-to-be.

We eat the food sent over from the caterer in relative silence, neither of us really knowing what to say. We should be dancing at Caterina's reception right now. Instead, we're sitting in our quiet dining room, eating the filet and crab cake that we should have been having at a white-covered table with violets in the center of it.

"I'm going to check with security once more before bed," Luca says when we've finished. "I'll meet you upstairs."

"Okay." I give him a small smile. "See you upstairs."

Halfway to Luca's—our?—bedroom, I pause in the hall. I have the sudden urge to do something different, something special for tonight. I don't know if it's the wedding ceremony, the interrupted reception, or something else altogether, but the thought of the look in Luca's eyes when he came back to tell Caterina that her wedding day had to be cut short makes me want to do something for him. Something to replace that look with a different one altogether.

I walk into the room that was mine, pushing open the closet door. Closest to it is the white lace-and-silk baby doll nightgown and robe that was part of the lingerie Luca had purchased for me. Then I'd seen it as a dig at the virginity I'd been clinging to, a spiteful way to remind me that if he'd wanted it, he could take it.

Now, looking at it hanging untouched in my old closet, it seems like a way to redo my wedding night. I could put it on for Luca, and tonight, on a night made for love, we could try again.

I slip it off of the hangar, carrying it into the master suite. In the bedroom, I strip out of the violet bridesmaid's dress, draping it over a chair as I kick off my high heels and take off my jewelry. And then, I slip on the silk nightie, sighing with pleasure as it slides over my skin.

It feels sensual just having it on. It falls to the tops of my thighs, fragile silk like the red dress I wore on that ridiculous date, and the feeling of having nothing on underneath it is both vulnerable and erotic all at once. There's eyelash lace along the hem, a delicate band of see-through lace at my waist, and more eyelash lace along the edges of the neckline. My nipples brush against the silk, hardening at the thought of Luca seeing me in this, the way I hope he'll react.

The robe is the same light, airy silk, and I leave it open as I shrug it on, walking into the bathroom. I leave my makeup on but undo my hair, letting it fall in heavy dark curls around my face. My lips are still faintly pink even after dinner, and even to my own eyes, I think I look sexy, more seductive than any virginal bride should be.

I hear Luca's footsteps in the hall and step out into the bedroom, feeling a sudden rush of nervousness. *What if he thinks this is stupid? What if he hates it?*

But when the door opens, he catches sight of me. The look on his face tells me a very different story.

SOFIA

21

"Sofia." He breathes my name, stepping into the room and letting the door close behind him. "What is this?"

I shiver a little as I meet him halfway, crossing the distance between us as Luca walks towards me. He reaches for me the minute I'm close enough, his hands slipping beneath the robe and sliding over the lace at my waist.

"I think this was supposed to be my lingerie for our wedding night," I say quietly, and I can feel myself flushing slightly at the memory. "I thought—I thought I could put it on, and we—we could try again." Even as I say it, I feel foolish. I can't lose my virginity twice. We can't undo the way that night went. Just like we can't undo everything we said and did before it. Pretending to be in Paris and movie nights at home can't change any of it.

But Luca isn't looking at me like he thinks I'm foolish. Instead, there's a heat in his eyes that I've never seen before, even in our most lustful moments.

"You look beautiful," he murmurs. "More beautiful than ever—" he trails off, and I reach up, smoothing my fingers down the v of skin where his shirt is undone.

"I wanted to do something special," I whisper. "Something different."

I've never undressed him before. Luca stays very still under my hands as I undo the shirt one button at a time, pulling it loose from his suit trousers and pushing the fabric off his shoulders. The sight of his muscled chest and carved abs, the flex of his arms as the shirt slides off, makes me shiver with desire. I can't imagine there's ever been a man as beautiful as Luca, as perfectly made. I want to touch him all over, so I do, giving myself completely over to my urges.

He sighs with pleasure as my hands run down his chest, my fingers tracing his rippling abs down to his belt. I undo it slowly, and Luca groans a little when I reach for his fly.

"We can slow down if you want," he starts to say, but I ignore him, pulling his zipper down and pushing his pants down his hips to pool around his feet.

He's already hard, as erect as I've ever seen him, his cock springing free and nearly touching his abs as it strains upwards, clearly aching to be touched. I shrug off my robe, letting the silk fall to the floor to join his clothes as I look up at him, sinking to my knees as I reach for his cock.

"Sofia—" Luca gasps my name as my hand wraps around his shaft, surprise coloring his tone. "You don't have to—"

"I know." I've wondered what it would be like to do this ever since he first went down on me that night that he teased me mercilessly, and now, tonight seems like as good a time as any to try. I want to give him the same kind of pleasure that he gave me, and I lean towards him, nervousness and excitement mingling as I flick out my tongue.

Luca groans when the tip of my tongue traces around the head of his cock, lapping up the bead of pre-cum already forming there, and I make a small noise when I taste him for the first time. Emboldened by the sound he makes, I run my tongue around it again, flicking it slightly beneath the head before I press my lips against it, pushing them forward as I take him in my mouth for the first time.

"Fuck, Sofia—" Luca wobbles a little, and I put a hand on his thigh to brace myself. "God, that feels so fucking good."

I can feel the tension in his thighs, and I know he wants to thrust more of himself into my mouth, to push it into my throat and make me take all of it. Just the thought of that scares and arouses me all at once, and I try to take more, feeling my lips stretch around his thick length as I take an inch more, and then another.

Luca lets me explore him, my fingers wrapping around the shaft as I start to try to move, bobbing up and down slightly as I run my tongue up and down, along his length and back up to the head, sucking in between. None of it is particularly skilled, I'm sure, but he doesn't seem to care. His fingers run through my hair as he groans above me, looking down at me.

"You look so fucking beautiful with my cock in your mouth," he murmurs, his voice thick with lust. "I pictured this so many fucking times, Sofia—" he moans my name again as I take him all the way to the back of my throat, slowly gaining confidence.

"If you keep doing that, I'm going to come." Luca's fingers tighten in my hair. "God, I want to come on your tits, in your mouth, on your face—"

I'm so turned on that I might have let him do any of those things, but I like the temporary control that I have from this. I like feeling in charge of his pleasure. I pull back slightly, feeling more daring than I ever have in my life as I look up at him, lips hovering just above his head as I whisper: "let's start with my mouth."

Luca stares at me in disbelief, but before he can say anything, I slide my mouth back down, sucking harder now, running my tongue up and down as I try to push him towards an orgasm. I want to feel it, taste it, desire rippling through my blood as I stroke his hip with one hand, running my hand over his thigh. The scent of his skin fills my nose, the taste and feel of him overwhelming me. I'm so into it that I almost don't hear his warning as Luca's back arches and his hand momentarily tightens in my hair.

The rush of it startles me at first. I feel his cock throb in my mouth, swelling and hardening even more as he groans above me with a sound of strangled pleasure, and then the first hot rush of his cum shoots over my tongue and down my throat.

I choke a tiny bit, and then I swallow, my throat convulsing as Luca shoots wave after wave of cum into my mouth, filling it as I swallow, again and again, still sucking until at last he gently pushes my face back, gasping and moaning as he pulls away.

"Holy fuck, Sofia—"

"Was that good?" I lick my lips, and an expression of pure lust crosses Luca's face.

"I'm about to show you just how good," he growls, reaching for me. Before I know it, I'm on my back on the bed, and he kisses me hard, seemingly not caring that he just came in my mouth. His hand strokes my cheek, running over my hair, and then he moves down my body, his hands skimming down my breasts and over my waist.

He takes one nipple in his mouth, licking my breast through the silk of my nightgown, and then moves further down, pushing the hem of it up as he leans down between my thighs, pushing them open so that he has the access he so desires.

The first swipe of his tongue makes me cry out, my back arching as his tongue delves into my pussy, licking all the way up to my clit, swirling and fluttering and sucking until I'm moaning helplessly, my hands tangling in his hair. There's no teasing this time, only his mouth driving me higher and higher until he thrusts two fingers into me, hooking them inside of my pussy and pushing against that spot that drives me wild until the combination of his tongue and his fingers are too much, and I feel my fingers knotting in his hair, my mouth falling open as my moan becomes a scream, my entire body tensing with pleasure so good that it almost feels like too much. Just like I kept going as he came in my mouth, Luca never stops, his tongue lashing against my sensitive flesh until I finally squirm away from him, gasping as I shudder with the aftershocks of the orgasm.

"I love how you taste," Luca growls as he moves up my body to kiss me again, and I taste myself on his lips. He's hard again, his heavy erection pressing against my inner thigh. "You taste so fucking good. I can't get enough of it. I can't get enough of you—" he kisses my neck as he reaches down, angling his cock so that the head pushes inside of me. But instead of thrusting in all at once, he starts to move slowly, sinking into me inch by inch so that I can feel all of it, every bit of him as he takes me slowly.

When he finally sinks all the way into me, Luca hovers above me, his hands braced on either side of my head. "I've rarely been with the same woman more than once," he says quietly, "and even then, it was only twice. I've never kept wanting someone the way I want you, Sofia. I've never felt so addicted to someone. So lost—as if I can't get you out of my head. As if I can't remember what it was like to not have you here."

He kisses me again, then, and the minutes blend into each other as we move against each other, all arching, straining bodies and damp skin, hands linking with one another as Luca thrusts into me in long, slow strokes that seem to go on forever, binding us together more closely than ever before. *This is making love,* I think dimly, and even as I remember that Luca told me that he couldn't love me, that we would never be in love, that this would never be that, my mind and body and heart and soul all soundly reject it. I can't imagine what love is if not this, two bodies straining towards pleasure together, locked in a tangle that neither of us ever want to escape from, breathing each other's breath, feeling each other's skin, our heartbeats pressed together until I've forgotten which is mine and which is his.

I feel him start to come as I do, my body tightening around him in a wave of pleasure that makes me feel as if I'm coming apart at the seams, dissolving entirely. I hear my high-pitched moans, my breathy gasps of his name in the same moment that Luca presses his mouth against my shoulder, groaning my name into my skin as his cock throbs inside of me, his orgasm spilling into me in a hot rush as we cling to each other, shuddering with pleasure that feels as if it might never end.

We stay like that for a long time, wrapped in each other's arms, Luca still inside of me as his cock softens slightly, still partially hard. When we finally untangle, it's only long enough for me to strip off the nightgown and toss it aside. Then Luca gathers me into his arms, pulling me against his chest as he sets his chin atop my head.

"I should take you on a honeymoon when this is all over," he says softly. "Anywhere you want."

I press my face against his chest, breathing in the scent of him. "That would be wonderful," I whisper, and I mean it. I can't imagine what it would be like to go on vacation with Luca, somewhere exotic and beautiful, just the two of us, but I suddenly want to find out. I want to escape this place more than anything with him, to go somewhere that the Bratva can't find us, where all of the dangers hanging over our heads vanish.

"Franco and I have to go try to handle the Russian problem tomorrow," he says quietly as if hearing my thoughts. "I might be gone for a few days. Promise me you'll stay here, Sofia. Promise you won't get into any trouble, that you'll do as I've asked, and be careful. If you want to see Caterina, she comes here. I'll have Carmen check in on you. It's dangerous right now," he adds as if I don't know that already. "I need your word that you won't do anything you're not supposed to."

Any other time, I might have bristled at being given orders, but I'm too relaxed and tired. *He's just looking out for me*, I think, my brain foggy with arousal and pleasure. "Okay," I mumble, curling closer to his chest. "I promise."

"Good." Luca leans down, kissing me softly, and he reaches for my leg then, pulling it over his as I feel his cock harden against me. "Let's do that again."

***

HE'S GONE when I wake up. There's a note for me letting me know that he didn't want to wake me and that he'll be back as soon as he can. For the first time, I notice how empty the bottom of the note looks with only his name signed. No *love*. Nothing other than his name scrawled across the bottom.

Last night felt like more. It felt like love. But I know better than to allow myself to think something like that. It's only going to lead to hurt in the end.

Enjoy what you have, I think to myself. *It's better than what you thought it would be.*

Caterina comes over a little while after breakfast. She looks tired and more sad than usual, and my chest tightens at the sight of her face. "Are you okay?" I ask, making her a cup of tea as she sits down in the kitchen. "Was last night—"

"It was fine," she says, her mouth twitching slightly. "Better than I expected, I guess? I don't know what I expected, exactly. Franco didn't seem too disappointed. He liked that I was a virgin, but that only works once, you know. So hopefully, he was happy enough to enjoy it again anyway."

"Was he nice?" I frown at her. "He didn't hurt you, did he?"

Caterina shakes her head. "He was gentle. It just—I don't know what I thought, really. I mean that. It was just more—detached, I guess." She takes the tea from me gratefully. "Maybe if things were more relaxed, if we could go on a honeymoon—" she shrugs. "But of course we can't, with the Bratva at our doorstep. And then my father is supposed to be released soon, but his condition still isn't great—and without my mother, I need to keep an eye on him." She pauses. "Which is why I came over, honestly, not just to talk about Franco."

"Oh?" I look at her curiously. "What did you want to talk about?"

"I wanted to ask you if you'd come to the hospital with me this afternoon. I'm supposed to go and talk to the doctor before they release him to go home, set up home health aide care until he finishes recovering from the surgery, and—" Caterina takes a deep, shaky breath. "I just can't go alone. I really can't. Please come with me?"

More than anything, I want to tell her yes. The thought of leaving her to handle all of this on her own cuts me to the core—but I remember the seriousness in Luca's voice last night. "I promised Luca I wouldn't leave," I say slowly. "He asked me specifically to stay here while he was gone, not to do anything I shouldn't. He'll be upset if—"

"It'd be different if he knew what it was," Caterina says insistently. I can see from her expression how desperately she doesn't want to have to be alone. "And besides, he doesn't have to know. I won't say anything, I swear."

BROKEN PROMISE

There's no way that Luca won't know. I'm positive he'll find out somehow. He always does. *But maybe she's right,* I rationalize. Maybe he would understand if he knew the circumstances. And besides, what could possibly happen? Caterina has as much security with her right now as I do. *It'll be fine,* I tell myself. *She needs you.*

"Alright," I relent. "I'll go."

Even as the words come out of my mouth, I know it's a bad idea. But the way Caterina's face lights up makes me certain I'm doing the right thing.

As long as Luca isn't too angry.

* * *

WHEN WE WALK into the hospital room, Rossi's eyes light up when he sees his daughter—the only real positive emotion I ever see from him—but his expression darkens just as quickly when he sees me. I hang back while he talks quietly to Caterina, feeling uncomfortably out of place. *I'm just here to support Caterina,* I remind myself as they talk, taking a seat near the window.

"I'm going to go talk to the doctor," Caterina says finally. "Wait here, Sofia? I don't want him to be alone."

Being alone in a room with Rossi is the last thing I would ever want to do. But I just nod, feeling stuck now that I've come here to help Caterina. I feel like I'm supposed to do whatever it is she needs from me, so I stay put, shifting in my seat as she walks out into the hall to find the doctor.

"You." Rossi's voice cuts through the silence in the room, cold and hard and rasping. "Come here."

"I'm just waiting for Caterina to come back," I start to say, and Rossi coughs, pushing himself up a little.

"You might be Luca's wife, but I'm still your elder." He clears his throat, his face flushing. "Come here."

It's the last thing in the world I want to do, but I don't want him to have a heart attack or something like that either, not when Caterina is already so fragile. So I stand up reluctantly, crossing the room to his bedside.

"What is it?" I try to keep my voice as calm as possible as Rossi turns towards me, his eyes dark and angry as they sweep over me.

"You're the cause of all of this, you know," he rasps. "Everything that's happened, this escalation with the Bratva, all of it is your fault. You and your filthy Russian bitch of a mother." He coughs, breathing with a rattle as he glares at me. "I should never have allowed Luca to follow through on your father's fucking promise. I should have had you killed when I had the chance."

"Vitto—" I should have known better than to use his first name. He looks almost purple with rage, his jaw working as he leans closer.

"You should hope that Luca doesn't find out the truth about why Viktor wanted you as his wife," Rossi hisses, and I stare at him, my eyes going wide with shock.

"He didn't want—"

"He did," Rossi says, satisfaction lacing his tone. "He wanted to marry you and fuck that tight virgin hole of yours every night until he put another Russian pup in you, the son he so desperately needs to take what he wants from us and keep it. But Luca got to you first. Even he doesn't know why you're so special, though."

"You're delirious." My voice doesn't even sound like mine to me, colder and harder than I've ever heard it. "You need to rest. You don't know what you're saying. Luca wouldn't appreciate you talking to me like this—"

"Luca is a fucking mistake," Rossi snarls, choking halfway through the sentence. "He's weak. I should never have given him—I should have fucking had you shot like the Russian bitch you are—"

I try to back away, chills running over my skin at the tone of his voice, the room suddenly feeling ice cold. But Rossi lunges towards me, yanking on his IV wires as he does and setting off the machine he's still tethered to. I dodge his hand, but it snags on the cross at my neck, snapping my mother's necklace and leaving it dangling in his fist.

"Give it back!" I exclaim, but he's already hiding it in his palm as a nurse and Caterina come rushing in, both of them wide-eyed.

"What's going on here?" the nurse demands, and Rossi lays back in bed, heaving and coughing.

"That girl—she's being cruel," he says, choking on his words. "I don't know why she's here; she doesn't belong here—"

"That's Sofia, you know her," Caterina says, her face deathly pale. "Dad, it's fine, she's just here to help me—"

"Get her out of here!" he roars, and I scramble backward, my heart racing in my chest as I push past the nurse. I almost make it out of the room, but before I can slip out, a sudden, awful wave of nausea grips me.

I barely make it into the bathroom before I heave over the toilet, everything I've eaten since last night emptying into it as I throw up again and again until my stomach is clenching painfully and my throat feels raw.

"Are you alright?" The nurse's voice makes me jump, and I nod, holding a hand out to keep some space between us as I wipe my mouth with a wad of toilet paper, my hands shaking.

"I'm fine," I manage. "It's just an emotional time right now, that's all. Everything is really stressful—"

But even as I say it, my mind is racing backward, making calculations that I hadn't bothered to think about. After all, Luca and I have been using protection—except we didn't, the night that he came racing home to me after the intruder broke in. And we didn't on the roof. And we didn't last night either—but it's that first night that's the culprit, if anything at all.

Because when I count, I realize something that makes me want to be sick all over again.

My period is a little over a week late.

LUCA

22

I've never enjoyed torture.

But I have to say, it hasn't been as difficult this time as it so often has been in the past. In fact, it's been almost harder to detach myself from it, to keep from going too far.

Whatever Viktor has threatened his soldiers with to keep them silent, it must be awful, because I use every method I know of, every trick I have, every painful thing I can imagine to try to pry out of them when and why and how they're attacking us, why Viktor insists on a bride as his price for peace, what they possibly hope to achieve. I even make Franco take over for a while, just to mix things up, but he can't get anything out of them either. By the time I exhaust the last of the Bratva men we managed to pick up, the warehouse floor is covered in blood and sweat, teeth and nails and piss. We're no closer to figuring out a way forward than we were before.

And it makes me question everything.

The one thing every single one of them made clear is that Sofia is at the heart of this. They're after her—Viktor's insistence on Caterina as his wife now is just his own personal desire—and they want her captured or dead. It doesn't really seem to matter which. But that's as much as we can draw out, no matter what we do.

You can't protect her. And you're getting too close.

That's the thought running through my head, over and over again, as I walk out to the docks. I hadn't meant to get in so deeply with Sofia. I'd meant to keep my distance, to tuck her away somewhere safely after the wedding and forget about her for the most part. For exactly this reason—because she's a distraction. My feelings for her are getting tangled up in the job I need to do, and it's making me unable to detach and do that job in the way that I need to. I didn't just have to hand things over to Franco for a little while as a means of mixing things up and trying to get them to talk.

I was also enjoying it too much. And I didn't want to stop.

I wanted to kill them, for ever thinking they could lay a hand on Sofia.

The night of Caterina's wedding, after Sofia and I finished for the second time, I knew I'd made a mistake.

I'd come damn close to telling her that I loved her. I'd been on the verge of it as I came for the second time, the words on the tip of my tongue, and I'd forced them back. Afterward, lying in bed next to her, I'd thought about the fact that since I'd rescued her from that hotel room, I hadn't so much as wanted to touch another woman. I thought about how many times we'd slept together, when before, I'd made sure to never come back more than once. I'd thought about the way she made me feel, almost addicted, craving her again even after I'd just come, thinking about her while I was away.

I knew then that whatever I felt for her—love, lust, addiction, obsession—it's too strong. Too powerful.

I need to step back. To put up the walls that were always meant to keep distance between us. Because nothing has changed. If I get close to her, if I let her close to me, if she starts to *matter*—if I'm being honest, she already does—then she can be used against me. Viktor, or anyone else, could manipulate me. Change my decisions, make me do things I wouldn't, otherwise. My head will never be completely clear again.

And if I'm being honest, I'm dangerously close to that already, if I'm not already there.

So when I head home, with blood still under my fingernails and my shirt still stained with it, I tell myself that however painful it might be, that last night with Sofia before I left needs to be the last time I ever touch her like that. If we do fuck, it needs to be colder, more practical, a means for satisfying lust, and nothing more. It can't be so intimate, so—personal.

And then, as if my mood weren't already bad enough, my emotions in an uncomfortable and unfamiliar tangle, I find out from Raoul that Sofia disobeyed me while I was gone. "She went to the hospital with Caterina," he tells me, and for a moment, I'm so intensely furious that I see red. I don't even hear the reason why, or another word that Raoul says, as I make my way towards the elevator up to the penthouse.

I'm almost shaking with fury by the time I walk in. *This is why*, I think, as I prowl the apartment looking for Sofia. This is why I can't allow myself to feel for her, why I can't allow that kind of intimacy, why it's better for her to fear me than care for me. I was an idiot to think that elaborate dates on the rooftop and nights spent laughing at movies together were possible for us, that I could somehow have ordinary pleasures like that while being a man who is anything but ordinary.

I'm the head of the biggest criminal organization in the world, not a husband who comes home every day for dinner. Not a soccer dad. Not a man who gets to have the trappings of a normal life. It's the price for the life I've led, the one I continue to lead, and I was always happy to pay it.

There's no reason to start pushing against it now.

The only way to keep Sofia safe is to make sure that she's too afraid to disobey me—for her to feel that my power over her is absolute, for her to know better than to ignore my orders. She can't think that we're equals, that there's an intimacy between us or a partnership.

It will only get her killed.

And if I allow that kind of closeness between us, and she gets herself murdered, it will shatter me. I know that. I'll do things I never would have otherwise, to save or avenge her.

I was never meant to have love. Never meant to have a wife that was anything more than a pretty trophy to take out occasionally and parade around, more than something to stick my cock into occasionally when I wanted to take my pleasure at home, with less effort than it took to pick up another woman. That was the mindset I'd clung to when I was told I'd have to marry Sofia to save her life.

I don't know when I lost it. But that changes today. Now.

Sofia is in the kitchen when I find her. She turns around with a smile on her face, only for it to die when she sees the expression on mine, the blood still spattering my skin and shirt. *Good*, I think, my brain feeling thick and slow with emotion, with the amount of discipline it takes to force myself to follow through on this. Her smile fades to a look of apprehension and then fear as I stalk towards her, and her shriek when I swing her up into my arms and toss her over my shoulder makes my chest ache more than it should.

"Put me down! Luca, what's going on—" she shouts, struggling in my grasp, but I hold on to her all the way to the bedroom. With a swift motion, I deposit her on the floor, trying to restrain the lust that rises up in me when I take in what she's wearing—a denim miniskirt and a white crop top made of some soft material that begs for me to run my hands over it.

"I know you went to the hospital." My voice is dark, gravelly, raspy from all the talking I've done today, trying to convince the Russians to roll over on Viktor so they could keep at least a few of their finger or toenails. "What did I tell you, Sofia?"

"You told me to stay here," she says in a small voice. "But Caterina—"

"I don't care." I see her recoil at the harshness in my voice, but I don't stop. "I don't care what your excuses are. Do you know what I did today, Sofia?"

Her eyes drift over me, over the blood, and I see her go even paler. "I can guess," she says in a small voice.

"This is who I am, Sofia. A bloody man. A killer. A murderer. A torturer. A man who will do anything to preserve what I've been given. A man who will do anything to protect you, since you're a part of that. You're *mine*, Sofia," I growl, taking a step towards her. "I think you've forgotten that."

"No, I just—"

"You just thought you could get away with it. You thought you could disobey me, and there would be no consequences. Look at me, Sofia!" My voice rises, filling the room, and she shrinks back. "Do I look like a man who can be disobeyed without consequences?"

I hate the fear that I see filling her eyes. I hate that I'm terrifying her, that I'm shouting at her, when all I want to do is take her into my arms and tell her that I need her to be safe, that the idea of her being killed because she couldn't listen to me makes me feel half-mad, feral with rage. That if I can't protect her, I don't see what the fucking point of all of this is anymore.

But I can't say any of that. Because I need to build the walls between Sofia and me so high that neither of us feels inclined to try to climb them again.

It's the only way to keep us both safe.

Her eyes are misting over with tears, threatening to spill over, but I ignore it. My chest feels tight, like it's hard to breathe, and just seeing her after being away for a few days makes me want her more than anything I've ever wanted in her life. I feel like an addict chasing his high, desperate for the heat of her body surrounding me, the blinding pleasure of sinking into her, the ecstasy of release.

With one swift motion, I stride forward, scooping her up and tossing her face-down onto the bed. She yelps, trying to turn to face me, but I push her skirt up over her ass, my arm pinning her down as I yank her thong off, leaving it tangled around one ankle as I push her legs apart.

"Luca!"

"Fuck, you're already so wet," I murmur, thrusting two of my fingers into her, hard. She moans, her ass pushing up into the air and back against my hand even as she wriggles in place. I'm already rock-hard, throbbing painfully with the need to come, and I drag my zipper down, releasing my aching cock. This is the only pleasure I can have, the only brief respite I get, and I fucking need it.

I need Sofia.

But it has to be in a way that pushes her away from me. Not one that brings us closer again, despite everything.

So I don't make her come first. Instead, I jerk my fingers free of her clenching pussy, angling my cock head at her entrance and thrusting hard.

The pleasure that washes over me at the feeling of her tight pussy clamping down onto my cock makes my toes curl. I start to thrust, hard and fast, intent on my own orgasm. Underneath me, I can feel her squirming, grinding back against me in an effort to come too, her fingers clawing at the blanket. I don't know if she's trying to get away or trying to get more, but I tell myself I don't care.

"Luca. Luca, please—"

"You want more? Good." I snarl out the words, fucking her harder, feeling half-mad with it as I drive into her again and again. "Take my cock, like a good wife. You can do at least that, right?"

"Luca—" Sofia whimpers my name again. "I'm sorry, I didn't mean—"

"Shut up," I growl. "Or do you want to swallow my cum, so you have something better to do with that mouth?"

Fuck. What am I doing? I don't want to speak to her that way, the way I treated her when we resented each other so much, when we did all we could to hurt each other and drive each other away. But if kindness and romance make her not listen to me, puts her in danger—my job is to protect her. To keep her safe, even if it's from herself. Even if it means being the don and not her husband. Even if the future we were trying for is impossible.

I can feel my balls tightening, my body throbbing with the intense pleasure of my oncoming orgasm. I thrust again, hard, and once more, wanting every bit of the sensation that I can get. I don't know when we'll do this again. Maybe never, and the thought makes me want to stay inside of her forever, keep her here until we drain each other to death. I can't imagine never being inside of Sofia again.

But there's no stopping it. Her body is clenching around mine rhythmically, and I can hear her moaning helplessly as she orgasms despite everything. Her back arches, and just as I feel myself reaching the point of no return, I do the only thing I can think of that will make her feel as if I'm just using her, that will push us apart even more than everything I've already done.

I pull out, gritting my teeth against the aching in my cock as I grab her waist and flip her over. And then, with her wide, surprised eyes looking up at me, I grab my throbbing length and start to jerk fast and hard, groaning with an almost painful sound, as I feel the first rush of my orgasm hit.

I've fantasized about coming all over Sofia since I first saw her. But not like this. She gasps with shock when the first spurt lands on her face, her hand going up numbly to touch her skin as my cum keeps shooting over her, landing on her breasts, her stomach, her pussy, her thighs. It seems to go on forever, shot after shot coating her skin as she turns away from me, the last spurts landing on her denim-clad hip.

She doesn't say anything to me. She just looks away, refusing to meet my eyes.

I feel worse than I ever have in my entire life. I feel—*heartbroken* is the only word I can come up with, even though that doesn't make sense. You have to love someone in order to have your heart broken. And I've never loved Sofia. *Right?*

I just got temporarily caught up. Addicted. But now I've put a distance between us that she won't soon try to cross. She'll go back to her room. I'll go back to avoiding her. We'll fight sometimes. Maybe we'll fuck. But we'll never have another night where I come close to making love to her, cuddling her against my chest as we fall asleep with me still inside of her.

That can never happen again.

It never should have happened at all.

So why does the thought hurt so fucking bad?

* * *

I NEED to talk to someone. And that leads me to a place I try to go to as infrequently as possible—the church. More specifically, the confessional booth.

I'm not actually confessing. I can't imagine saying out loud to Father Donahue the things that I've done—that I just did—to Sofia. Besides the fact that I don't want to admit it, it seems kind of cruel to talk to a priest about coming on a woman's face—something he'll never get to do.

What I can do is talk to him about everything else, though—and I do. In the end, it winds up with us sitting in one of the pews, with me looking up at the spot where not all that long ago, I married Sofia.

"Rossi and I are at odds," I tell him flatly. "I want peace. I want to come to terms with the Russians, to find some way to bring this conflict to an end. But Viktor refuses all my attempts. And Rossi thinks I'm weak because I refuse to go straight to killing."

"You know my opinion on that," Father Donahue says. "I've always believed that you had the potential to be a good man, Luca. Your father was a good man for all his flaws."

"And how, exactly, do I do that?" I can hear the traces of bitterness in my voice. "I want peace when everyone around me wants war. I try to protect my wife, and she won't obey me. I'm trying to do all I can to bring in a new era, one without bloodshed, and everywhere I turn, I feel as if they're all against me."

"You're in an unenviable position," the priest admits. "But I have faith in you, Luca. I see what there is between you and Sofia. She's young, but she's stronger than you know. She could be a good wife to you in time. Perhaps even now, she's what you need, without you knowing it."

"I don't need a wife. I need to push back the threat. I need the Bratva off of my doorstep. I only ever married her to keep Rossi from killing her, but the wolves keep howling for her, and I don't know why."

"You should talk to Sofia about that," Father Donahue says gravely. "There are things about her family that you should know. But it's not my place to share the Ferretti secrets."

"Even if I need to know in order to protect her?"

"Even so." Father Donahue frowns. "Luca, I know I'm a priest. You'll say that although I bless marriages, I have no idea what goes on in one, what it really means to be married day in and day out. And I would tell you that while that's true, I do know the meaning of commitment. I made a vow to this church, and I kept it. I made a vow to Vitto Rossi's father, and I have kept it. I made a vow to your father and Sofia's, and I have kept it. I've tried to keep the peace among the factions as best as I could for all these years. I've been a priest, a counselor. I've presided over funerals and weddings and baptisms. I was there to bless you as a baby just as I was there to join you in marriage. But Luca—" he pauses, his expression more serious than I've ever seen it. "I don't want to see the day that your coffin goes into the earth. I don't want to be the one who performs that funeral."

"I don't want you to outlive me, old man," I say dryly. "But I don't see what this has to do with my marriage. I didn't want to make that commitment. I said vows, but in my heart, the only vow that mattered was the vow to protect her. Everything else was just words I had to say."

"Still, you said them. And you will be stronger together than alone, Luca." Father Donahue looks at me, his face still grave. "Listen to me, son. You can fight them separately or together. But if you're fighting each other as well, how can there ever be peace? Even if the Bratva can be pushed back, there will never be peace for you as long as you go on like this."

He stands up then. "Go home to your wife, Luca. Let her comfort you. Be the man I know you can be."

"And who, exactly is that?" I can't keep the sarcasm out of my voice, but Father Donahue doesn't seem to notice.

"One who isn't afraid."

I don't move for a long moment after he disappears into the back of the church. I don't entirely know what he means by that, and I most certainly have no idea what secrets he thinks Sofia has that I don't know.

But the one thing I know for certain is that there's no way I'm going home tonight.

SOFIA

23

I wake up the next morning in my old bed in the guest room, my stomach knotting with nausea and my head hurting from crying. My whole body aches, and I want to believe that everything that happened yesterday was a bad dream.

As the memory of all of it comes rushing back in, though, I know that it wasn't. My stomach turns over again, and I barely make it out of bed and to the bathroom in time to make it to the toilet, my insides turning out again as I vomit profusely.

I sink to the floor, covering my mouth with my hand as I try not to burst into tears. I feel so overwhelmed, and this is just one more thing that I don't know how to begin to deal with. The conversation with Rossi in the hospital was bad enough, the loss of my mother's necklace after he ripped it off of me and the way he made it sound as if I'd been the one antagonizing me. The embarrassment and fear of throwing up in front of everyone and realizing that my period was late.

I'd thought for sure that when Luca got home, at least that would be one thing that would be better. I'd been looking *forward* to him coming back. And then he'd walked into the kitchen, bloody from—what, exactly? Torture? I could only guess at what he'd been doing.

Without bothering to clean up first, he'd hauled me into the bedroom and fucked me without the slightest concern—and come all over me. My hair. My breasts. All over my body and clothes. On my face.

And then he'd just walked away.

It left me feeling terrified. The way he'd acted—the way he'd talked to me, the things he'd said, the things he'd done. The blood on his hands and clothes while he'd fucked me, as if he hadn't cared that he still had other men's blood on him while he was inside of his wife.

I was wrong about him. It's the only thing I can think of, over and over again. The man who took me up to the rooftop, who gave me a diamond bracelet while I was sitting in a bubble bath, who watched movies with me and made love to me—that wasn't Luca. That was—some kind of temporary insanity, maybe. A brief flash of him being another kind of person. But not him.

Tears rise up in my throat, hot and thick, choking me. Those two men are so different from one another. Even if both were real—the Luca who can be cruel and brutal, the bloody man who tortures and kills, *and* the man who is tender with me, who held me and whispered sweet things to me, who gave me pleasure beyond anything I ever imagined—I don't know how to reconcile that. I don't know how I could love both.

That's the hardest part of it all—but I can't ignore it. The Luca who was kind and gentle—I was beginning to fall for him. I know that I was. And it feels as if that tender, new emotion has been crushed. Destroyed.

I feel destroyed.

And then there's the other problem to deal with.

I'm terrified to take a test. I know what the answer will be—there are only so many reasons I could be vomiting all times of the day with no other symptoms other than exhaustion and a missed period—especially when the timing of Luca flying home to me lines up so perfectly. I'd lost count of how many times we'd had sex that night and the morning after—and we hadn't used a condom even once. Not a single time.

If I am pregnant, the ramifications of it are astronomical. I can see the contract I signed as if it's floating in front of my eyes now, the paragraph that clearly stated in no uncertain terms:

If at any point in our marriage, I become pregnant, whether the child is the legitimate product of my union with Luca Romano or the result of infidelity, the pregnancy will be immediately terminated as soon as it is confirmed. If the pregnancy is not terminated, I understand that it effectively voids this contract. Luca Romano will no longer be responsible for, nor can he ensure, my safety or that of my child. My child nor I will receive financial support or protection. Luca Romano will not accept paternity of the child at any time. If an effort is made to establish paternity in the event of a non-termination, the child will be removed from custody and placed elsewhere.

It didn't take a genius to know that "placed elsewhere" was a way of saying that any child I insisted on having that I tried to prove was Luca's, or who later found Luca and insisted on being recognized, would be killed as quickly and efficiently as I would have been. It was just a means of not saying "murder" in a legal contract.

But we'd be lucky to make it that far. As soon as I tried to escape, my life and the baby's life would be forfeit, immediately on the list to be eliminated. Luca had said that he had no desire to kill me if I tried to escape our marriage, only to bring me back, but would that extend to a circumstance in which I was pregnant? A condition of our marriage was that we would never have children.

And now I've broken that. *We* have, but Luca will never have to accept responsibility. I know enough about how this family works to know that.

I still need to take a test, but I already know. And I'm terrified of the confirmation because then I have to make a choice.

Even as I think it, though, I can't see how there is any choice. A few days ago, I would have had hope that Luca might have had a change of heart, that he wouldn't follow through on the terms of the contract. I don't even fully understand *why* it's there, and I'd hoped I could get him to clarify before I knew for sure. But after what he did yesterday, how he talked to me, I can't trust him not to force me to follow through. That Luca was the old Luca, the one who treated me so roughly before our wedding, who was hard and cold towards me. Who tried to be my master, not my husband.

I feel betrayed by that short time where things were different, where *he* was different. I feel unloved and abandoned, completely alone. And as I touch my still-flat stomach, I think of the reality of having a child of my own, a little son or daughter.

Someone I can love unconditionally. Someone who could love me back.

Suddenly, with that thought, I can't bear the idea of losing this baby.

I remember before the wedding, my last conversation with Father Donahue. I remember what he said to me.

Sofia, in the presence of the Lord and the Holy Mother, in memory of your father, I will do all I can to protect you and keep you safe. If there comes a day when you wish to leave Luca, all you need to do is walk through those doors, and I will find a way.

The next thought that I have is sharp and immediate, and absolutely certain.

I have to get out of here. I have to get to the church.

I saw Caterina put in the elevator code yesterday, and I'm almost certain that I know what it is. If I can get outside, I can hail a cab and get to the church. And after that, Father Donahue will help me.

I know he will.

* * *

IT'S RAINING when I get outside. The code worked, despite my shaking fingers and uncertainty, but the numbers I thought I saw Caterina type in were the right ones. And now I'm out on the Manhattan street, cold rain soaking through my thin t-shirt as I wave down a cab.

My wrist catches the light as I do, and I realize I'm still wearing Luca's bracelet. I don't know why. A part of me is tempted to take it off and throw it into the gutter, but I don't. *I might need to sell it later,* I tell myself, but even I know that's not the whole reason.

I just can't look at it too closely after everything that's happened.

It's late, but Father Donahue answers the door when I pound on it, leaning against it exhaustedly. I'm soaked through now, and when he opens the cathedral door and sees me there, drenched with rain and with red-rimmed eyes, a strange expression crosses his face.

"Sofia?" I can hear the concern in his voice. "Is everything okay? I mean—it must not be, for you to be here like this. What's happened?"

I look up at his kind, worried expression and promptly burst into tears. And then, after a few minutes, I explain everything.

Well, not *everything*. I definitely don't go into explicit detail. But I tell him about my fights with Luca, about how he rushed home to me after the intruder nearly killed me, about our dates, about how I thought things were getting better. About how I realized that my feelings for him were growing. And then I explain about the baby—how I'm almost certain that I'm pregnant, and the contract that means I absolutely should not be.

"And you think Luca will force you to honor this contract?" Father Donahue frowns deeply. "What he is insisting on is a grave sin. But it won't be you who bears the burden of it if he insists on it."

"I don't want that. I want my baby." As I say the words out loud, I feel more assured than ever that that's true. "But I don't think Luca will give in on this. I don't know why it's so terrible for us to have children. But even that reason doesn't matter so much as the fact that I can't trust him not to force me into terminating the pregnancy."

"You said things had changed between you, though. Softened."

"Until yesterday." I take a deep, shaky breath. "He came home, and he was—different. I think he'd hurt some people. Tortured someone, maybe, to try to get information. He was cold and cruel to me. I'd gone to the hospital with Caterina, even though he'd asked me not to leave while he was gone. But he was so angry. It was like how things used to be, at first. I was terrified of him all over again. He's not—" I shake my head, trying not to cry again. "He's not the man that I thought he was."

"Perhaps." Father Donahue looks thoughtful. "Perhaps not."

"I need a way out." I look at him desperately. "I need a way to escape with my baby. Some way that he'll never find us. You promised you would help if I ever needed you—"

"I did. And I'll keep that vow," Father Donahue looks at me carefully, his face serious. "If you're certain."

"I am."

"Well, it will take a little time to set things up. But I can get you new papers, a fake ID, the things you would need to start over. You can stay in the rectory until—"

There's a cracking sound. I reel backward, startled as his eyes bulge in his head, a trickle of blood running from his mouth as he lurches forward in his seat, cracking his forehead on the pew in front of him.

Standing behind him is a man all in black, with a mask over his face. Just like the intruder in the apartment—except this man is holding a crowbar.

One that he just used to knock Father Donahue out cold.

I start to scream, but a gloved hand comes from behind me and clamps over my mouth. I'd been so focused, so intent on my plans for escape that I'd never even seen them sneaking up in the shadows. My eyes blur with tears as I look at Father Donahue slumped in the pew, and my blood runs cold. Did they kill him? Oh my god, what if he's dead? I'll never forgive myself—

Deep down, I know they're here because of me. I don't know why, but I know they came for me, that they would never have been here otherwise. Father Donahue is unconscious, bleeding, maybe dead because of me.

It's my fault. All of it. My fault.

I try to scream, to bite, gnashing my teeth at the gloved hand over my mouth, kicking wildly as the strong arms holding me haul me backward over the pew and out into the aisle. I try to fight, but I'm nowhere near as strong as the man holding me.

The hand loosens for just a second as if my kidnapper is trying to grab something, and I seize the opportunity. "Help me!" I shriek, squirming madly in his grasp, but it's useless. He presses his hand harder over my mouth, yanking my hair back with his other hand so that my face is tilted up.

"Shut up, bitch," he snarls, and to my shock, the voice isn't Russian. There's no thick accent like I expected, and my heart starts to race as I realize what it *did* sound like.

The accent was faint, that of someone who has spent most of their life in the States.

But it was an accent I'm familiar with—I've spent my whole life around it.

Italian, I think frantically as a wet cloth covers my mouth and nose, forcing me to breathe in the sickly scent of whatever is soaking it. *Why the fuck would they be Italian?*

And then, as my vision starts to blur, *I'm being drugged. Oh god, I'm being kidnapped, and they're drugging me, I can't get away—*

The last thought that goes through my head as I slump in my captor's arms is fear—fear for myself, but mostly fear for my baby.

My baby, who only moments ago I was trying so desperately to save.

I try one last, desperate attempt to wrestle free, but it's far too late. The drug is already taking hold, and my vision goes dark as I cling to that last thought, that I have to survive this somehow.

For my baby, if no one else.

THE FINAL BOOK in the Promise series. Ruthless Promise Releases 10/29/2021. You can purchase here. Don't forget to join the M. James reader group for exclusive updates and giveaways here.

ABOUT THE AUTHOR

Join the Facebook group for M. James' readers at
https://www.facebook.com/groups/531527334227005

Printed in Great Britain
by Amazon